MARRIED BY THE MILLENNIUM

Ten Ways To Say "I Do" by 2000

by Sally Trent

Is your heart's fervent desire that you ring in the New Year with a ring on your finger? Here are ten ways to find the hero of your dreams in time to say **I Do** before the year 2000 countdown begins!

1 ***Go Where the Guys Are*—aka *Home on the Range.*** Get a job, start socializing in a place that's full of eligible guys...like a ranch!

2 **Find a Single Daddy Club—aka *Saturday in the Park.*** Single dads populate the park playground on weekends, so how better to meet one than find an excuse to be there, too!

3 **Get Personal—aka *Truth in Advertising.*** Personal ads are a bit like opening Door Number 3: you just never know who you'll find—but he might be Mr. Right!

4 **Join a Gym—aka *Fit to be Found.*** Nothin[g] ... hormones spinning like ... local gym.

SHARON SALA

Sharon Sala realized that she was meant to be an author when she found herself loving to read, hating her job and constantly daydreaming. "I joined the Romance Writers of America and never looked back." Sharon has published eight books for Silhouette and, more recently, *Sweet Baby* (02/98) and *Reunion* (02/99) for MIRA Books. Born and raised in Prague, Oklahoma, Sharon still lives in the state she has always called home, with her two grown daughters nearby. She describes her writing style as "instinctive. I rarely have to sit down and think of a plot or character for a new book. They are always floating around inside my head, waiting to come to life."

MARIE FERRARELLA

Marie Ferrarella swears she was born writing, "which must have made the delivery especially hard for my mother." Born in West Germany of Polish parents, she came to America when she was four years of age and settled with her family in New York. Marie wrote her first romance novel when she was eleven years old. After receiving her English degree, Marie and her family moved to Southern California, where she still resides today. Marie, who has written over 100 novels, including more than ninety with Silhouette Books®, has one goal: to entertain, to make people laugh and feel good. "That's what makes me happy," she confesses. "That, and a really good romantic evening with my husband."

BEVERLY BARTON

Beverly Barton has been in love with romance since her grandfather gave her an illustrated edition of *Beauty and the Beast.* An avid reader since childhood, Beverly wrote her first book at the age of nine. After over thirty years of marriage to the "love of her life," Beverly is a true romantic and considers writing romances a real labor of love. The award-winning author of over twenty-five books, Beverly is a member of Romance Writers of America and helped found the Heart of Dixie chapter in Alabama.

SHARON SALA

MARIE FERRARELLA

BEVERLY BARTON

3, 2, 1... Married!

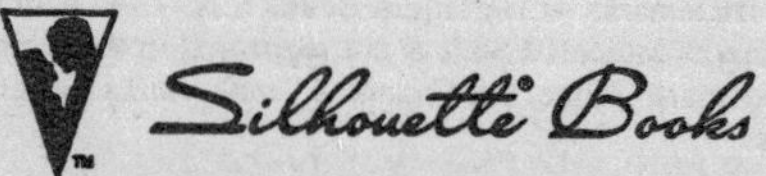

Published by Silhouette Books
America's Publisher of Contemporary Romance

If you purchased this book without a cover you should be aware that this book is stolen property. It was reported as "unsold and destroyed" to the publisher, and neither the author nor the publisher has received any payment for this "stripped book."

3,2,1...MARRIED!

Copyright © 1999 by Harlequin Books S.A.

ISBN 0-373-48385-6

The publisher acknowledges the copyright holders of the individual works as follows:

MIRACLE BRIDE
Copyright © 1999 by Sharon Sala

THE SINGLE DADDY CLUB
Copyright © 1999 by Marie Rydzynski-Ferrarella

GETTING PERSONAL
Copyright © 1999 by Beverly Beaver

All rights reserved. Except for use in any review, the reproduction or utilization of this work in whole or in part in any form by any electronic, mechanical or other means, now known or hereafter invented, including xerography, photocopying and recording, or in any information storage or retrieval system, is forbidden without the written permission of the editorial office, Silhouette Books, 300 East 42nd Street, New York, NY 10017 U.S.A.

All characters in this book have no existence outside the imagination of the author and have no relation whatsoever to anyone bearing the same name or names. They are not even distantly inspired by any individual known or unknown to the author, and all incidents are pure invention.

This edition published by arrangement with Harlequin Books S.A.

® and TM are trademarks of Harlequin Books S.A., used under license. Trademarks indicated with ® are registered in the United States Patent and Trademark Office, the Canadian Trade Marks Office and in other countries.

Visit us at www.romance.net

Printed in U.S.A.

CONTENTS

Dear Reader,

I think you'll agree with me that every woman who plans to marry dreams of finding Mr. Right. But finding him and marrying him are two different things. Sometimes your right is his wrong. And sometimes our vision of right is blurred by good looks and pretty words, rather than clarified by the depth of character and sincerity we should be looking for.

I think you'll find that the women in these stories had their own special sets of issues to work through, yet I'm certain that you'll rejoice with them as they finally find their happy ever afters.

The only advice I would give you in searching for love is to trust your instincts and to remember that, most often, true love finds you, rather than the reverse. I guess what I'm trying to tell you is—you can't *make* love happen. But when it's time, it *will* happen to you.

Enjoy the romance, and my best wishes to you all. I love to hear from my readers. You can write to me at P.O. Box 127, Henryetta, OK 74437.

Sharon Sala

Miracle Bride

Sharon Sala

I dedicate this story to my three granddaughters,
Chelsea, Logan and Leslie Sala,
with the prayer that, when they grow up,
they each find their way to true happiness.

Chapter 1

"Aunt Hallie doesn't have any boobs."

"She does, too. All girls have boobs."

Five-year-old Dustin stuck his tongue out at his cousin, Chelsea.

"Then why don't they bounce?" he asked.

Six-year-old Chelsea wasn't sure why she felt the need to defend her aunt, but just to be on the safe side, she gave Dustin a punch in the stomach.

"You're such a baby," she said, as he set up a howl. "Aunt Hallie has boobs. They're just a little bit flat, and everyone knows the flat boobs don't bounce."

Hallie O'Grady stood in the middle of the hallway with a tray full of sandwiches, trying to decide if she should laugh or cry. Her mother had always told her that no good ever comes of eavesdropping. At the age of thirty-one, she now understood why.

She looked down at her chest. Compared to her sisters, she was flat, although she'd been telling herself for years that a borderline B-cup bra was perfectly normal. So, she wasn't all that endowed. And so she was the only one of her sisters who wasn't married. So what?

The same little niece came darting past her, now sporting a stunning piece of bosom, compliments of two balloons she'd thrust beneath her sweatshirt. Hallie grinned in spite of herself. So she wasn't built like a stripper. At least she still had her dignity. But, she reminded herself, dignity was a cold bed partner.

The whole incident made her think of a piece she'd read in an old issue of *Prominence Magazine* the other day. According to the article, even if she was in the market for a suitable mate, she was going about it the wrong way. She couldn't remember the exact title of the article, but it had to do with ways to meet the man of your dreams and be married on New Year's Eve 1999. According to the article, she needed to put herself in the proverbial line of fire. She should go where men congregated, like ball games and golf courses…and bars. But for Hallie, there was something too clinical about setting out to intentionally snag a mate. She wanted love at first sight. She wanted to be bowled over—knocked off her feet—or however one chose to categorize the moment. She wanted the whole nine yards.

And while she was still considering her situation, two more of her nieces came barreling through the hallway, one with a Barbie doll, the other with a Ken doll. One niece was screaming, the other was giggling while making kissing motions with Ken toward the Barbie her sister was holding. Hallie grinned wryly as she sidestepped their raucous play. Even the kids were getting in on the act. So what was it about falling in love that was so difficult for her? Was it her attitude, or just her lack of opportunities?

"Hallie, where are the sandwiches?"

Her mother's voice jerked her back to the reality of the moment, and that was feeding this rowdy crowd before it got any rowdier. At that moment, she realized she'd forgotten to put the olives on top of the sandwiches. For two cents, she'd just let it go, but her mother would comment.

"Just about done," she yelled, and made a neat pivot back to the kitchen.

In Moira O'Grady's world, it was the little touches that counted. Moments later, Hallie was stabbing olives with toothpicks and poking them into the tops of the sandwiches while contemplating the society of the times. What was it about people who felt the obligation to push single men and women to meet and marry? As far as she was concerned, there were far too many people looking over her shoulder as it was.

She poked the last toothpick into a sandwich and then went to the sink to wash. As she did, she caught a glimpse of her reflection in the window over the sink.

As the eldest of Sean and Moira O'Grady's four daughters, it only stood to reason that she should have had first pick of the good family traits. Instead, she was the odd one out. Her mother called her a changeling. Her sisters, Evie, Dana and Petra, were tall, curvaceous, green-eyed, redheads. Between them, they'd given their mother and father three fine sons-in-law, and to date, eight grandchildren to love, including the two precocious ones who had been discussing Hallie's lack of physical attributes, and the one yet to be born that Petra was carrying.

Compared to her sisters, Hallie looked like an elf. She was small-boned, with straight black hair and brown, almond-shaped eyes. At only four inches over five feet tall, she had nephews who would outgrow her within the next couple of years. And while she'd missed being marked an O'Grady by her father's red hair and green eyes, she had inherited his stubborn streak.

Independent to the point of obstinate, Hallie was cognizant of her weak points, but also aware of her strengths. For the better part of six years, she had been supporting herself as a successful author of children's books. Her father fumed and muttered on a daily basis that his beloved eldest would die an old maid and constantly thrust what he considered eligible suitors into her path.

And, while Hallie longed for a husband and family as her sisters had, she wasn't willing to trade off her independence for second best. She disposed of the suitors as deftly as she ignored her father's interference. If there was a man for her, then, God willing, they would someday find each other. Until then, she was calling the shots regarding her life, flat boobs and all.

With a wry grimace, she picked up the tray and carried it into the dining room where her family was beginning to gather.

"There you are!" Sean O'Grady boomed. "Where the hell have you been hiding yourself, girl?"

Hallie elbowed her way through the crowd with the food and gave her father a glare as she set the tray on the table.

"I haven't been hiding and you know it," she said, then eyed the crowd with cool intent. "And I'd better not be seeing any strange faces here today, or your name will be mud, Father dear. This is my birthday party, not another round of your blasted dating game."

Everyone burst into laughter as Sean's face turned a dark, hearty red.

"I don't meddle," he blustered.

"Right," she said. "And my name is not Hallie O'Grady."

"Come on you two, no fighting today," Moira said, pushing her husband toward the plates at the end of the buffet as she gave her eldest daughter a wink. "It's Hallie's birthday and I won't have anyone messing it up." Then she gave the tray a quick glance and patted Hallie on the arm.

"Your sandwiches look marvelous," she whispered. "And I just love those little olives, don't you?"

Hallie grinned.

Moira turned, waving at the crowd of family spilling through the rooms of the O'Grady house.

"Dinner is ready," she called. "Everyone grab a child. We'll fill their plates first."

And they did as their mother had directed. Within a few minutes, the eight grandchildren were scattered about the room with their plates on the floor between their legs, eating to their hearts' content. Petra, who was the next oldest to Hallie, leaned over and gave her a hug as she stood in line at the buffet.

"Happy Birthday, Hallifax."

Hallie snitched an olive from the tray of sandwiches and popped it into her mouth.

"Lose the nickname, Petra, or I will tell your children you used to wet the bed," she muttered, chewing around her threat.

Petra laughed, but held up her hands in a gesture of defeat.

"I concede," she said, and then chuckled. "Besides, you never did play fair."

Hallie snorted beneath her breath. "Don't give me fair. I'm the one who got shortchanged. If you don't believe me, ask your son. He just told Chelsea I didn't have any boobs."

Petra flushed. "Oh, Hallie, I'm so sorry. I'll speak to him about—"

Hallie laughed. "Don't bother. Chelsea punched him in the stomach."

Evie gasped as she overheard the last of their conversation and pivoted toward the children, eyeing her eldest with a gleam in her eye.

"Don't," Hallie said. "They've already sorted out their problem. Besides, truth is truth."

Evie glanced at her husband, who was tending to their brood, then took Hallie by the arm and pulled her aside. As always, the other sisters followed.

Sean was the first to notice his daughters' absences and looked up to see them in a huddle on the far side of the room.

"What's going on over there?" he asked.

Evie's husband, Sam, scooped himself a generous helping of lasagna and then handed Sean the spoon. "Here, Sean. You should know by now that when those four get together, the best thing to do is leave them alone. Trust me, have some of Evie's lasagna and mind your own business."

Sean frowned, but did as his son-in-law suggested.

"What's up?" Dana asked, as Petra pulled her close.

"Hallie's on one of those self-deprecating kicks again," Evie said.

Dana rolled her eyes. "Hallie, if you complain one more time about your tiny butt or your B-cup bra, I'm going to throw up. Ever since baby number three, I can't fit into a single pair of my slacks and the cup size of my bras has gone to a D. I feel like a six-foot, redheaded version of Dolly Parton—without the glamour."

Hallie shrugged. "Look. I'm not complaining. I'm just facing facts. I'm thirty-one years old today and I have never even been in love. You three are curvy redheads with husbands who adore you. You breed children faster than Daddy sprouts gray hair."

Petra rolled her eyes. "Breeding? Oh, thanks. Now I feel like a rabbit."

"But an adorable rabbit," Hallie added.

"Just because you don't look like us doesn't mean you're not pretty," Dana said. "You're just different and from where I'm standing, different is better."

"Yeah," Evie said, and punched Dana lightly on the arm. "At least when you fall in love, you'll know that the guy wasn't using you to settle for second best."

Dana laughed. Evie's sixth-grade boyfriend had been besotted with Dana, but upon learning that

Dana wasn't interested, he had settled for Evie instead.

"That's old news," Petra said. "This is a new day for Hallie." Then she hugged her. "And, because we love you madly, we went together to get you a very special birthday present."

"You're going to do this now?" Evie asked. "I thought we were going to make the presentation after we ate."

Petra looked at Hallie, then frowned. "Now's better."

"Goody," Dana cried. "I've been dying to tell her for days."

"Do you have it?" Petra asked.

"Right here," Dana said, pulling a long, white envelope from her jacket pocket.

"What's this?" Hallie said.

"You'll see. Just open it," they chimed.

Hallie tried to smile, but she kept remembering a similar event a few years back and the "exciting" surprise her sisters had sprung. It had taken her the better part of five months to get over the "day of beauty" they had given her. She'd come out of the spa looking like a short version of Cher, complete with spiked hair and a fake mole near the right-hand corner of her upper lip.

"I'm not changing the color of my hair," she warned.

They laughed. "Just hush and open it," they urged.

She did, eyeing the plane ticket and the brochure with mild surprise.

"A trip?"

"Not just any trip," Evie said. "It's a two-week, all-expenses-paid stay at the Miracle Guest Ranch in Cold Water, Texas."

Hallie's eyes widened. "Texas? That's halfway across the country from California."

Evie sighed, and pointed toward the brochure. "You don't know anyone interesting here. Besides, look what's waiting for you when you get there."

Hallie's gaze followed the direction of her sister's finger. A dark flush suddenly stained her cheeks as she looked up at her sisters in disbelief.

"You aren't pointing at scenery. You're pointing at those cowboys. You three are getting as bad as Dad."

"Now, Hallie, it will be fun," Evie muttered.

Hallie glared. "How do you know? I can't ride. I don't like to camp and I have a deadline on a book."

Petra folded her arms across her chest and glared right back. "They will teach you, you have a cabin all your own, and you own a laptop."

Hallie sighed. "It's not that I don't appreciate the gesture, but I just can't see myself in jeans and boots."

Evie's eyes narrowed thoughtfully. "Oh, I don't know. I think you'll look quite nice. If I had a tight little rear and long legs like you do, I might wear slacks more often myself." Then she lowered her voice. "Besides, you *have* to see yourself in jeans and boots because that's what Mom and Dad got you."

Petra rolled her eyes. "My Lord, Evie. Why don't you just spill the rest of the surprises now and we can all go home?"

Evie sniffed. "She had to be warned."

Hallie's eyes widened perceptibly. "Warned? Why do I have to be warned?"

"You can return them before you go. You don't leave for a couple of days, yet," Evie added.

"Return what?" Hallie muttered.

The sisters pulled their circle a little tighter. "The boots," they hissed. "Mom picked them out. I swear to God, they look like they came off a clown."

Hallie groaned.

A short while later, she was thankful for the warning. It was the only thing that kept the smile on her face when she opened the boot box. It wasn't so much that they were red. Red cowboy boots were a little flashy, but she could have lived with the color. It was the silver tabs on the toes and white fringe around the top that stunned her. All she could think was, what in hell had my mother been thinking?

She looked up, a wide smile on her face. "Mom! Dad! I don't know what to say!"

Moira smiled, pleased with herself. "See there, Sean. I told you she would like them!" Then she added, "Of course, if they don't fit, you can exchange them. It's a little risky buying shoes for someone, you know."

Hallie's smile widened. There was her out. "Right! I sure don't want an uncomfortable boot."

Sam slapped her on the back. "So, kiddo, when are you leaving?"

Hallie looked around the room, sighing in silent defeat. The expectation on her loved ones faces was impossible to ignore. It might prove to be the biggest waste of her time she'd ever made, but she didn't have it in her to disappoint them. Not when they'd gone to so much trouble and expense.

"According to my ticket, day after tomorrow."

"Enough!" Moira suddenly announced. "Let's cut the cake."

As the family began gravitating toward a three-layer banana cream cake on the sideboard, Dana leaned over and whispered in Hallie's ear.

"That doesn't give you much time to exchange those damned boots."

"Trust me," Hallie said. "I will find the time."

Jake Miracle lifted the glass of ice water to his mouth, drinking thirstily. It was twenty minutes after three in the afternoon and dark would come none too soon this day. He set the glass down with a thump, then took off his Stetson and combed his fingers through his hair, lightly massaging a knot of tight muscles at the back of his neck. He had the makings of a headache and as usual, he'd missed lunch. But these were small prices to pay for the solvency of his family home.

Ten years ago, he and his brothers, Luke and John, had been facing bankruptcy after the untimely deaths of their parents. Luke had just turned sixteen and at fourteen, John had just begun his second year of high school.

At twenty-five, Jake had been on his own for the better part of five years. His college was behind him. His job as a surveyor for the State of Utah was all that he'd hoped it would be. And then the unbelievable had happened. He'd gotten a frantic phone call from Luke and hopped the first plane he could get back to Dallas. The journey home had been hell. He'd alternated between disbelief that his parents—two vital, fun-loving people—could so swiftly cease to be. But they'd walked into a convenience store in the middle of a robbery and wound up the only victims. The robber had gotten $172 and a carton of cigarettes and then had been captured before he got out of the parking lot. The only casualties of the incident were Frank and Helen Miracle.

For Jake, the ensuing month was pure chaos. Besides the fact that the ranch was in debt and his father's bank account probably wouldn't sustain them six months, child welfare had intruded with full intent of removing Luke and John from the home. That's when Jake snapped. He insulted the caseworker, cussed the sheriff who'd come with her, and quit his job to stay home.

That night, the Miracle brothers gathered at the kitchen table, a long-time problem-solving ritual, and began voicing ideas. It was John who came up with the idea first. Paying customers on a real Texas ranch. At first Jake had scoffed at the idea, claiming no one in their right mind would pay money to do something he'd worked so hard to escape. But the longer he thought of it, the more the idea grew. Long after the boys had gone to bed, he was up making lists and spreadsheets, figuring monetary outlay and necessary renovations. By morning, he had a plan.

Now, the plan was ten years old and had been running in the black for almost eight of those years. And a strange thing had happened during the process. Along the way, he'd discovered how deep his roots ran in Texas soil.

However, there were days, like this one, when the pressure of the guests got to him. Yes, he and his brothers had stayed on their family ranch. And no, child welfare had not taken them away, but they were paying a dear price. Every year, from April to October, they shared their home, their time and their lives with total strangers.

Jake was settling his Stetson back on his head when the shrill peal of the ranch phone made him pause. The phone was little more than an intercom, but it connected the main house and office with every separate cabin and outbuilding on the ranch.

It rang a second time and he wondered why the secretary hadn't picked up, when he remembered she'd taken the afternoon off to take her daughter to the dentist. He grabbed it before it could ring again.

"Office."

"Jake, it's me, John! That Denison kid in cabin five let all the colts out. They're heading in three directions at once. I need help."

"Call Shorty on the two-way. I just sent him to the canyon to set up the hayride. He can't be far. And call Luke. He'll have his radio with him. I think he's in the machine shed working on a tractor. I'm on my way."

"Will do," John said, and disconnected.

Jake shoved his hat tight on his head and headed for the door. He was halfway out when he caught a glimpse of something pink from the corner of his eye, but was too late to stop his momentum. He collided face on with the person just entering.

"I am so sorry," he gasped, and grabbed at the kid before she could fall. He had a fleeting impression of big eyes and dark hair and a small, slender build. "Sorry to rush, but I've got an emergency. Go on inside, kid. Someone will be with you shortly."

Then he bolted off the porch and jumped into his truck. Moments later, he was headed toward the corrals in a cloud of dust.

Still trying to catch her breath, Hallie watched his disappearance in disbelief. About all she'd seen was a man with big shoulders, tanned skin and a black cowboy hat. What was worse, she hadn't exactly bowled him over. In fact, it had been the reverse.

"Well, that was encouraging," she muttered. "My sisters send me halfway across the country to meet men and the first one I see thinks I'm a kid."

With a backward glance at the disappearing pickup, she swatted at a fly buzzing about her nose and slipped into the office to wait. A short while later, a young woman came into the room on the run.

"Hi, I'm Carol," she said. "I'm sorry you had to wait. The regular secretary is out and all hell—" she hesitated at her choice of words and blushed "—and most of Jake's colts just broke loose down at the barns. But if you will bear with me, I'm sure I can locate your reservation and get you moved into your cabin in no time."

Hallie smiled. The girl reminded her a little bit of her sister, Evie.

"I have a reservation...Hallie O'Grady."

Carol's smile widened. "Hello, Miss O'Grady. Welcome to Miracle Ranch. Now let's get you to your cabin so you can settle in before night."

"What's happening tonight?" Hallie asked.

"An outdoor barbeque and barn dance. The food is great! The music is better! Do you know how to two-step?"

Hallie shook her head.

Carol grinned. "It won't take those cowboys long to teach you. You're going to love it."

A short while later, Hallie was settling into cabin number ten, unpacking her clothes and sipping on a cold soft drink she'd gotten from the cabin refrigerator. Her itinerary for the two-week stay was on the table and there was a bounce to her step as she went from bed to closet and back again, hanging up her clothes. For the first time in as long as she could remember, she had a plan that did not include meeting a deadline.

Over the hum of the window unit air conditioner, she heard a man shout, then the nicker of horses. Curious, she glanced out the window just in time to see a couple of cowboys with lassoes in the air, trying to catch some horses. It occurred to her then that this was the "hell" that Carol had spoken of. She grinned. It didn't look all that serious, just terribly dusty. From where she was standing, she could see several guests watching and laughing, cheering the men on as they continued to round up the young colts. Moments later, she focused on one man in the middle of the dusty scramble and her heart skipped a beat. The broad shoulders. The black hat. It had to be the one who'd almost knocked her down. He was leading two colts with one hand and one with another, and there was a calmness about him in the midst of the mess that intrigued her. If that had been her father, he would have been cursing and ranting at the top of his voice, and everyone would have been scurrying to do his bidding.

She leaned closer to the window, watching until the man disappeared from her view. Then she stepped back with a sigh and returned to her unpacking, reminding herself not to get too interested. He'd already put her in her place.

As she emptied the last of her underclothes into the dresser, she paused and looked up, absently studying the unremarkable features on her face. Then she frowned and stuck out her tongue.

"Quit trying to be something you're not," she told herself, and slammed the drawer shut with a thump. Then her gaze slid to her chest, and her slight, slender build. "And don't sweat the small stuff, especially when it's all you've got."

Chapter 2

Hallie could smell the barbeque smoke from the porch of her cabin as she stepped outside. The faint strains of music were drifting through the air as she tucked her key in her pocket and followed the sounds. Before she'd gone far, she was joined by a middle-aged couple, and then a family of four. By the time they reached the barn, introductions had been made all around. The food smelled good—the raucous noise sounded better. It reminded her of O'Grady dinners.

"Hey there, little lady," someone said, and took her by the hand. "Welcome to Miracle Ranch."

She turned. The pair of smiling cowboys had to be brothers. The green eyes and teasing smiles were too similar to ignore.

"Why, thank you," she said. "Are you two the official welcoming committee?"

They laughed. "You could say that," one said. "I'm John Miracle. That poor ugly thing is my brother Luke." Then he winked. "It's too early for Christmas, so you can't be the Christmas angel, but darlin', you sure are a pretty thing, all the same."

Hallie stood with her mouth open, her eyes glittering with surprised delight. Then she threw back her head and laughed. It was a belly-roll of a sound that shattered the momentary silence between them.

Both men wore sheepish grins, aware that their normal banter had not connected in quite the manner they had envisioned.

"I don't think she bought it, do you, Luke?"

Luke Miracle grinned. "For once, little brother, I think you're right."

Hallie was still chuckling as she held up her hands in a gesture of defeat.

"Sorry, boys, but I'm Irish, and you'll have to kiss a bigger Blarney stone before you can make me believe all of that."

Luke's grin widened. "I hear you, Irish, but I'm thinkin' it isn't a Blarney stone you should be trustin'. This is Texas. Down here, we kiss women, not rocks."

Hallie laughed again, then let herself be led toward a massive buffet being laid across the room.

Jake heard her laugh before he saw her face and the sound sent a shiver up the back of his spine. He looked up from the side of beef he'd been carving, searching for the owner. There was an anxiety inside him he didn't recognize. It was almost as if he'd been listening for that sound all his life.

He saw his brothers at the doorway. As usual, they had one of the young female guests cornered. All he could see was her back, but he had to admit his brothers seemed to have good taste. She wasn't tall, but she was leggy, and what she did for a pair of jeans should have been illegal. He started to look away, when he heard the laughter again. It was then he realized it was coming from her.

A lump formed in the back of his throat and he held his breath, watching as she began to turn. Black hair fanned as she pivoted. She looked vaguely familiar. When they started toward him, he tensed.

"I'd like some well-done."

He jerked, then looked down at the short, heavy-set man in front of him.

"I'm sorry, what did you say?" he asked.

The man held out his plate, pointing to the roast Jake was supposed to be carving.

"The roast. I'd like a slice well-done, please."

"Coming up," he muttered, and laid a slab on the man's plate the size of his hand.

By the time he looked up, he'd lost track of Luke and John, as well as the mysterious woman. Disappointment niggled. He wanted to see her close up—to hear her voice—and if by some great stroke of fortune—hear that wonderful laugh all over again.

Then he frowned and gave himself a mental shakedown.

Get hold of yourself, Miracle. She's one of the guests, so she's not going anywhere. Besides, you should know by now that nothing is ever as good as it looks.

"Excuse me?"

He looked up. It was her! She was standing before him with a plate in her hand and all he could think was, my God, her eyes are as dark as her hair. She kept looking at him. Waiting. Waiting. What the hell was he supposed to do?

"Dang, Jake, are you going to make her beg for it?"

Luke's voice broke Jake's concentration. He blinked, then slid a practiced glare at his younger brother.

"What are you talking about?"

Luke pointed to the carving knife and fork in Jake's hand.

"I think Miss O'Grady wants a piece of meat."

Jake's focus shifted and he found himself locked into that dark, bottomless gaze again. O'Grady. Her name is O'Grady.

"Miss O'Grady," he said softly.

"Please call me Hallie. Besides, I don't think it's necessary to be so formal, since we've already met."

His eyebrows knitted in a frown. "No, ma'am, I'm sure I would have remembered."

"On the porch...this afternoon. We sort of ran into each other." Then she extended her plate again. "You called me kid."

He groaned beneath his breath. This was proof he'd been working too hard. The woman before him was as far from being a kid as he was, and packaged as neatly as any female he'd ever seen. Tiny waist, slender hips. She reminded him of a leggy colt. And her face. He couldn't quit staring at the beautiful, exotic face.

"Jake!"

Again, his brothers' voices turned his attention.

"What?" he growled.

They pointed toward the meat. He gritted his teeth, then slid a look at Hallie O'Grady.

"How do you like it?" he asked.

Hallie stared at his lips.

"How do I like what?" she muttered.

"The meat. How do you like your meat?"

"Oh...um, well done, please, I suppose."

Jake angled the carving knife over the roast and started to slice.

Luke elbowed John. John wiggled his eyebrows back at Luke.

"Just give her some food, big brother. Luke and I will furnish the rest," John said.

Jake stopped in the middle of a cut and lifted his

head. The look he gave Luke and John wiped the smiles off their faces.

"I trust you are looking after our other guests as diligently?" he asked.

They nodded.

Jake laid a perfect slice of beef on Hallie's plate.

"Miss O'Grady, I hope you enjoy your stay at Miracle Ranch."

Hallie shuddered, and made herself smile. "Thank you. I'm sure I shall."

She moved down the buffet, choosing bits and pieces of other dishes—anything to take her mind off what had just happened. By the time she found herself a seat, food was the last thing on her mind, although she managed to introduce herself to her table companions and ordered iced tea from a passing waitress.

A short while later, she was still picking at the food on her plate when a hand touched her shoulder.

"First dance is mine."

She turned, masking her disappointment when she realized it was Luke, and not his big brother Jake, who was asking her to dance.

"I don't know how to two-step," she warned him.

Luke grinned and winked. "Oh, that's all right. I'm a real good teacher."

Hallie grinned back. This kind of sexual banter was easy to handle.

"Now, why does that not surprise me?"

Luke laughed as he pulled her to her feet.

Moments later, he had her out on the dance floor, taking her through the motions.

Jake watched from the sidelines, his gut in a knot. When she looked up at Luke, his breath caught in his throat. And when something Luke said made her laugh, he unconsciously doubled his fists. Stunned that he was reacting so strongly to a woman he didn't even know, he pivoted sharply and walked out of the barn, getting lost in the dark Texas night.

Hallie woke abruptly. Still locked in the dream she'd been having, she turned toward the door, expecting to see Jake Miracle standing there. Only after she realized she was alone in her cabin, did she begin to relax.

It was morning.

She lay there, absorbing the quiet and staring through the parted curtains to a clear, sunny sky. The leaves on the tree outside her window were turning. Every now and then, one would give way and fall, drifting toward the ground like a bird with a broken wing. Outside, a car horn honked and someone yelled a response. She couldn't hear what was being said, but she knew that the business of the day was already in hand.

She rolled over on her side, hugging a pillow to her breasts. The urge to close her eyes and sleep in was strong, then she thought of Jake Miracle. It was enough to get her out of bed and digging through clothes for something to wear.

Day one of her stay was just beginning.

"Hey, Luke, where are you going?" Jake asked.

Luke paused at the doorway to the office, his hat in his hand, and looked back at his brother behind the desk.

"To meet Hallie O'Grady. I promised her a riding lesson."

"That's Dobber's business. You promised me day before yesterday that you'd go into Cold Water and get a load of feed," Jake said shortly, then slipped an invoice into a file.

"But I—"

Jake never batted an eye. "Business first, Luke. Business first."

Luke sighed. "Yeah, okay," he muttered. "I'll just go tell Hallie I can't—"

"We don't disappoint our guests,' Jake said. "I'll find Dobber and have him do it. Where are you supposed to meet her?"

"At the corrals. She wanted to go on the trail ride, but I told her it would be better if she knew how to ride a little before she spent the day on a horse. Besides, the rides go out every other day. I promised her she wouldn't miss anything."

"Just go get the feed and quit worrying about who's going to teach your latest honey how to sit a horse," Jake snapped.

Luke stared. The anger in his brother's voice was unexpected. He began to grin. The longer he stood there, the wider it became.

"You think she's pretty, don't you?"

Jake glared.

"You're attracted to her, aren't you?"

Jake didn't answer. He'd never been good at lying.

Luke laughed and slapped his hat firmly on his head. "I never thought I'd see the day. Last night we suspected you were interested... Hot damn, wait until I tell John we were right—"

"Don't you have some place to be?" Jake snapped.

"Yeah," Luke drawled. "And so do you. Don't keep Hallie waiting, okay?"

Jake reached for his hat and stalked past Luke without answering. His brother's chuckles were ringing in his ears as he strode off the porch. Besides, Luke didn't know what the hell he was talking about. *Attracted* was hardly the word.

From her perch on a nearby fence, Hallie watched the group mounting up for the trail ride, then waved to a young couple she'd met over breakfast. A twinge of envy dug deep as she watched them laughing at each other's antics. As far as she knew, she was the only single guest at the ranch and she was beginning to feel out of place. Not that she wasn't having a great time, but still...

"Miss O'Grady."

Hallie jumped, her seat on the rail suddenly unsure as she teetered for balance. Suddenly, a hand centered on her back while another grabbed her arm. She looked down. Jake Miracle was looking up at her.

"I didn't mean to startle you," he said.

Hallie thought she smiled. She knew she was trying.

"It's okay. I was just lost in thought and didn't hear you come up."

Jake had to remind himself why he'd come.

"My brother wanted me to tell you that he's sorry he couldn't make the riding lesson. He's on his way into town to bring back a load of feed."

Hallie's hopes fell. If she didn't learn how to sit a horse, she wouldn't be able to go on the trail ride.

"That's okay," she said. "I'll find something else to do."

She started to jump down when Jake suddenly stepped in front of her and grabbed her by the waist with both hands.

Instinctively, she grabbed his shoulders, bracing herself to keep from falling, then looked down—straight into a pair of the bluest eyes she'd ever seen—and forgot what she'd been going to say next.

Jake found himself caught in a dark, endless gaze and going down for the last time when a horse nickered nearby. He blinked, realized what he'd been thinking, and mentally took a step back.

"Let me help you down," he said, and lifted her from the rail as if she was a child. The moment her feet were on firm ground, he set her free and turned around. "If you'll follow me, I'll introduce you to Dobber. He's been with the family for years and knows as much about horses as anyone you'll ever meet."

"I don't want to be a bother," Hallie said.

Jake paused, then turned. "Nothing is a bother for our guests."

Hallie felt as if she'd been kicked in the stomach. The reminder that she was nothing more than a paying customer hit hard. At that moment, she realized what she'd been thinking. She blamed herself—and her sisters—for letting all this nonsense go to her head. In spite of the fact that she felt like crawling in a hole, she made herself smile.

"Why, thank you," she said, and folded her hands in front of her like a perfect child.

The mental wall that sprang up between them was impossible for Jake to ignore. He didn't know what had happened, but he felt it, just the same.

"You can thank me tomorrow, if you still feel like walking," he said, and pivoted, resuming his trek toward the stable.

Hallie frowned as she hurried to catch up. Jake Miracle was a strange man. He went from hot to cold faster than she could keep up.

A short while later, she was making fast friends with a mare named Sugarfoot, while Joe Dobbs, the wrangler, was teaching her the fundamentals of mounting a horse. He gave Hallie an instruction to mount, and then had to grab her arm before she wound up under the horse instead.

"No, ma'am, don't never get up on that side of a horse," Dobber said, and guided Hallie to the other side of Sugarfoot.

"Why?" she asked.

He shoved his hat to the back of his head, scratching at the sparse growth of hair beneath.

"Well, just because," he muttered, and then he squinted against the sun, his expression drawn and serious. "If you was drivin' a car, would you get in on the side without a steerin' wheel?"

Hallie paused. The image made her smile.

"No."

"All right, then," Dobber said. "There's your reason."

Hallie grinned as she climbed into the saddle.

Joe Dobbs's analogy didn't really hold water, but he was too endearing to argue with.

"Now then," he said. "You just hold on to that pommel. I'm gonna lead you around the arena a bit until you get the feel of the saddle."

"What's a pommel?" Hallie asked.

Dobber grinned and pointed. "That thing you're holdin' on to."

"Oh."

"All right now, little lady. You just hang on. Let

yourself feel the rhythm of the horse and as they say, go with the flow."

They started to move, and Hallie clenched the pommel with both hands, resisting the urge to lean forward and wrap her arms around Sugarfoot's neck. But the longer she rode, the more comfortable she became. When Dobber glanced back to see how she was faring, she grinned and dared a wave.

He grinned back.

A few minutes later, he handed her the reins, with a few terse instructions about how to turn a horse from right to left and how to make it stop. Hallie was stunned to learn it wasn't the word *whoa* that did the trick. It was the tug on the reins and the pressure of a bit inside the horse's mouth.

"Won't it hurt her?" Hallie asked.

Dobber shook his head. "Nah. Their mouths are pretty tough. 'Sides, that's the point. You pull on the reins. She don't like the pressure. She stops walkin' so you'll stop pullin', get it?"

Hallie laughed. "Got it."

"All righty, then. You have a go at it by yourself, and don't panic none. The corral is round, so Sugarfoot ain't goin' nowhere and I won't be far."

The world looked different from the back of a horse. Hallie nodded, then took the reins with the confidence of a woman who'd been riding for years and nudged the horse's flanks as she'd been taught. Sure enough, Sugarfoot started to walk.

Hallie laughed aloud.

* * *

Jake was coming out of the tack room with a handful of bridles in need of repair when he heard the sound of her laughter again. He stopped in midstep, searching the area. Then he saw her in the corral on the back of old Sugarfoot and smiled. For a tenderfoot, she sat a horse real fine. Her back was straight, her legs gripping the sides of the horse's belly as old Dobber had told her to do. The reins were loose in her hands and she was riding the horse's rhythm almost perfectly.

A natural.

He wondered if loving came as easily to her and then took a deep, shuddering breath.

Where the hell had that come from? The woman was here for two weeks and then she would leave, just like the other paying guests. Jake didn't mind his brothers flirting with the single ladies. In fact, he knew some came expecting it. But he drew the line at casual, recreational sex. Besides the fact that it wasn't his cup of tea, he didn't want the guest ranch getting the wrong kind of reputation. So then, why did he fantasize about kissing her—and taking her clothes off that dynamite body?

Slowly.

One button, one item, at a time.

He shuddered, then stood in the drive with the bridles trailing in the dust, staring at the dark-haired rider while his stomach tied itself in knots.

* * *

On the fourth day of Hallie's vacation, she was up at dawn and although it was more than an hour before breakfast, she was already dressed. She was wearing a pair of form-fitting jeans, a long-sleeved shirt and light jacket, and her new, but very dusty, brown cowboy boots. Excited about the ensuing trail ride, she bolted out of the cabin, heading toward the stables to tell Sugarfoot hello.

The day was cool, but the air held a promise of later warmth. Dust poofed on the toes of her boots as she ran, eager to feed her horse the bits of apple she'd saved from last night's supper.

A wrangler was coming out of a stall with an empty bucket as she rounded the door.

"Mornin' ma'am," he said softly, and tipped his hat. "Somethin' I can do for you?"

Hallie gave him a tentative smile. "Um, I was just going to see Sugarfoot...if it's okay."

He grinned. "Third stall down on your right," he offered.

Hallie started on past.

"You be real careful when you feed her," he said. "She has a tendency to take fingers along with her treat."

Hallie flushed. So, her early-morning trips weren't so secret after all.

"Is it okay...to feed her, I mean?"

The wrangler smiled and his eyes disappeared in the wrinkles.

"I reckon so. A little treat never hurt anyone now and then."

A horse nickered behind her. She spun around. Sugarfoot was poking her head over the stall door.

"Well, good morning to you, too," Hallie said, and started digging in her jacket pocket for the apple she'd cut up.

Moments later, she and the horse were head to head, passing the time with a little fruit and a little love. She couldn't remember ever feeling so satisfied with herself or with the world.

Jake came around the corner of the stables with a cup of coffee in one hand and a biscuit in the other. Today was Stenson's day off, which meant Jake would be taking the riders to the line camp for the picnic lunch. His mind was on the trail ride and the equipment they would need until he heard the sound of a woman's voice. He looked up and then stopped.

It was Hallie. She had her arms around a horse's neck and her cheek against its forehead. The communion of woman to animal was stunning. For a second, he wished he could trade places with that horse, and then frowned and took a big bite of his biscuit. He was going to have to find a way to get over fantasizing about a woman who was just passing through his life. For all he knew, she could be married. At the least, she was bound to be in a serious relationship. No one who looked like that could be free.

He chewed angrily, washing the bite down with a sip of coffee, then took a deep breath and started toward her.

"Morning, Miss O'Grady. You're up early."

Hallie spun. Even though his silhouette was all she could see, she knew him by the swagger in his walk and the tilt of his hat. Her heart skipped a beat.

"I uh...I mean the horse..."

"You've taken quite a shine to Sugarfoot, I see."

Hallie relaxed and turned back to the horse, running her hand up the blaze on Sugarfoot's head.

"Yes. She's wonderful," Hallie said softly.

The tenderness in her voice, as well as her touch, cut the ground from under his feet. *Look at me, Hallie O'Grady. Touch me like you're touching that horse and I'll show you wonderful.*

Hallie was still smiling as she looked up.

Jake groaned beneath his breath.

"So, you're from California, right?"

She nodded.

"It's a long way to come by yourself to have fun," he said.

She gave him a considering look, then answered. "It was a birthday present."

"From your husband?" he asked.

"I'm not married."

"Boyfriend?"

She leaned against the wall of the stable and

stuffed her hands in her pockets so he wouldn't see them shaking.

"Not one of those, either. The trip was a present from my sisters."

He nodded and took another bite of biscuit to keep from saying something stupid—like hallelujah.

Hallie sighed. Her initial excitement about his questions was tapering off. What's wrong with you, she thought. He isn't interested. He's just being polite, which in spite of her disappointment, didn't surprise her. The men she liked weren't usually attracted to her. Why should this one be any different?

"That biscuit looks good," she finally said. "I suppose I'd better head for the dining room to breakfast. I don't want to be late for the trail ride."

Jake stifled another groan. He hadn't seen the sign-up sheet for the trail ride, although he should have suspected she would be going. She'd taken to her riding lessons with a diligence his father would have been proud of.

"Think you're up for the ride?" he asked.

Hallie nodded. "Oh, yes," she said. "Dobber says I'm a natural."

Jake knew he was staring. "I'll just bet you are," he muttered beneath his breath.

"What did you say?" Hallie asked.

He blinked. "Uh…I said, we're not going far."

She grinned and nodded. "Yes, I know. That's why I signed up for this ride, rather than the overnight one. I figure half a day on horseback is enough for a start."

"Yes, ma'am."

"Please call me Hallie."

His voice was quiet, just above a whisper as he repeated her name.

"Hallie," he said, then exhaled softly, watching as she gave Sugarfoot one last pat.

"I'll see you soon," Hallie said, and smiled as she moved past him.

"Yeah, soon," he muttered, turning to watch as she hurried toward the mess hall.

He watched until she was completely out of sight, then looked down at his hand in disbelief. The biscuit he'd been eating was crushed between his fingers. He opened his hand, letting the crumbs fall into the dirt.

"I've got to get a grip," he admitted to himself, then downed the last of his coffee and headed for the tack room to get ready for the ride.

Chapter 3

The day was clear and cool. Earlier, gentle digs about saddle sores and greenhorns had been rampant. Just into their second hour in the saddle, the riders' excitement was beginning to dim.

But not Hallie's. Sugarfoot had a smooth, steady gait, and nothing could quell her delight. She kept wishing she'd brought a tape recorder along to record her impressions of the country through which they were riding so she could use them in her stories. But she hadn't, and so she tried to capture it all in her memory, from the scent of sage and the ever present mesquite, to the smell of the horses and the creak of saddle leather, even the way dust tasted on her lips.

A swift gust of wind shifted the hat she was wearing and she grabbed at the brim, pulling it down a little bit tighter. Every now and then the sound of Jake Miracle's voice would drift back to her from where she rode, and she would listen to the deep, steady nuances of his speech. The calm reassurance in his voice and the gentle praise and coaxing he gave the timid riders who were with him was almost hypnotic. More than once, she would blink to realize she had no idea of the scenery they'd been passing. Reminding herself that this trip wouldn't last forever, she made herself focus.

She rode next to the last in the group of twelve. Not because she couldn't keep up, but because she was, by nature, an observer. And it was because of her proximity that she noticed the woman just ahead of her seem to be in pain. Although Hallie had seen her around the ranch with her husband, for some reason, he hadn't come on the ride. But when the woman suddenly doubled over the saddle, Hallie urged Sugarfoot forward.

"Ma'am, are you all right?" she asked.

"My name is Cheryl," she said, and managed a grin. "And, yes, I'm fine."

But Hallie didn't agree. The woman was pale and sweating, her eyes glazed with pain.

"Are you sure? I could ask Jake to stop and—"

"No!" Cheryl cried. "I'm fine. I insist."

Hallie sighed. "If you say so, but I'm right behind you, okay?"

She managed a smile and nodded as Hallie dropped back into place.

Minutes passed, during which time, Hallie's thoughts shifted to contemplating the width of Jake Miracle's shoulders. When he suddenly reined up and turned sideways in the saddle, she found herself staring directly at his face. Jake's gaze shifted subtly as he surveyed the riders behind him, but she knew that she'd been caught. She pulled back on the reins. Thankfully, Sugarfoot stopped.

"We're going to take a fifteen-minute rest here," Jake said, pointing to a small stand of mesquite and an adjoining patch of shade from an overhanging bluff. "Within the next hour, we'll be moving steadily upward. We should get to the line cabin for lunch just before noon."

A chorus of appreciative grunts and groans met his announcement. He grinned, and swung down from his horse, letting the reins trail in the dust as he turned to face the riders.

"Tie your horses to the mesquite and rest your bones," he ordered.

No one argued.

Hallie dismounted, grateful to be able to stretch her legs, and pretended not to notice that Jake was heading her way. But when he took Sugarfoot's reins from her hands and deftly tied them to a nearby mesquite, she was forced to look at him.

"Thank you," she said. "But I could have done that myself."

Jake felt like a teenager—all hands and feet and a big, stupid grin he kept trying to hide.

"Just helping, Miss O'Grady."

She smiled back at him and reached for her canteen. He lifted it from the pommel and handed it to her.

"Making it okay?" he asked.

She nodded, then opened the cap and lifted it to her lips, drinking thirstily. A droplet of water was still clinging to the edge of her mouth as she lowered the canteen. She licked it off as she replaced the cap, then hung it back on her saddle.

"How much farther to the line camp?" she asked.

The moment her little pink tongue had snaked out from between her lips in search of the water, his focus had locked on it, and the pearly sheen it had left behind. In the midst of considering what kissing her would be like, he completely missed the question she'd asked.

"Jake?"

He jumped, hoping a guilty conscience wouldn't show. "I'm sorry, what did you say?"

"I asked how much farther we have to go."

As far as he was concerned, not damn far enough. He was sorely tempted to drag her off into the bushes and kiss her senseless, but there were too many witnesses.

"Before we do what?" he muttered.

Hallie put her hands on her hips in a gesture her family would have recognized as one of impatience.

"Eat. I'm getting hungry."

Jake's gut knotted as the wind suddenly gusted, blowing a strand of her hair across his face. He stood mute before her as if he'd been slapped.

Hungry? Woman, you don't know the meaning of the word.

His silence only fed her growing frustration. Muttering something to herself about good-looking men with no brains, she plopped herself down in some shade. Before he could redeem himself, one of the other riders called out to him, diverting his attention. He touched the brim of his hat and then nodded.

"Excuse me a minute," he said, and strode away.

Hallie's belly knotted as she watched his easy swagger. Never in her life had she been around a man who exuded so much masculinity without even trying. Disgusted with herself, she tossed her hat to one side, then leaned back and closed her eyes, thankful for the solidity of earth beneath her backside and the cool feel of wind against her scalp.

Almost at the point of dozing, she heard a low moan and looked up. It was Cheryl again, only this time, she was lying on her side and doubled up in obvious pain. Within seconds, Hallie was on her knees at her side.

"Cheryl, are you sick?"

"Hurt...stomach hurts," Cheryl moaned.

Hallie looked up, searching the area for Jake and saw him a distance away, tightening the girth on a saddle.

"Jake!"

The fear in her voice pulled him around. When he saw her on her knees and the other woman on the ground, he started to run. Within seconds, he was beside her.

"What happened? Did she fall?"

The woman grabbed her side and moaned even louder.

"No," Hallie said. "She's in pain. I thought so earlier, but she denied it. Now..."

Jake's face was clouded with concern. "Mrs. Packston?"

Hallie touched Jake's arm. "Cheryl. Her name is Cheryl."

Jake nodded a thanks as he brushed his hand across the woman's forehead."

"She feels a bit feverish," he said.

"Maybe it's appendicitis. One of my sisters had an attack like this last year. She had to have surgery."

"I hurt," Cheryl said. "Please, I need to get to a doctor."

"Don't worry," Jake assured her. "We'll get help." Then he looked at Hallie. "There's a two-way radio in my saddle bag."

Hallie was off and running before he had time to ask her to get it. She returned moments later with the rest of the group behind her. She dropped back to her knees and handed it to him.

Jake took it thankfully. Seconds later the radio crackled, then came to life.

"Luke? John? This is Jake. Are you there? Over."

Static again, then the familiar sound of John Miracle's voice filled the air.

"This is John, big brother. What do you need? Over."

"I've got a rider down. It's Cheryl Packston. She's sick and complaining of severe abdominal pain. I'm about halfway to the line camp. Over."

The jest in John's voice was noticeably missing. "You want an ambulance or do you want me to come get her? Over?"

Jake glanced at Hallie. The concern on her face mirrored his own.

"I think that will take too long," he said. "Get me a helicopter up here, and fast. She may have a hot appendix. Over."

"Will do, big brother. Over and out."

"We should get her out now," a man said. "If we wait, she could die."

"No! If you move her, it could be worse!" another argued.

Jake stood abruptly. "Is anyone here trained in the medical profession?"

"No," a man grumbled. "But I still think we—"

Jake put his hand on the man's shoulders. It was at once a comfort and a warning that he was the one in control.

"Sir, it would be a big help to me if you could take everyone here back to the shade. The quieter it is for Cheryl, the better she will probably feel, don't you think?"

Shamefaced, the man nodded, then straightened as he turned to the crowd.

"Come on, people. Let's give her some room."

The woman groaned, then grabbed at Hallie's wrist.

"Please…Miss, someone needs to tell Paul."

"Is that your husband?" Hallie asked.

Tears seeped from the corners of the woman's eyes. "Yes. We've been married twenty-one years this week. This trip was my anniversary present."

Jake touched her cheek. "Don't worry, Mrs. Packston. John will tell him."

She closed her eyes. Jake saw her biting her lip to keep from crying aloud.

"Is it bad?" he asked.

"Let's just say I'd rather be in labor," she muted, then rolled as a fresh wave of pain bent her double.

Hallie pulled off her jacket and rolled it up, fashioning a makeshift pillow to get Cheryl's head out of the dirt.

"There, that should feel better," she said.

"Don't leave me," Cheryl moaned, and grabbed at Hallie's hand.

"Don't worry, sweetheart," Hallie whispered. "They couldn't beat me away with a stick."

Jake touched Hallie's shoulder, then motioned

that he was moving away to use the radio again. She nodded, understanding that there were some things he might need to say to John that Cheryl Packston didn't need to hear.

He walked a short distance away. "John, this is Jake. Are you there? Over."

"Jake, it's me, Luke. John's gone to get Mr. Packston. Mediflight is on the way. Should be there in less than ten minutes. Over."

Jake breathed a sigh of relief. "Thank God. Over."

"Is there anything else we can do from our end? Over."

Jake's voice came through to Luke loud and clear. "A prayer couldn't hurt. Over and out."

Eight minutes later, the familiar sound of an approaching helicopter sent everyone scrambling to their feet. They began waving their arms to make themselves visible in the midst of the rocky terrain.

When Hallie saw the chopper beginning its decent, she made the sign of the cross, then bent over Cheryl's body, protecting her as best she could from the flying debris stirred up by the downdraft of the blades.

"What is it?" the woman muttered, barely aware of the noise.

"Cheryl, help is here. You're going to be all right," Hallie said, and gave her fingers a squeeze.

Within minutes, the chopper had lifted off, taking the ailing woman to safety. They watched it go until it disappeared from sight, and then Jake called the group together. He could tell by the expressions on their faces that the joy of the day had dimmed considerably for them.

"Okay, my friends, we've got a decision to make. Do you want to continue on to the picnic, or do you want to go back to the ranch?"

It was almost a unanimous consensus to go back to the ranch.

No one grumbled or complained as they mounted up and headed back in the direction that they'd come.

Once again, Jake reached for his radio.

"Luke, this is Jake. Come in. Over."

Again, static crackled before Luke Miracle's voice came over the airways.

"This is Luke. Over."

"They're on their way to the hospital at Waco. Make sure someone goes with Mr. Packston. Over."

"Already done. Over."

"Good," Jake said. "I need you to notify the line camp to pack it in. The group took a vote. We're coming back to the ranch. Over."

"Will do, Jake. Anything else? Over."

Jake sighed. "No, little brother. See you later. Over and out."

Then he grabbed the reins of the extra horse and looped them across the pommel of his saddle as he started to mount.

"Need any help?" Hallie asked.

Startled by the sound of her voice, he paused, and turned. "No, honey, I don't," he said softly, taking pleasure in the soft flush that slipped up her cheeks. "But thank you for asking."

Hallie nodded, then retraced her steps to where she'd left Sugarfoot and mounted as well. The aftermath of the trauma was catching up with everyone. The isolation in which they'd been riding, as well as the lack of what society called luxuries, had become blatantly noticeable. Suddenly, there was nothing more important than getting back to civilization.

Jake was anxious to get back to the ranch and check on Cheryl Packston's condition. Even though what had happened to her was not his fault, he still felt a certain amount of responsibility. When the rooftops of the ranch finally came into view, he breathed a quiet sigh of relief.

Jewel Franklin's disappointment in finding Jake Miracle absent on her arrival had been tempered by the knowledge that he was en route back to the ranch with a group of riders. Three days ago in Dallas, her date had taken her to dinner and then taken her for a ride she hadn't counted on. She had awakened the next morning with a hangover and a missing credit card to boot. Now, the police were on the trail of the wayward gigolo while she was forced to face the fact that she'd been had. For a day she'd moped and stewed, then had decided to soothe her injured pride by retreating to her favorite getaway, the Miracle Ranch. But it wasn't the fresh air and clean living that kept drawing her back. It was Jake. In all her life, he was the first man she hadn't been able to control, and bedding him had become her ultimate goal.

"Ooh, there they come now," she squealed, and climbed down from the fence on which she'd been sitting as a group of riders topped a distant hill and started toward the ranch.

"Careful, Miss Franklin. You don't want to bust them britches you're wearin'" Dobber said, then turned and spit a stream of tobacco into the dust.

Jewel Franklin's baby-doll features puckered as she frowned at the little man.

"That's a disgusting habit," she muttered, as she brushed at the seat of her too tight pants and checked the buttonholes in her red western shirt, making sure that all the buttons were safely in place. With her buxom body, one never assumed.

"Yes, ma'am, it sure is," Dobber said, but he stayed his ground.

All the hands at the Miracle Ranch had their orders from the boss when it came to this woman. Jewel Franklin was in no way, ever, to be encouraged. Yet constantly being thwarted had not deterred her. She'd set her mind on Jake Miracle, and no matter how many times he had politely refused her overtures, she kept coming back to try again. She was as aggravating and persistent as a flea on a crippled dog.

Jewel shaded her eyes with her hand, trying to find Jake in the midst of the riders. If they were only a little closer, she would be able to tell. She knew everything there was to know about him, right down to the fact that he ate his pancakes with sorghum molasses and his biscuits without butter. All she had to do was find a way to remind Jake that blondes really did have more fun.

When she started moving toward the stables, Dobber stepped in front of her.

"Say, Miss Franklin, if you don't hurry, you're gonna miss lunch. The chef is fixin' a real good meal all special. Fried chicken, cream gravy and all the trimmins'."

Jewel wrinkled her nose as she pushed past him. "I'll wait and eat with Jake," she said, and headed toward the stables at a trot.

Dobber rolled his eyes and threw up his hands, muttering to himself as he walked away.

John Miracle came around the corner of the barn just as Dobber started inside. He took one look at Dobber's face and started to grin.

"What's wrong with you?" he asked.

Dobber pointed back toward the stables. "It's that Franklin woman. She's back and movin' in on Jake like one of them heat seekin' miss-iles. I tries to head 'er off, but you know how she can be. She saw the riders comin' and headed for the stables, probably plannin' on givin' Jake one of her welcomes, if you know what I mean."

John paled. The last time she'd come, she'd greeted Jake like a long-lost lover, and not her host.

"Oh, man, not now," John muttered.

Dobber frowned. "Jake done told us he didn't want nothin' to do with her. What's so different about now?"

"I think Jake might be sweet on that O'Grady woman."

"Jake? Are you sure? He ain't never...uh... indulged like that before."

"Well, all I can say is, he gave Luke and me go-to-hell looks at the dance the other night for flirting with her, and he's been dogging her footsteps all over the place. I catch him looking at her all the time."

Dobber spit again. Jake was a notorious loner. It was difficult to imagine him smitten by anyone.

"Well, I'll be damned." Then he spun suddenly. "What if she's the one? Lordy, that Jewel woman could be messin' up a real good thing."

"Exactly," John said, and made a run for the stables, hoping he could head Jewel off before the riders came in.

Less than a quarter of a mile from the ranch, Jake dropped back until he was side by side with Hallie. The tentative smile she gave him was all he needed to see. He gave the brim of her hat a teasing thump then winked at her.

"You did real good back there," he said.

Hallie felt herself smiling. His praise was unexpected, but oh so welcome.

"Thank you. I suppose being the oldest of four girls has its benefits. My sisters think I'm bossy. I like to think I'm forthright."

He laughed, and the sound felt good. On the contrary, he'd found her easy to be around. In fact, he couldn't remember when he'd felt so relaxed around a woman.

"Yeah, I know a little about that eldest child thing myself."

They rode a few more feet in silence, and then both spoke at once.

"Sorry," Hallie said. "You first."

Jake shook his head. "No way, honey," he said gently. "Out here, ladies are always first."

If she hadn't been so high off the ground, Hallie would have done a little dance. Honey. He called her honey, again. Was that just a Texan way of being friendly, or did it mean what she wanted it to mean?

"Okay. Then here goes. I was just curious. How long have you been doing this job?"

"About ten years. It was John's idea. Saved the family ranch from bankruptcy after our parents died."

Her face crinkled with concern. Even at her age,

she couldn't imagine what it would be like without her mother and father.

"I'm sorry. That must have been a tough time for you."

He shrugged. "It's past."

"Now, it's your turn to ask a question," she said.

He glanced up at the riders ahead, making sure that everyone was still okay, then gave her a slow, considering look.

"I was just curious," he said.

"About what?"

"Why you aren't attached?"

She frowned. "Attached?"

"Why you're single. Footloose. You know... available?" Then he realized how personal he'd become and quickly apologized. "Sorry," he muttered. "I suppose none of this is my business."

Hallie's heart skipped a beat, but she refused to let herself hope that this was more than idle chatter.

"No, it's okay," she said. "I suppose it's because I'm probably too independent and too particular."

He nodded. "Nothing wrong with that."

They rode in silence a minute or two longer. Finally, Jake tried again.

"So, you're planning on coming to the dance tonight, aren't you?"

She nodded. "I'm still learning some of the steps, but it's a lot of fun. All your employees, including your brothers, have been very helpful in teaching me."

"I'd consider it an honor if you'd save a couple of dances for me," he said.

Hallie's heart skipped a beat, but she kept reminding herself he was just being courteous. This didn't have to mean a thing.

"Sure," she said. "But I didn't know you liked to dance. I've never seen you out on the floor."

"I like it just fine...with the right partner."

Her heart skipped another beat. *Oh, Lord, is he really flirting...with me?*

"Besides," Jake added. "It'll give me a real good excuse to put my arms around you, which is what I've been thinking about for most of the morning."

This time she made no pretense of hiding her shock. *He is! Jake Miracle is flirting with me!*

In spite of her excitement, she managed to maintain her composure. She gave him a long, slow look, taking note of the gleam in his eyes and the muscle jerking at the side of his jaw and then shook her head.

"I don't know whether to believe you or not," she said.

"Why?" he asked.

"Because in my experience, men aren't usually interested in a woman like me."

A dark flush spread up his neck and he gave her a sidelong glance. "I don't know where you come from," he finally said. "But the men must all be fools."

Hallie let herself grin. "Why, Mr. Miracle, is that a compliment?"

The gleam in his eyes disappeared, leaving them completely unreadable.

"Do you want it to be?"

She held her breath, almost afraid to answer. And then she reminded herself that coming here had been a gift, and she'd been brought up to believe that it was a sin to refuse a gift. The least he deserved was her honesty.

"Yes, Jake, I believe that I do."

He reached for her hand. "Then I've—"

But before he could finish, a shrill feminine squeal drifted into the air. Startled, he looked up.

"Oh, holy hell," he muttered.

Hallie followed the direction of his gaze, staring in disbelief at the curvy blonde running toward them and calling Jake's name. Even from here, the bouncing breasts and flyaway hair were impossible to miss. It was Hallie's worst nightmare all over again.

Jake reined up, then turned in the saddle to look Hallie square in the face.

"Look, Hallie, this is not what it seems."

She reined up, too, then dismounted. "You mean that woman is a hallucination?"

Jake dismounted as well, grabbing at her arm before she could move away. A dark flush spread up his neck.

"No, but—"

"Jake! Darling! I didn't think you'd ever get back!"

They turned. Jake tried to move, but he was a little too late. Before he could say anything, the blonde had wrapped her arms around his neck and planted an open-mouthed kiss in the middle of his lips.

Disgusted with herself for believing that anyone like Jake Miracle would ever be seriously interested in someone like her, Hallie took Sugarfoot's reins and led her toward the stables. In the background, she could hear the woman's lighthearted giggles and Jake's husky growl. She just bit her lip and kept on walking.

Chapter 4

Hallie strode toward the stables with her chin held high. The smile on her face was as fake as the bounce in her step as she handed Sugarfoot's reins to a wrangler and headed toward her cabin.

"Hey, Missy, how did the ride go?"

Hallie looked up. It was Dobber. She made herself smile and wave, but she kept on walking. Even though she felt like a coward, she didn't have it in her to face anyone. She kept seeing that curvy blonde with her arms around Jake Miracle's neck and her mouth upon his lips.

You're stupid, stupid, stupid, Hallie O'Grady. It's your own fault for believing his lies.

But the mental castigation she was giving herself

didn't help the pain in her heart. For a short while, she'd let herself believe that Jake liked her. It hurt like hell to know he'd just been fooling around.

"Hallie, aren't you going to eat lunch?"

She looked up to see the couple who were staying in the cabin next to hers.

"I'll be along later," she said. "I want to wash up."

She kept on walking. Food was the last thing on her mind. A sudden film of tears blurred her vision and she stumbled, then started to run. She had to get to the cabin. The last thing she wanted was for someone to see her cry. Moments later, she reached the porch, fumbled in her pocket for the key and then let herself in. Only after the door was shut and locked behind her did she let herself go. Tears slid from her eyes and ran down her cheeks as she dropped onto the side of the bed.

"Oh, Lordy," she muttered, and tossed her hat across the room.

It landed on the floor next to her tennis shoes. The incongruity of the items hit her like a fist to the belly. Tennis shoes and cowboy hats didn't match and neither did she and Jake.

She lay back onto the mattress and flopped an arm across her eyes, willing herself to stop crying. It hurt to accept, but Jake Miracle had led her on and she'd believed him. The worst of it was, it was her own fault. She'd come here looking for love, and as the old country song went, in all the wrong places. She should have paid attention to her good senses instead of her heart. There was no such thing as making love happen. If it wasn't spontaneous, it wasn't real.

In the midst of her misery, her stomach suddenly growled. The traitorous sound made her laugh. So, her heart was a little bit broken, but obviously not enough to stifle her need to sustain life.

She dragged herself up from the bed and stalked to the bathroom, sloshing water on her face and then scrubbing it dry with a towel. She glared at herself in the mirror. Her eyes were red, her hair was a mess, but what the hell. So she got a little dust in her eyes and she looked like she'd been rolled in the hay. She was on vacation. This time next month, these people would be nothing more than a memory. With a heartfelt sigh, she ran a brush through her hair and tucked her shirt into the waistband of her jeans. Her daddy had taught her to face her disappointments as readily as she faced her enemies. It was one lesson she'd learned all too well.

Jake was beside himself with frustration. By the time he'd unwound himself from Jewel's arms, Hallie was nowhere in sight. He handed the reins of his horses to one of the wranglers, all too aware of the woman still clutching his arm.

"Jake, we must sit together at lunch. I have tons of things to tell you."

He looked at her in disbelief. What the hell would

it take for this woman to get the message that he just wasn't interested? It was all he could do not to throttle her.

"I'm sorry," he said. "But I have to tend to some business. One of the riders was taken ill during the ride. I need to check on her condition."

"Oh, no! How awful for you." Then she leaned a little closer, pouting her lips and lowering her voice. "Then we'll touch base at the dance later tonight."

Before he could argue, she winked and blew him a kiss, then sauntered off.

He headed toward the office, cursing fate every step of the way. Why did she have to show up now? As he walked, he caught himself listening for Hallie's laughter, hoping to catch a glimpse of her face. He groaned, remembering the stiff set to her shoulders as she'd walked away from him at the barns.

He wanted—no—he needed to explain. He didn't want to lose Hallie's good graces—and anything else that might have developed. She was the first woman in years who'd stirred his interest and by damn, he wasn't going to lose her before he found out if she felt the same way.

"Jake! There you are. I've been looking all over for you."

He looked up. The concern on Luke's face made him panic. What if Mediflight had been too late?

"Cheryl Packston. Is she all right?"

Luke nodded vehemently. "Yeah, didn't mean to

scare you,'' he said. ''In fact, her husband just called. It *was* her appendix. They caught it just before it ruptured. She's in recovery and doing fine. He said to tell you thank you a hundred times over for sending the helicopter. It probably saved her life.''

A burden lifted from his heart. ''That's good, but the diagnosis wasn't mine. It was Hallie O'Grady who made the guess. I just followed suit.''

Luke rolled his eyes and then snapped his fingers.

''Speaking of women,'' he muttered. ''That's what I was coming to tell you. Jewel Franklin is back.''

Jake gritted his teeth. ''I know.''

Luke grinned wryly. ''Sorry, but what do we do?''

''Wipe that damned smile off your face,'' Jake muttered. ''She's here, so we'll just have to deal with her. But you better spread the word. If she calls for a reservation again, tell her we're all full up.''

Luke chuckled. ''And what if we're not?''

Jake poked a finger against his little brother's chest.

''All I'm telling you is, the next person who takes her reservation is fired.''

Hallie would have sworn she'd never be able to eat a bite of food again. But that was before she'd seen the spread at lunch. Besides fried chicken, there was corn bread, brown beans and ham, cole slaw, fried potatoes and what looked like enough peach cobbler to feed the Dallas Cowboys football team. She dug into the food with abandon, certain she'd never tasted anything so fine.

Halfway through her meal, she got up to get a second helping of corn bread and found herself face-to-face with the buxom blonde. Through chatty table partners and an overzealous waitress who'd identified the newcomer in the dining room as a regular to the ranch, Hallie now knew her name.

Jewel Franklin.

Jewel recognized Hallie as the woman who'd been riding beside Jake and eyed her somewhat like she might have a dirty-faced child.

"Excuse me!" she drawled, and stepped aside, as if standing too close to Hallie might in some way contaminate her.

"Oh, that's okay," Hallie said. "You're not in my way."

She reached in front of Jewel for a piece of corn bread, broke it open and slathered a huge hunk of butter between the slabs. Then, licking her fingers, she headed back to her table. She couldn't see Jewel's stare, but she felt it just the same.

Dobber sauntered by Hallie's table on his way back to the buffet table for seconds. He glanced at Jewel and then gave Hallie a wink.

"Better watch your step, little one. If looks could kill, you'd be toes up in the dust."

Hallie plopped her corn bread onto her plate, then

covered the entire hunk with a dollop of sorghum molasses.

"Whatever," she muttered, forking a big bite of the food. "But I'm not going anywhere, not even to hell, until I've finished my food."

Dobber grinned. He liked this one more and more every day.

"For whatever it's worth, I'm in your corner," he drawled, and then headed for the beans.

The woman across the table frowned as she leaned forward.

"That's an odd little man, don't you think? And whatever did he mean by 'if looks could kill?' Is someone angry with you?"

Hallie swallowed her bite and washed it down with a sip of iced tea before answering.

"He doesn't seem odd to me. In fact, I think he's sort of cute, but then my family believes in leprechauns, you know, so I could be prejudiced."

The woman laughed. "I suppose so." She gave Hallie's arm a squeeze. "I don't know what's going on, and as my husband so fondly likes to remind me, I suppose it's none of my business. But if you need a friend, you know where we are."

Hallie laid down her fork and gave her table companion a smile.

"Thanks, but I'm sure it's nothing."

Then she saw movement at the door. It was Jake, and he was looking around the room, obviously in search of someone special. Probably Jewel Franklin, she thought, and ignored the twinge in her heart. But when he suddenly saw her and headed her way, she froze.

"I've been looking all over for you," Jake said, and then slipped into the empty chair next to her.

Hallie's mouth dropped. "You have?"

He nodded at the other people around the table, then focused on her. "I thought you would want to know that Cheryl Packston came out of surgery just fine. And you were right. It was her appendix."

"Wow," Hallie said, and leaned back in her chair. "Thanks for telling me. I've been thinking about her ever since the helicopter took her away."

Jake smiled, then absently glanced at her plate, focusing on the corn bread she'd been eating. A surprised grin spread across his face as he pointed at her food.

"So...you like that, do you?"

Hallie knew she was gawking at Jake, but for the life of her she couldn't quit. And to her dismay, she could see Jewel Franklin staring at them from across the room. The last thing she wanted was to get in the middle of a lover's tiff.

"Like what?' she mumbled.

"Sorghum molasses."

She managed a grin. "As my five-year-old niece often says, it's my new best thing."

He laughed, and without thinking, reached over and wiped at a tiny smear of sorghum on her lower lip and then licked it off of his thumb.

"I'm with you all the way on that," he said. Then he stood abruptly. "Save me a seat," he said. "I'll be right back."

Shocked by what he'd just done, it was all Hallie could do to speak.

"But what about her?" she asked.

Jake didn't have to look to know who she was talking about. He could guess.

"What about her?"

"I thought you...I mean, aren't you two...?"

He stared her straight in the eyes. "No."

She waited for further explanation. It didn't come.

"I'm going to get some food. Are you still going to be here when I get back?" he asked.

Still reeling from the feel of his thumb on her lip, she managed a nod.

Jake hid a huge sigh of relief and walked away.

The woman across the table giggled at Hallie. "Oh, honey, I think he's sweet on you."

Hallie rolled her eyes. "At my age, I have learned not to put credence in fantasies."

An elderly man at the end of the table cleared his throat and then stood.

"If you kind people will excuse me, I feel a nap coming on."

One by one, the other people began to leave until Hallie found herself alone. At that point, something inside her began to quiver. Was it hope? Or could it be that last piece of corn bread threatening to come up? Either way, the feeling was unnerving.

She reached for her tea and took a long drink. By the time Jake got back to the table, she had her emotions under control.

Jewel was livid and doing a poor job of concealing the fact. Not once had Jake ever sought her out as he had that skinny little bitch. She'd spent the better part of two years trying to land that man, if only for a night, and the best she'd gotten out of him was a couple of dances. Before, he'd at least been courteous enough to accept her company, but not today. Less than an hour ago, she'd invited herself to his table and he'd declined. Now she knew why. Certain that all the employees were laughing at her behind her back, she flung her napkin onto her plate and stood up with a jerk, storming out of the dining room as if she'd been set on fire.

Neither Jake nor Hallie saw her go, but Dobber did. He shook his head and took another bite of peach cobbler. They'd better be watching that one, all right. She reminded him of a dog he'd once had. That dog would lick your boots clean and then bite you in the butt when you weren't looking. Yeah, that woman would cause trouble before she was through, or his name wasn't Joe Dobbs.

Hallie was beside herself with anxiety as she dressed for the dance. Blue jeans and boots were the standard, and she'd chosen a long-sleeved white shirt to go with them. Although the walkway between cabins and outbuildings was well lit, it was already dark outside. In deference to the evening chill, she left her hair down. The weight of it brushed against her collar as she leaned forward toward the mirror, peering at a spot on her face. When she realized the spot was on the mirror and not her, she burst out laughing.

And that was what Jake heard as he stepped up on her porch. He paused, then took a deep breath, wondering if she laughed like that when she made love.

"Hell," he mumbled, and made himself focus as he knocked on her door.

Moments later, Hallie was standing in the doorway with the remnant of her laughter still on her face.

"Jake!"

He thought about pushing his way inside and kissing that smile off her face. Instead, he yanked off his hat and managed a smile of his own.

"I thought I might walk you to the dance?"

Hallie's heart skipped a beat. "I'd love it," she said. "Just give me a second. I was about to put on some lipstick."

"Yeah, sure," Jake said, and leaned against the doorjamb, watching as she darted into the bathroom.

He glanced around the cabin, taking note of her neatness, and how everything was hung up and put away. The only thing out of place in the room was a laptop computer in the middle of her bed. He frowned. It just occurred to him that he didn't know what she did for a living.

"Hey, Hallie."

She took a step backward so that she could see him as she ran a brush through her hair one last time.

"Yes?"

"As I was coming up on the porch, I heard you laugh. What was so funny?"

She grinned. "The best jokes are the ones on ourselves."

He nodded slowly, taking careful note of everything about her, from the way she rocked back on the heel of one boot when she was talking, to the haphazard way she was brushing her hair. He'd never met a woman so at ease with herself.

He pointed toward the laptop. "Don't tell me you're one of those people who brings work on a vacation?"

She tossed her hairbrush on the counter and sauntered back into the main room, tucking in her shirt as she went.

"I'm a writer. I never leave home without it."

His whole face lit up. "Really? Are you published?"

She nodded.

"Tell me some titles," he asked. "Maybe I've read some."

She grinned. "Umm, the most recent ones are *Cricket Takes a Vacation*, and *Howie at Mystery*

Mansion.'' Then she added, ''I write children's books.''

The relief on his face was priceless as he absorbed the explanation for the childish titles.

''Then that explains why they're not on my shelf.''

She chuckled. ''Scared you, didn't I?''

He groaned inwardly. Scared? She didn't know the half of it. He wasn't sure, but if he had to hazard a guess, he was halfway to falling in love.

''Never mind,'' Hallie said. ''You don't have to answer.'' Then she gave him a smile. ''Come on, Mr. Miracle. Take me to that dance before you really put your foot in your mouth.''

He grabbed her hand, stopping her motion.

Hallie looked up, the smile still on her face. ''Did we forget something?''

''Just this,'' he said softly, and before she could stop him, he leaned down and brushed his mouth across her lips.

At the moment of contact, Hallie's eyes automatically closed and Jake could have sworn he heard her groan. When he broke contact, she inhaled sharply. He stood, waiting to see if she would slap his face or let it pass.

''I'm not going to apologize for that,'' he warned.

Hallie's eyes were dark with emotion, yet she managed to insert just enough levity into the moment to keep them both on an even keel.

''And your decision was wise, Mr. Miracle. I do

not suffer men who can't make up their minds. You kissed me. I liked it. Let it stand."

He grinned. "You're something, you know that, Hallie?"

"That's what my father says right before he announces that he's washing his hands of me, this time, for sure."

Jake chuckled. "Something tells me he probably says that a lot."

She pretended an insult. "And why would you be saying something like that?"

He grabbed her by the hand and dragged her off the porch. "Does the phrase, 'I refuse to answer on the grounds that it may incriminate me' sound familiar?"

"This is me ignoring you," Hallie said, as she started toward the barn without him. To her delight, he quickly caught up and took her by the hand.

"Considering you are one of only two single women on the ranch tonight, you will not be short of partners, but I'm asking for the first and last dance just the same."

At that moment, she remembered Jewel Franklin. A frown furrowed her forehead and she stopped. The intimacy of darkness gave her the courage to say what she had to say.

"I know a dance is just a dance to you, but if you and Jewel Franklin are having some sort of a fuss, I won't like being used."

Then she looked away, suddenly embarrassed at having been so abrupt.

Jake sighed. After the way Jewel had wrapped herself around him at the stables, it was inevitable that she might think that.

"Look at me," he begged, tugging gently on her hand.

She did as he asked, waiting. He had no way of knowing how much of her hope was riding on his answer.

"Miss Franklin is a guest here. That's all she's ever been, although I will admit that's not what she would like." He could feel the tension in Hallie's hand, and he rubbed at her knuckles with the ball of his thumb, trying to assuage her uneasiness. "There is nothing between us—not now—not ever. I don't have flings and especially not with my guests."

Hallie felt as if he'd thrown cold water on her. But before she could speak, Jake suddenly cupped the side of her face.

"Hallie, don't."

"Don't what?" she muttered.

"Don't look like I just kicked your feet from under you. It makes me feel like hell. Whatever is happening here is not a fling. I like you, Hallie. That hasn't happened to me in a long, long time."

She exhaled slowly, wondering if she looked as faint as she felt. This seesaw of emotions was too hard on her heart. She slid her hand over his, feeling his strength as well as his gentleness.

"Cowboy, that just bought you the first and last dance, and any you so choose in between."

Jake grinned. "That'll do for starters," he drawled, and then took her by the hand. "Come on, honey. Let's go find some people before I forget my manners."

She paused, giving him a pointed stare. "Just don't forget I'm Irish. When it comes to hugging and kissing, manners can well cramp your style."

Then before he could answer, she pulled on his hand and dragged them both toward the light spilling out of the huge barn ahead, following the sound of the music drifting out into the night.

Jewel Franklin had been lying in wait for Jake. But when she saw him coming into the barn dance and holding that woman's hand, she went sick with fury. She set her cup of punch down with a thud and turned her back toward the door, struggling to regain her composure. This, added to the mess she'd left behind her at home, was, as they say, the last straw. She didn't know how, but before she left here again, she would make Jake Miracle sorry he'd shamed her this way.

"Miss Franklin, would you care to dance?"

She looked up to find herself face-to-face with one of the wranglers. It took everything she had, but she made herself smile.

"I'd be delighted."

The wrangler's name was Danny. In Jewel's opinion, he was a poor substitute for Jake Miracle, but he would serve his purpose. She needed to get as close to Jake and Hallie as possible, and what better way than to be danced into their paths? To her dismay, Jake didn't immediately take the woman onto the dance floor, and she was forced to dance through two more dances before things started falling into place.

The band struck up a waltz. At the sound, Jake took Hallie's glass of punch out of her hands and then took her into his arms.

"Miss O'Grady, I believe this dance is mine."

She looked up. His expression was unreadable, but the glitter in his eyes revealed more than he probably knew. She stepped into his embrace as if she'd been doing it all her life.

They circled the floor once, then twice, lost in the music and the heady feeling of being in each other's arms. Just as the music was coming to a close, Jake happened to look up and over Hallie's head to the couple dancing toward them.

"Hang on to your britches, honey. We've got a bogie at six o'clock."

Hallie couldn't help but laugh. "She's just a woman, not a bomb. Besides, none of this would be happening if you weren't such a hunk."

"This isn't funny," he muttered, and then it was too late to do anything but stand his ground.

As Jewel and her partner danced past, she suddenly hauled him to an abrupt halt. Danny the wrangler looked startled, but it was nothing to the hackles that rose on Hallie's back as she took the brunt of Jewel Franklin's stare.

But Jewel refused to acknowledge Hallie's existence, and after a perfunctory glance, she turned her attention to Jake.

"How about trading partners," she asked, and started to slip between Jake and Hallie when Jake stopped her with a shake of his head.

"I don't think so," he said. "The song is over."

Color rose high on Jewel's cheeks. She couldn't believe he would turn her down in such a public manner.

"There'll be others," she insisted, still refusing to let go of his arm.

"I'm sorry," Jake said, "but I've got to relieve Luke at the buffet table."

Jewel was so angry now she was shaking. "There was a time when you weren't so casual with me," she said, and gave Hallie a pointed look, as if to insinuate they had some sort of past.

Jake's chin jutted. Had Jewel known him better, this would have been when she cut her losses and left. But she didn't, and her humiliation was just beginning.

"Miss Franklin, there has never been a time when

I was anything *but* casual with you." Then he gave Danny a pointed look. "I think Miss Franklin looks thirsty."

Thankful for a reason to leave, Danny bailed out of the situation without hesitation.

"I'll be right back," Danny said quickly.

"Don't bother," Jewel said. "If I want something to drink, I'll get it myself."

The wrangler nodded and quickly disappeared.

Hallie was almost as uncomfortable as Danny had been. "Well, I'm thirsty," she said. "I think I'll check out the punch bowl."

Jake reached for her, but she was already moving away.

Jewel sneered, taking no care to lower her voice. "I never would have figured you for the flat-chested, little-girl type."

Hallie froze. Suddenly it was one snide remark too many, and from the wrong quarter. Slowly, she turned, fixing Jewel with a cool, calculated stare. Then she looked at Jake.

"If you walk her back to her cabin tonight, make sure she doesn't stumble and fall." She pointed at Jewel's bountiful breasts. "She might smother herself."

Stunned by her own temerity, she headed for the punch bowl, thankful that neither one of them could see her face.

Jewel hissed. It was the only way to describe her reaction.

Jake grinned before he thought, which only added to Jewel's rage. He tried to regain control of the situation, but it was too late.

"Look," he began. "There is no need to involve Miss O'Grady in your misconceptions about—"

But Jewel didn't stay around to hear what he had to say and Jake found himself alone in the middle of the dance floor, wondering how in hell he'd gotten himself into such a mess.

"I think that went rather well, don't you?"

Jake pivoted to find himself face-to-face with his brother, John, who was grinning from ear to ear.

"Just shut the hell up," he warned, and strode off the dance floor in search of Hallie.

Chapter 5

Hallie's fists were doubled and her cheeks were burning as she made her way out the door.

"Hey, Missy, you better slow down 'fore you hurt someone," Dobber said, and grabbed her by the shoulders just before they collided. The fury in her eyes dampened when she realized it was him.

"Sorry, Dobber. I didn't see you."

"Yeah, I noticed." He looked closer. "Them ain't tears in your eyes, are they?"

She lifted her chin. "Not in this lifetime," she muttered.

He nodded, but when she started to walk past him, he threw out one last remark that stopped her cold.

"I never figured you for a quitter."

She turned, glaring angrily. "I'm not!"

"Then where were you goin'?"

Her shoulders slumped.

"Get back in there and give 'em hell."

She sighed. "Can I ask you something?"

"Shoot," he said.

"Is Jake Miracle for real?"

He scratched the edge of his jaw as he gave her a considering look.

"If you're askin' if he means what he says, then yes. If you're wantin' to know if he's inclined to sweet-talk all the pretty ladies who come through here, then 'scuse my French, but hell, no. I think the boss likes you, and I think you like the boss. Am I right?"

She shrugged, unwilling to bare her heart. "Maybe."

He grinned. "Then fight for what you want, girl. Don't let some duded-up female outgun you, if you know what I mean."

Her voice softened. "What if I'm wrong? People come and go through Jake's life all the time. What makes you think I would be any different to him?"

Dobber shrugged. "I don't know, Missy. Maybe you'd better ask him."

Hallie spun. Jake was coming toward her. She stiffened.

"Stand your ground, girl."

She stood.

Jake had been in a panic until he'd seen her, and

only after he had her by the hand did he breathe a sigh of relief. Then he glanced at Dobber, suddenly aware he'd interrupted more than idle chitchat. He arched a questioning eyebrow. Dobber only shrugged. Jake exhaled slowly. He got the message. If he wanted to know what was going on, he was going to have to ask Hallie.

"Evening, Dobber," Jake said.

"Evenin', boss." Then he hitched up his pants and yanked down on the brim of his Stetson. "Well, now, I reckon I'll be getting' me somethin' to eat and a good seat to watch the rest of the dance." He winked at Hallie. "Evenin', Missy. Remember what I said."

"Thank you, Dobber."

Impulsively, she threw her arms around the old wrangler's neck and gave him a hug. Dobber blushed, but he didn't pull back.

"What was that for?" he asked.

"I don't have to have a reason. I'm a woman, remember?"

Dobber glanced at Jake and then nodded. "That you are, Missy, that you are." He walked away.

It was the glimmer of unshed tears in Hallie's eyes that was Jake's undoing.

"Hallie, I'm sorry."

"For what?" she muttered, and looked away.

But Jake wouldn't let her ignore him. He cupped her cheek, forcing her to meet his gaze.

"For putting you in the middle of something that's not your fault."

She took a deep breath, remembering one of her Grandmother O'Grady's favorite sayings about, in for a penny, in for a pound. *Okay, Jake Miracle, here's where you show me what you're made of.*

"I want to know something," she said shortly.

"Anything."

"Am I really in the middle, or am I just passing through?"

"Honey, that's strictly up to you," he said softly.

Something shifted inside her chest, relieving a persistent knot of misery. She wanted to believe him, but there was too much at stake to take him at his word.

"Come back inside with me," he urged. "You haven't eaten and you still owe me a dance."

She hesitated, frowning. "Okay, but I'm giving you fair warning. I will only take so much from that woman."

He grinned. "God help us all from the wrath of the Irish."

She arched an eyebrow. "Don't push your luck, Miracle. I have a large family with far worse tempers than mine."

He tried not to grin. "Is that a warning, or an invitation to meet them?"

"What do you want it to be?"

His eyes darkened. "A promise."

She paused. "Promise of what?"

"That this isn't over when you leave."

This time, she smiled. "We'll see," she said softly, and let herself be led back inside.

To her relief, Jewel Franklin was nowhere in sight. Time passed in a whirlwind of music and magic. When she wasn't dancing with Jake, she was aware of him watching her from the sidelines, his expression unreadable. As midnight grew nearer, she grew nervous, then anxious. Would he walk her back to her cabin? And if he kissed her again, would once be enough? She alternated between cursing her sisters for putting her in such a fix, and blessing the ground they walked on for setting her in this man's path. When the band leader announced the last song, she turned in place, searching the dance floor. And then she saw him coming toward her—moving in that slow, sexy walk without taking his gaze from her face. She didn't realize she was holding her breath until he reached for her.

"I believe this is my dance."

She exhaled slowly. "Yes."

He swept her into his arms. Hallie assumed there must be music. Other people were smiling and talking as they waltzed around the floor, but she didn't hear it or them. All she could hear was the frantic thump of her heart as Jake waltzed her out the door and into the dark.

"I hope you know where you're going," she said, as they moved farther and farther into the night and away from the light spilling out of the doorway behind them.

Jake stopped, his arms still around her, his mouth only inches away from her face.

"Honey, I haven't known straight up from sideways since I first heard you laugh. I'm scared as hell that I'm feeling something you're not, and that you're gonna walk away from me in five days without a backward glance."

Hallie froze. "I don't—"

He put his finger on her lips, then replaced it with his mouth.

"Please," he whispered. "Give me this much."

His mouth was hard, relentlessly coaxing the shock on her lips until she gave way. She sighed, then she groaned, then she wrapped her arms around his neck.

Jake picked her up off the ground, her feet dangling in midair. Suddenly, her back was against the wall of a building and her breasts were crushed against his chest.

And the kiss went on.

It wasn't until a loud rumble broke the quiet between them that he set her down on her feet and looked up at the sky.

"It's going to rain."

Hallie shuddered. That might be good. She could use a cold shower.

"I'd better get you back to your cabin," he said, and took her by the hand.

They started walking hastily. Halfway there, the first drops began to fall.

"You up for a run?" Jake asked.

Hallie nodded.

A minute later, they reached the porch of her cabin as the rain began to fall in earnest.

"Just in time," Hallie muttered, and fumbled in her pocket for the key.

"Here, let me," Jake said as he took the key from her trembling fingers and unlocked the door.

She stepped inside and turned on the lights, shivering, not from the cold, but from nerves. A flash of lightning suddenly lit up the night and at the same time, all the lights flickered, then went out.

Jake frowned. "Damn," he muttered. "Power's gone. I'd better go check on the guests to make sure they all got back to their cabins."

Hallie sighed. She didn't know whether to view this as a reprieve or a disappointment. She'd wondered how they were going to end this night. Mother Nature had ended it for them.

"I know where a flashlight is," Hallie said. "I'll get it for you."

"Wait here," he offered. "They're all in the same place in the cabins. I'll get it."

He came back with the flashlight and carrying a candlelit hurricane lamp for her.

"Here, this should help, and hopefully the power outage won't last long."

"Thanks," she said.

Bathed in candlelight and shadows, her fragility was even more pronounced. He hated to leave her, but he had a duty to the others, as well.

"Will you be all right until I get back?"

She caught her breath. "You're coming back?"

"If you'll let me."

She hesitated, then sighed. Let him? Lord, yes, she'd let him. She'd let him come back, and hold her, and kiss her, and—

"Yes."

"Hold that thought," Jake said.

She could have sworn he winked and grinned, but then he was gone. She closed the door, started to lock it then hesitated. He said he'd be back. She shrugged and started toward the bedroom.

But what could she do while she waited?

Her gaze fell on her laptop computer. That's what. She could write. It ran on batteries, as well as electricity, and the screen was well lit. It would be like watching TV in the dark.

Jewel had been waiting outside the dance, knowing that when the evening was over, Jake would be one of the last to leave the building. Then, to her dismay, he'd come waltzing out the door with that woman in his arms, and it had been all she could do to stand still. When they'd disappeared into the shadows, she'd followed instinctively. She saw him stop, then heard their whispers, then almost cried aloud when he took the little bitch in his arms. Hate spilled, burning away whatever sense of fair play she might have, in her need for some sort of revenge.

When it thundered suddenly, she jumped, startled by the sound. Sprinkles of rain began falling on her face, and she started to leave, but moving now would reveal her presence, so she was forced to wait for them to make the first move.

Finally, they began to run toward shelter, with her following a distance behind. But when Jake went inside Hallie O'Grady's cabin, something inside Jewel Franklin snapped. Rain was falling harder now and still she stood at the cabin's perimeter, waiting to see if he would come out. When the lights suddenly went out, she groaned aloud, unable to believe that woman had accomplished something in only a few days that she'd been trying to do for two years. It took several moments for her to realize that Jake hadn't turned out the lights in her cabin, but that the power was out everywhere.

Her shoulders slumped. It was time to give up. Although she'd planned to stay a full five days, it wasn't going to happen. Not now. Rain poured down her face, streaking her carefully applied makeup and plastering her hair to her head.

"Damn, damn, damn," she muttered, and started to leave when she saw a small orb of light in Hallie's cabin.

Moments later, Jake came out on the run with a flashlight in his hand. She stepped back against the cabin wall, watching as he ran past her. Again, she started to leave when she saw another light, only this time, it stayed inside the cabin.

It was her.

Jewel paused, staring through the window to the woman beyond. When she was honest with herself, which wasn't often, she would admit that the only thing that had ever been between her and Jake Miracle was her own persistence. But coming here again had been a last resort. She'd craved reassurance that she was desirable, but all she'd gotten was another rejection. She must have Sucker tattooed on her forehead. Why else did she keep picking the wrong men to fall for? Back home, she'd been screwed, then screwed up. The police had warned her that the chances were slim of ever finding the gigolo who'd stolen her credit card. And here, only a few yards away, was the woman responsible for ruining what was left of her dreams. She might not be able to do anything about the creep back home, but she could do something about Hallie O'Grady. She glanced around the area, making sure that no one was in sight, and then stepped up on the porch.

The rain was loud upon the roof and Hallie was focused on the story unfolding on the screen before her. She didn't hear the footsteps on her porch, or the slight squeak of hinges as Jewel Franklin slipped inside. It wasn't until a cool draft of air hit her face that she thought to look up.

"What are you doing here?"

"I'm going to teach you a lesson, you little tramp," Jewel cried, and came at her with her fists doubled.

She landed belly first on the bed on top of Hallie. Although Hallie was undersized, both in weight and height, her Irish blood was up. For every blow she took, she gave one back. In the midst of flailing arms and kicking legs, they rolled off of the bed, taking part of the bedspread with them.

Hallie's head hit the floor only seconds ahead of her laptop. The corner of the laptop hit the back of her head and she went limp.

It was the absence of light, rather than sound and motion that stilled Jewel's anger. The shattered lamp was on the floor, but the candle was nowhere in sight. Lightning flashed outside the window, giving her a brief, but startling, look at what she'd done. Hallie O'Grady was facedown on the floor—and she wasn't moving.

"Well, hell," she muttered, and leaned down, making sure the bitch was still breathing.

She was.

Satisfied that she'd gotten her point across, she dragged herself to her feet and ran to the door. Without looking back, she ran out into the night, slamming the door behind her.

Lightning flashed again, revealing a thin tendril of smoke coming from beneath the bed, but Hallie was in no condition to see it.

A minute passed, and then another and then another.

Jewel Franklin was in her cabin, considering the wisdom of packing it in. Now that the heat of the moment had passed, she knew she would be found out. So she'd probably blacked the little bitch's eye—so what? She wasn't anxious to leave now, in the dark, in the rain, but it was more enticing than facing Jake Miracle's wrath.

The thunderstorm was passing, but the gray tendril of smoke beneath Hallie's bed had grown until the room was full of it—thick, acrid and black as a devil's heart. Hallie came to consciousness choking and coughing. She opened her eyes just as the nearby mattress exploded into flames.

She screamed out in horror, then rolled to her knees, suddenly gasping for air. She had to get out! She had to get out! But her head hurt so bad, and oh God, oh God, where was the door?

Disoriented and in danger of passing out again, she ran, but when she felt the cool, slick surface of the porcelain sink instead of rain-washed air, her chances of survival dropped. She'd run through the wrong door.

The scream was faint, but it was enough to bring the couple next door outside. Within seconds of seeing the flames through Hallie's window, they started to shout.

Jewel heard the commotion and ran to the window.

"Oh, no," she mumbled, and bolted outside, moving with the others who were congregating at the fire. This wasn't what she'd meant to happen. All she intended to do was make a point, not kill her.

Jake was on his way back to Hallie's cabin when the security lights above him suddenly flickered, then came on full force. Before he had time to rejoice in the return of power, he heard screams and shouts and the sound of breaking glass. He'd just left his brothers in the house, so he knew they would still be awake. He grabbed his radio and started to run.

"Luke! John! This is Jake! We've got a problem. Over."

"This is John. What's up? Over."

Jake came around a shed on the run. When he saw the flames and realized the location, his heart nearly stopped.

"There's a fire at cabin ten. You know what to do?"

Twice more the radio crackled, but the messages weren't for him. He knew his brothers would follow procedure. The men would be roused. The old pumper truck in the shed was kept full and waiting for the occasional grass fire that ranchers had to contend with. But this was far worse. Flames were coming out a window. All he could think was, please God, don't let her be inside.

He was almost there when Jewel suddenly appeared before him, grabbing at his arm and screaming incoherently.

"I didn't mean...it was all her..."

"Not now," he said, and shoved her aside.

There was a wet washcloth on the edge of the bathroom sink. Hallie plastered it to her face and dropped low to the floor on her belly. She tried to stay calm, picturing the floor plan in her head, then began crawling on her elbows and knees toward what she thought was the door. Except she crawled into a table, then moments later, a chair toppled over on top of her. The faster she crawled, the more lightheaded she became. When she bumped into a wall and the door wasn't there, she groaned inwardly. The heat inside the cabin was becoming intense. The shirt on her back was starting to smoke and she could smell her own hair beginning to scorch.

Oh God, oh God, don't let me die...don't let me burn.

She was past needing help. What she needed was a miracle. She reached out, feeling along the baseboard and trying to reorient herself within the room when suddenly something came crashing in over her head. Glass shattered around her as a heavy thud vibrated the floor near her feet.

She screamed out Jake's name, and then suddenly

he was there, lifting her in his arms, and passing her through a window to someone outside. People were shouting and running in all directions as she was carried away from the fire to the porch of a cabin across the way.

Her eyes were burning, her lungs were filled with smoke. She kept choking and coughing as tears washed down her face, and in the midst of it all, she felt Jake's arms around her, lifting her up, then carrying her away.

"Jake!"

Jake turned. Luke was running toward him.

"Ambulance is on the way," Luke said. "Is she all right?"

"I don't know," Jake said. "She took in a lot of smoke."

Suddenly, Hallie's fingers were around his wrist.

"Okay," she gasped, then coughed again.

The sound of her voice was such a relief he started shaking.

"You handle this," Jake said. "I'm taking her up to the main house."

He moved as quickly as he could, aware that his brothers were as capable of coping with this as he would have been, maybe even more so, considering his state of mind.

"Oh, God," Hallie gasped, then coughed again. "Thought I would die."

"Don't talk," Jake said, as he rounded the corner and hurried up the porch steps of the main house.

Moments later, they entered. She was vaguely aware of moving through rooms and hallways, and when he laid her on a bed, she started to cry.

Her tears were nearly Jake's undoing. He ran into the bathroom, liberally dousing a bath towel with water and carried it dripping back to the bed.

"Mess," she moaned. "Making a mess."

"Just shut up, woman," he muttered. "The only thing that matters is you. Do you hurt? Are you burned?"

His words were harsh, but his touch was gentle as he laid the wet towel on her skin.

"My head hurts."

Jake felt through her hair, frowning when he felt a large knot.

"What happened? Did something fall on you?"

And then she remembered. "It was Jewel."

He rocked back on his heels, stunned.

"What the hell do you mean, it was Jewel?"

"After you left...she burst into my cabin. She—"

Jake grabbed her arm. "Are you telling me that she came in uninvited and started a fight with you?"

Hallie nodded.

The expression on Jake's face went flat.

"She hit you?"

"Yes. Then we rolled off the bed. I don't remember anything after that until I woke up in a room full of smoke."

Jake stood.

"I left something in the truck. I'll be right back."

Before Hallie could blink, he was gone. He needed his two-way, but he'd given it to someone at the fire just before he'd broken in her window. Seconds later, he was at the truck. He reached inside, retrieving the extra he kept inside.

"Luke! John! This is Jake. Over."

"This is John, go ahead. Over."

"I want Jewel Franklin brought to the house immediately. I don't give a damn what she says, just get her up here. Over and out."

The ambulance arrived only moments ahead of John and Jewel. John was grim-faced and silent, and Jewel was blubbering at the top of her lungs as the paramedics raced through the house toward the bedroom where Hallie was lying.

It was obvious by the disdain on John Miracle's face that she'd already confessed to the fight, but she kept swearing she'd meant her no harm. Certain that she was being brought to the house to be arrested for murder, she fell to her knees with relief when she saw Hallie was still alive.

"I didn't know...I didn't know," she kept sobbing. "It must have started from your lamp when we rolled off of the bed. I didn't know."

Jake looked at Hallie. "It's up to you," he said shortly. "If you want my opinion, at the least, file charges of assault."

Hallie shook her head and then moved the oxygen mask aside long enough to speak her piece.

"Take her away. I don't ever want to see her again."

Jewel crawled to her feet, shaking with every breath.

"No...I mean, yes...I won't...I mean, you won't."

The paramedic took the mask out of Hallie's hands and put it back over her mouth and nose.

Hallie inhaled deeply as Jake leaned down and brushed a kiss across her soot-stained forehead. For a second, their gazes met and locked, and in that moment, Hallie knew her life had just taken a turn.

Then Jake pulled back and stared Jewel straight in the face. When he took a step toward her, she shrank back in fright.

"Get," he said.

"I was leaving tomorrow anyway," she began.

"Now."

Her eyes widened apprehensively. "Please, just let me—"

He doubled his fists.

She turned and ran.

John started after her, then turned to Jake.

"The fire is out."

"Not all of them," he muttered, and turned to Hallie.

His shoulders slumped as he watched them carrying her out of the house on a stretcher. There was a knot in his belly that had nothing to do with pain. Tonight he'd come too close to losing something precious. Unconsciously, he splayed his fingers across his chest, willing his heartbeat to a slow, steady pace.

Then the paramedics stopped and one of them called out.

"Hey mister, she wants to know if you would come with her."

Jake blinked and then shuddered. "Oh, yeah," he said softly, then thought of the mess they had to deal with here.

"Go on," John said. "Luke and I can handle whatever comes up."

Moments later, they were gone.

Several hours and a bath and a shampoo later, Hallie was thanking God for being alive. And after hearing a doctor announce she'd suffered no lasting effects of the smoke, she'd ordered Jake not to call her family, then drifted off to sleep. Against his better judgment, he'd done as she asked. And even after she'd gone to sleep, he couldn't bring himself to leave. She looked so small and helpless lying there in that bed, and he'd come to so damn close to losing her before they'd had a chance to begin. Needing to touch her, if only to assure himself she still breathed, he lifted her fingers to his lips.

"When you wake, honey, we've got some talking to do," he whispered.

Hallie sighed in her sleep. For Jake—for tonight—it was answer enough.

* * *

"I had Carol get you some clothes, since all your belongings were destroyed. Hope they fit," Jake said, and laid the bag on the side of her bed.

Hallie shoved a shaky hand through her hair and managed a smile.

"Thanks, but I don't suppose you thought to get a hairbrush, too?"

He dug through the bag, then came up with one in his hand.

Hallie reached for it and then winced.

"Let me," Jake pleaded.

She sighed and turned her back, giving him full view of her head.

"It's a mess of tangles," she warned him.

"I'll be easy," he said, and he was.

Slow, easy, stroke after stroke, he brushed until the tangles were gone. Then he pulled a pair of jeans and a sweatshirt from a sack.

"Need any help with these?" he asked.

She blushed. "I think I can manage."

"There's some underwear in there, too," he added. "Carol went by the sizes of everything you had on, which, by the way, went in the trash."

Hallie sighed. "Even my boots?"

"No, they're in the closet. If you're sure you don't need help, I'll wait outside. When you're dressed, I can take you back to the ranch." Then he added. "I'm so sorry this happened to you. Please know that you'll be receiving full restitution for all your lost belongings. Just give my secretary a list and I'll see that the insurance company gets it."

She nodded.

Then he groaned and took her in his arms. "Maybe this isn't the time or the place, honey, but I don't intend to let another minute pass without telling you something. For a while last night, I thought I'd lost something very precious—something I was just beginning to explore."

"Oh Jake, I—"

"Wait," he begged, then took her hand. "I think this is where I need to make a formal statement of intent."

She grinned. "Why?"

He leaned closer until his breath was fanning her cheek.

"Because if you stay, I intend to make love to you. I figured you deserved, at the least, fair warning, so this is it. And if you're not interested, then say the word, and I'll have you on the next plane to your home."

It was all Hallie could do to remember to breathe.

"Well?" he asked.

"Well, what?" she muttered.

"What'll it be—a plane ticket or the ranch?"

"I don't want to go home," she said.

He sighed. "Thank God."

"So I'd better get dressed."

He gave her a lingering look, then nodded. "I'll be waiting."

Chapter 6

Hallie slid into the seat of Jake's truck and leaned back with a sigh, watching as he ran around to the driver's side and got in. She kept trying not to stare at the man who'd saved her life, but he was too much man to ignore. His shoulders alone spanned almost half the length of the seat and the muscles in his legs strained at the denim fabric of his jeans. His dark hair was cut short and only half-visible beneath the brim of his gray-belly Stetson. His profile seemed solemn, almost angry, and she wondered if his anger would spill over onto her.

"Jake?"

He turned. "Yeah? You okay?"

She nodded. "It's not that. It's just that there's

something I've been thinking about all morning...something I should have said to you last night."

"What?"

"Thank you for saving my life."

The knuckles on his fingers turned white as he tightened his grip on the steering wheel. When he spoke, he heard anger in his voice.

"You should never have been put in that situation to begin with."

"She's gone. I'm satisfied with that."

His expression was grim as he started the engine. "You're more forgiving than I am." Then he cleared his throat. "If anything had happened to you, I don't know—"

"But it didn't," she said, interrupting him before it went any further. "Let's go, okay?"

He managed a smile. "You're right. Everyone is anxious to see you. A couple of guys got some minor burns trying to get to you, too. They deserve as much thanks as me."

Her eyes widened. "I didn't know."

"There's a lot you don't know," he said softly, then put the truck in gear. "One being, for the rest of your stay, your new room is in the main house."

"Oh, but—"

"You have to," he said. "No other vacancies and your cabin was a total loss."

She leaned back in the seat, contemplating the fact that she would be spending her days—and her nights—under the same roof as Jake. The idea was enticing—and just the least bit frightening, as well.

"Is that okay with you?" he asked, as he maneuvered them into the traffic. Although he dreaded asking, there was an offer that still had to be made. "God knows I don't want you to leave, but please know that after all of this mess, if you would rather be home, I'll see that you get there."

"I don't want to go home," she said. "And, the better question would be, is my staying in your home okay with you?"

He paused at a stop sign and then gave her a cool, studied stare.

"Oh, yeah," he said softly. "It's more than okay."

Hallie shivered and then looked away. The closer the inevitable moment came, the more disconcerted she became. If she let him, they would wind up in bed, of that she was certain. But was she willing to settle for a fling, or would it only exacerbate the pain of leaving him? She sighed, then frowned. The best thing for her to do was just cross that bridge, when and if they came to it.

A short while later, their arrival at the ranch was the spark to start her welcome party. An impromptu shower had been organized and Hallie was moved to tears by the thoughtfulness of strangers as they replaced the things that she'd lost—from something as simple as hair spray and hand lotion to a brand-new cowboy hat from Luke and John. But it was the small, unwrapped gift Dobber laid in her lap that touched her the most. It was a band-new, sky-blue bandanna.

"Every good cowgirl needs herself a bandanna," he said, and then stuffed his hands in his pockets, suddenly embarrassed.

Hallie looked up in surprise. "Am I really a good cowgirl?"

His eyes twinkled. "Purty near the best I've ever seen," he drawled.

She beamed.

"Okay, everybody, party's over. I think she's had enough excitement for now. The doctor told her to take it easy for another day or so," Jake said.

Hallie was tired, but it was a good kind of tired. "Thanks to all of you for being so thoughtful. I'll see you later." Then she caught Dobber by the hand as he started to leave. "Would you do me a favor?" she asked.

"Just ask," he said.

"Would you make sure Sugarfoot gets a treat today?"

He grinned and then winked at Jake. "Anytime you get a woman who worries more about her horse than herself, she's a keeper."

Before either Jake or Hallie could respond, they found themselves alone.

"I guess I'd better get this stuff out of your living room," she said, and began gathering up her gifts.

"Leave them," Jake said, and scooped her into his arms.

"You don't have to carry me," she protested. "I can walk."

"Humor me."

She leaned back in his arms, trying to calm a racing heart as he carried her down the hall to her new room, then laid her in the middle of the bed. Before she could move, he had taken off her boots and gotten an extra blanket from the closet. He paused at the foot of the bed, trying not to focus on the fact that she would be sleeping across the hall from his room.

"Need anything else?"

She hesitated a moment too long. A muscle jerked at the side of his jaw.

"Hallie, I—"

"Thanks for everything," she said softly.

He shrugged. "No big deal. Get some rest."

He was almost out the door when she called him back.

"Jake?"

He turned quickly, eagerness in his voice. "Yes?"

"See you at supper?"

Masking his disappointment, he nodded. "I'll save you a place."

She smiled to herself as he closed the door. A few minutes later she was fast asleep. She never saw him peek back inside, or walk to the foot of her bed and stand quietly within the room, watching her sleep.

But she slept through supper. In fact, when the second bout of thunderstorms began building just after dark, she was still fast asleep. The Miracle brothers were in the living room, watching the news and weather and discussing the next day's events, when a belch of thunder suddenly rattled the windows. Luke got to his feet and walked toward the window, looking past the perimeter of the security light to the darkness beyond.

"Looks like it's going to storm again tonight," he said.

Jake's thoughts were on Hallie and the fact that she was still asleep. He barely nodded, which didn't matter, because Luke wasn't paying any attention to him, either. His worries were on his favorite mare.

"Runner is due to foal any day now. I've got a gut feeling tonight's the night. Think I'll get my sleeping bag and spend the night in the barn."

John jumped up from the sofa. "I'll go with you," he said. "Give me a couple of minutes to get my stuff."

This finally got Jake's attention. He glanced out the window to the approaching storm, then back at his brothers.

"You've never spent a night in the barn with a horse in your lives," he muttered.

Luke shrugged. "Well, big brother, you've never spent a night under the same roof with Hallie

O'Grady, either. The way I look at it, there's a first time for everything. Come on, John, let's hustle."

Jake's eyes narrowed with an unspoken warning. Wisely, neither brother chose to make further comment. A few minutes later, they were gone. Jake walked through the house, checking locks on windows and doors, then turned off the television and turned out the lights. He had a big day ahead of him tomorrow. It was time to get some rest. But before he did, he would check on Hallie, one more time.

Smoke drifted through Hallie's dream, wrapping itself around her legs, then her arms, then sliding up her nose in insidious silence. Fear suffocated her as she rolled onto her side, struggling to breathe.

Hot! Hot! Everything's hot! Can't breathe! Can't see! Jake, don't let me die!

The last bit of her dream came aloud in her mind, then spewed from her lips into an ear-piercing scream. Even as she was waking up, she felt Jake's arms around her—just as they'd been when he'd carried her from the fire.

Then his voice broke the thread between reality and sleep just enough to know that she was in his arms.

"Hallie, it's me, Jake. You're dreaming, honey. Wake up. Wake up."

His touch was gentle as he pushed the hair from her face. Sweat had beaded her clothes to her body and she was trembling from head to foot.

''Oh, Lord,'' she moaned, and hid her face against his chest.

Jake laid her down and hurried into the bathroom, returning moments later with a wet cloth.

''What are you doing?'' she mumbled, as he swiped the cloth across her face, then down her neck and arms.

''Something my mom used to do for us when we were kids. I'm wiping away the bad dream.''

She looked up at him then, hovering above her with a look of concern on his face. At that moment, everything became so suddenly clear. If she'd died last night, she would have never had a chance to tell Jake Miracle what was in her heart. Before she hadn't had the guts, believing that it was far too soon to believe she was in love. For fear of rejection, she had almost lost her chance. She wasn't going to waste it again.

''Jake, how do you feel about me?'' she asked.

He inhaled slowly, watching the way the terror on her face give way to passion.

''What the hell do you want me to say?'' he growled. ''That you make me ache in all the right places? Well, you do.''

She sat up in bed, then tossed the washcloth on the floor.

''If I asked you, would you do something for me?''

''Ask,'' he said.

"Make me ache, Jake Miracle...in all the right places."

His answer was a groan as he took her in his arms and fell back with her onto the bed. Clothes came off, adding to the pile with the wet washcloth underneath, until they were lying face-to-face, arm in arm, shaking from anxiety and need.

Jake caught her lower lip between his teeth and tugged just enough to make her groan.

"You sure about this?" he asked.

Her dark eyes narrowed as she raised up on one elbow and raked a fingernail down the middle of his chest—then lower. This time he was the one who groaned. The discussion was over.

The beauty of her body stunned him as he began his exploration, sweeping delicate curves and taut limbs with both his hands and his lips. When he cupped her breasts, he felt an involuntary flinch and remembered her reaction to Jewel Franklin's slight. He kissed the tip of each nipple, then raised up on one elbow long enough to whisper, "Hallie, don't do that."

She looked away, well aware of what he meant.

"Look at me, woman. I'm about to make love to you and there's something I think you better hear first."

Her eyes widened.

He traced the shape of her mouth with a fingertip and watched the pupils in her eyes slowly dilate. "You are about as beautiful a female as I've ever seen in my life, both inside and out. And...just for the record, in my opinion, anything more than a handful is a waste."

She sighed and dug her fingers into the hair at the back of his head.

"Okay," she said softly. "Then just for the record, if you're as good at making love as you are at sweet talk, I'm a goner."

"Try me," he said.

So she did.

Sometime during the night, the storm came and went, but it was nothing to what had gone on inside Hallie's room. Dawn wasn't more than a couple of hours away when Jake finally rolled over onto his back and fell asleep. Hallie lay cuddled in the crook of his arm, her cheek upon his chest, her arm around his waist. Her worst fears had been answered. She was, indeed, a goner.

Five days later, she was packing to go home with an ache in her heart and tears in her eyes. Every night since that first one, she'd slept in Jake's arms with no apologies to the rest of his family. They seemed to take it as a matter of course that she was "Jake's woman." But what that entailed had yet to be seen. She tossed the last of her clothes into a new suitcase and slammed the lid shut just as Jake appeared in the doorway. His expression was blank, his posture stiff and unyielding.

"Are you ready to go?" he asked.

She bit her lip to keep from crying again and nodded.

"I'll carry that," he said, and took the bag from her hand. The look on her face was killing him. He knew what she wanted to hear, and God help him, he wanted to say it worse than anything he'd ever wanted in his life. But he was all too aware of holiday romances. They were passionate but brief, and rarely lasted. Theirs had definitely been brief and passionate, but damn it, he wanted more. He wanted her to love him—at least forever. Longer if she really cared.

She hesitated, unable to believe he would let her go without a word, although she kept remembering last night, and the panic with which they'd made love. Maybe that had been his way of saying goodbye. She was heartsick and angry with herself for believing he loved her, and for him, for pretending it was true.

"Jake, I—"

He dropped the suitcase, then took her in his arms. "I don't know whether you want to hear this or not," he said harshly, "but I'm going to say it anyway. I love you, Hallie O'Grady. I don't know how I'm going to ever sleep again without your breath on my chest and your head nestled under my chin."

A weight rolled off of her.

"Oh, Jake, so do I, but I thought you—"

"Don't say anything more," he warned. "Just

know this. We're not over. Not yet. You've been on vacation. Now I want you to go home and take a deep breath. Stand back from the drama of everything that happened and take a real good look at your heart. I don't want your gratitude, honey, I want you. I have your parents' address from the registration you filled out. You said your family always spends the holidays together there. So...on Thanksgiving Day I will be at their house. I will meet your family and I will tell your father that I'm marrying his little girl. I don't give a damn whether he likes it or not. All that matters is if you say yes."

Hallie started to laugh. "Yes," she cried. "Yes, yes, yes."

Her joy was like a knife in his gut. "Tell me that again on Thanksgiving," he growled.

"But Jake..."

"You heard me," he warned. "Go home and take a deep breath. If you don't want this as bad as I do, then stop me before I get there."

Later, leaving him at the airport was the hardest thing she'd ever had to do. During the entire flight, she kept seeing his face and the fear in his eyes. But what he didn't understand was that she was afraid, too. She wasn't the only one who might suffer a change of heart. Anything could happen between now and Thanksgiving. Time enough for his ardor to cool and rationality to return. She closed her eyes and said a quick prayer. She didn't want him cool and rational; she wanted him crazy in love—with her.

Petra sidestepped a crawling baby as she carried two pumpkin pies to the sideboard in the dining room.

"Hey, Dana, move your urchin before he gets squashed," she yelled.

Dana picked up her son and headed for the playpen in the corner of the room.

"How did he get out, anyway?" she muttered, as she walked away.

In the other room, a loud roar of male disapproval suddenly sounded. Evie grinned as she came out of the kitchen with a bowl of mashed potatoes.

"Sounds like the wrong team just scored a goal," she said.

Petra rolled her eyes. "Men. They're nothing but overgrown babies. They are helpless when sick and have the memory of a gnat."

Evie giggled. "So...it sounds to me like Wayne forgot and left the toilet seat up again."

Petra made a face. "It was just after three in the morning. I fell all the way in."

Evie chuckled. "I know just how you feel."

Hallie came out of the kitchen with a basket of hot bread for the table. The smile on her face hadn't made it as far as her eyes. As soon as she was gone, both sisters dropped into the whisper mode and started to speculate.

"See, I told you the other day something was wrong. She hasn't been the same since she came back from her trip. Has she talked to you? Did she have a good time?" Evie asked.

Petra shook her head. "I don't know. I just assumed she'd talked to you."

"Who talked to who about what?" Dana asked as she slipped into the huddle.

"Hallie," they echoed. "What did she say to you about the trip?"

Dana looked startled. "Well, nothing. I just supposed she'd talked to you guys. I've been so busy with the baby's earache and all, I just assumed..."

The trio turned, casting a speculative glance toward Hallie, who was coming back out of the kitchen with another hot bowl in her hands.

"What's going on?" she asked.

They looked at each other than shrugged. "Nothing," Petra finally said. "Just bitching about men and toilet seats...stuff like that."

Hallie went pale. To their shock, she reacted angrily.

"Shut up. Just shut up," she muttered. "You don't know how blessed you are. At least you've got a man to gripe about."

Then she shoved the bowl she'd been carrying into Petra's hands and pivoted sharply, heading back to the kitchen for more.

The sisters' mouths dropped. Stunned into momentary silence, they looked at her departing figure, and then back at each other.

Evie was the first to grin. "She met a man."

"You're wrong," Dana hissed. "If she had, why would she be so mad?"

Petra sighed and set the bowl aside. "Because she came back alone, that's why."

They sighed in unison. Before they had a chance to mend fences, a child shrieked in anger as another erupted with a scream. They spun around, racing to cool baby Irish tempers before disaster followed.

Hallie was sick to her stomach and sick at heart. It was almost one o'clock and Jake Miracle was nowhere in sight. The past twenty-something days had been nothing but pure hell. She couldn't sleep, she couldn't eat, and she hadn't been able to write. Everywhere she turned, she kept seeing Jake's face. She missed the vast open spaces of Texas and the man who lived there. All day she'd been jumping at shadows, listening for sounds of a knock that never came. Thank God she hadn't made a fool of herself by racing home and announcing her love to the world. At least now she could suffer in silence—at least, it would be silent when she went home. Right now, focusing on family chaos rather than her pain was all that was keeping her together.

"Hallie, darling, carry this to the table, will you?"

Hallie blinked, then looked up. Her mother was pointing toward the twenty-pound turkey her father would soon be carving. She lifted her chin and took a deep breath.

"Sure," she said, and started to pick it up, when the doorbell suddenly rang. She froze, and then made the sign of the cross and closed her eyes.

Moira O'Grady gasped. "Hallie, darlin', are you all right?"

But Hallie wasn't talking, she was praying, as hard as she'd ever prayed in her life. Moments later, Evie dashed into the kitchen.

"Hallie, there's a man at the door. He says you were expecting him. He says he's staying for dinner."

"Praise God," Hallie gasped, and flew out of the room.

Mother and daughters paused only long enough to wipe their hands, then they were right behind her.

Jake stood in the doorway wearing blue jeans and boots and a western-cut coat. Impatiently waiting with his Stetson in hand, he was holding his own beneath the stares of the family beginning to congregate. He nodded at the men, and smiled at the women, but he was watching for Hallie.

Suddenly she was there, pushing her way through the crowd and laughing out loud. Right then, every anxious moment he'd had just faded away. He opened his arms and held out his hands.

"Come here to me, woman," he said, and caught her in midair, kissing her soundly in front of everyone assembled with no thought of what they might think.

"Here now, Hallie," Sean O'Grady mumbled, suddenly remembering his place. "Just who in blazes is this stranger you're kissin'?"

Laughter bubbled up between her words as she looked up at Jake.

"So, exactly how should I be introducing you to my family?"

Jake handed her his hat, then grabbed her hand and slid a ring on her finger. "Hallie, darlin', this is sort of public, but something tells me you're not going to mind."

She was shaking with joy. It was all she could do to stand still.

"I don't mind," she whispered, looking down in disbelief at the solitaire.

"It's beautiful," she whispered.

"Just like you."

Tears sprang to Hallie's eyes. She clasped the ring to her breasts.

"Oh, Jake."

"Just a minute, here," Sean sputtered.

Jake looked up. "Sir, I've come to tell you that I love your daughter, and that we're getting married New Year's Eve, 1999."

Moira O'Grady squealed, then gasped. "Saints preserve us! That's only six weeks away. How will I manage?"

Sean spluttered, then sighed. He'd known Hallie

far too long to know that argument would only fuel her fire. He caught Jake's hand in his own, taking the big man's measure, but finding nothing outwardly wanting.

"Calm yourself, Moira," he muttered. "You'll find a way—you always do." Then he gave Jake a hard look. "So you want to marry my daughter, do you?"

Jake didn't flinch. "Yes, sir, I do."

Sean stared back. When the man's gaze never wavered, he began to relax. Never trust a man who wouldn't look you in the eyes. But this man seemed forthright enough. He finally shook his hand.

"That's all well and good, I suppose." Then he turned to Hallie. "Don't you think it would be a kindness to the family if you told us his name?"

"Yes," Hallie said, and shyly threaded her fingers through Jake's. He squeezed them gently, then lifted them to his lips for a kiss. It was all she could do to remember what she'd been about to do.

"Uh...Jake...this is my family. My mother, Moira. My father, Sean. Those are my brothers-in-law, Sam, Wayne and Frank. We'll sort out last names and who they belong to later." Then she pointed at the roomful of children behind them. "Suffice it to say that none of those little beggars are mine. They belong to those poor dumb, but beautiful redheads who are standing with their mouths agape. Pity for me, but those wretches are my sisters. The tallest one is Evie. The pregnant one is Petra. The other one is Dana." Then she took a deep breath, and turned to her family. "Everyone, I want you to meet Jake Miracle."

A few seconds of stunned silence enveloped the group, and then Evie suddenly giggled.

"Gee, Hallie, you always said it would be a miracle if you ever got married, but I didn't think you meant it so literally."

Hallie grinned. "Trust in the power of prayer." Then she turned to Jake. "Jake, darling, understand I'm only asking, not complaining, but why so soon, and why New Year's Eve?"

"Soon? Excuse my language, but these past weeks have been hell. As for the date, it's the day before the millennium, and I'm not too good at remembering dates. I figure if we get married on New Year's Eve, then it's a sure bet I'll never forget our anniversary."

Hallie threw back her head and laughed. Jake grinned. God, but he loved to hear her laugh.

Sean O'Grady chuckled. "That's a smart man. Say...there's a rousing game of football on the TV. By any chance, do you like the game?"

Jake grinned. "Next to women and oil, I don't think there's anything a Texan likes better." Then he noticed the frown on Moira O'Grady's face and the food cooling on the table. "But, it looks as if I got here just in time to help put food on the table."

The sisters gasped, then sighed in unison.

"My God, you don't suppose he also puts the toilet seat down?" Petra muttered.

The three husbands groaned. "Now you've done it, Hallie. You've gone and picked yourself a gentleman and we'll never hear the end of it."

Jake laughed. This family was something. Now he knew where Hallie got her spunk.

"Don't let it worry you," he said. "We'll live far enough away that maybe it won't rub off."

The women groaned again, only this time in dismay.

Hallie's heart gave a twist, but just for a moment. As much as she loved her family, she loved this man even more.

Moira O'Grady gave Jake a long look, but she'd made up her mind. If Hallie loved him, then it was good enough for her.

"Young man...if your offer to help is still open, come with me. There's food to eat and plans to be made. I won't have my daughter standing before a justice of the peace. I'll see her married in a church before you take her away, and that's a fact."

Jake shrugged out of his coat and laid it on a nearby chair. Then he grabbed Hallie's hand.

"Come on, honey. Let's make your mama happy."

Evie piped up again. "Oh, that's easy," she said. "Just have some babies. After that, she's yours for life."

Hallie blushed, but Jake never missed a beat.

"It would be my pleasure," he said. "And we'll start right in on the process, but not until I've tasted your mother's cooking. If it's as good as it looks and smells, I'm in heaven." Everyone was laughing as they started toward the kitchen, when something occurred to Jake and he stopped.

"Hallie, honey, can you cook?"

Someone gasped. Everyone stopped. Hallie was beginning to look nervous. Then Jake shrugged.

"It really doesn't matter. I can."

The men groaned again, only louder.

"Somebody feed him to shut him up. He's ruining us," Sam said.

Hallie did a little dance in the middle of the floor, turning around and around like the ballerina in a child's jewelry box, then to Jake's delight, threw her arms around his neck and kissed him soundly.

"Cowboy, I am yours for life."

He grinned. "Shoot, honey, I already knew that, but what convinced you?"

"Because you love me, not for what I have, but in spite of what I'm missing."

Suddenly, he understood and grinned. As his daddy always said, anything more than a handful was a waste—and only the good Lord knew what a handful Hallie O'Grady really was.

The good news was, now she was his.

* * * * *

Dear Reader,

Well, here we are, standing on the threshold of a brand-new century. The last time people did this, LA had no smog, New York had no [illegible] traffic. Anywhere else, in the greater part of the world, romance was more likely to be used in reference to languages or an era in literature than to what went on between two people. Think of the progress we've made these last hundred years. We [illegible] coughing and terminally stuck in traffic. But our hearts are free to fall in love, and that, to me, is what makes the world go around.

I've never been to a New Year's Eve party, not even once, but I wouldn't trade any of the New Years I've had with anyone, because all my New Year's Eves were spent with the people I loved most, my parents and brother, and later, my husband and children. That last evening of the year is a time that always seems to remind me just how very blessed I am.

I hope that when the ball comes down that last minute of this year, that you're at a huge party or at least a private one for two, and have someone to hug and kiss as you welcome in a brand-new century. I wish you all health and happiness and, most of all, someone to love and to love you in return.

With all my love,

[illegible]

Dearest Reader,

Well, here we are, standing on the threshold of a brand-new century. The last time people did this, L.A. had no smog, New York had no midtown traffic (or traffic anywhere else, for that matter) and the word *romance* was more likely to be used in reference to languages or an era in literature than to what went on between two people. Think of the progress we've made these past hundred years. We might be coughing and terminally stuck in traffic, but our hearts are free to fall in love, and that, to me, is what makes the world go around.

I've never been to a New Year's Eve party, not even once, but I wouldn't trade any of the New Years I've had with anyone, because all my New Year's Eves were spent with the people I loved most: my parents and brothers, and later, my husband and children. That last evening of the year is a time that always seems to remind me just how very blessed I am.

I hope that when the ball comes down that last minute of this year, whether you're at a huge party or an intimate one for two, you have someone to hug and kiss as you welcome in a brand-new century. I wish you all health and happiness and, most of all, someone to love and to love you in return.

With all my love,

Marie

The Single Daddy Club

Marie Ferrarella

To everyone in my life
and to everyone within sight of this book,
Happy New Century

Chapter 1

"There they are, just like clockwork. They gather together there every Saturday and Sunday."

Rachel Collins leaned forward in the wheelchair she'd temporarily adopted, thanks to an unceremonious spill last week while taking advantage of an early snowfall at Lake Tahoe.

Finally, Rachel thought, something good was going to come out of having this wretched accident. She glanced over her shoulder at her sister, K.C., to see if she was listening. K.C. didn't even seem to hear her.

Determined, Rachel continued, raising her voice just a little. "Sundays they meet an hour later." She turned in her chair to face K.C. What did she have to do, hit her over the head? "This is just like in that article in the magazine."

K.C. shoved Mr. Fuzzy-Foo, a ridiculously named bear with an endearing face, under her arm as she busily cleaned up after Gracie, Rachel's exuberant two-year-old and her beloved niece. K.C. didn't even bother turning around. A registered visiting nurse by profession, she'd offered to use her vacation time to help out until Rachel was back on her feet. But Bryan, Rachel's husband, had insisted on employing her instead. His shrewd reasoning was that it kept the agency happy, K.C.'s vacation intact and K.C. at Rachel's beck and call, something that Rachel had delighted in since they were children.

K.C. was beginning to wonder if she'd somehow gotten the shorter end of the stick in this deal.

"What's just like in that magazine?" K.C. shoved a myriad of stuffed animals into Gracie's overflowing toy box, then paused to look at her sister. She knew that expression. Rachel was up to something. Maybe she had better pay closer attention before Rachel got carried away with whatever it was that she thought she was cooking up. "Rachel, what are you talking about?"

Ever since Rachel had read the article in the August issue of *Prominence Magazine,* she had been searching for a way to get K.C. to try this newest avenue for meeting single men. In her opinion, it was high time K.C. started going out again.

Swinging the wheelchair around completely so

that she could face her sister, Rachel beckoned her over. "Come here."

The family room window offered an expansive view of the park across the street. In passing, Bryan had mentioned encountering the group to Rachel the other day. It was comprised of several single fathers who gathered together twice a week in the park to exchange information and support in this maze called parenthood. He'd been mistakenly invited to join their ranks when he'd taken Gracie to the park one Saturday while Rachel had been nursing a stubborn cold.

Seeing them as she had just now, everything fell into place for Rachel. It was perfect. A smorgasbord to choose from. K.C. had to get out there before some woman took it upon herself to snap up the dark-haired one, Rachel thought. The one who looked as if he could double as a romantic spy in a James Bond movie.

"See those men?" She pointed to the bench in the foreground. "With the kids?"

K.C. saw the children first, then noticed the men clustered on the bench and casually sprawled out on the grass on either side of it. They seemed to be having a good time. There were five of them. Friends from the looks of it. It was a heartening sight, she supposed, but nothing for Rachel to get excited over.

"What about them?"

Rachel hesitated a moment. If she told K.C. that

she knew all about the group and that Bryan had talked to some of them, then K.C. might decide to be perverse, not go out and ruin everything. She searched for the right way to present this.

"Just that I've seen them out there before. Five single men. Kids. No women hanging on their arms. I'll bet they're part of a 'Single Daddy Club' of some kind." Her face was the picture of innocence when she looked at K.C. "What do you think?"

"I think you landed on your head as well as your leg when you took that tumble down the ski slope, that's what I think." Both hands filled with crayons she'd picked up from all four corners of the room, K.C. deposited the booty next to Gracie. The little girl was sprawled out on her stomach, determined to leave her mark on every single page of the new coloring book she'd been given this morning. "'Single Daddy Club,'" K.C. echoed. "Is this something you just made up?"

It was obvious that K.C. had completely ignored the magazine she'd given her to read. It was still lying on the coffee table, untouched like the others. Rachel wheeled herself over to the table, found the issue she wanted and held it up.

"No, it's in the magazine." When K.C. made no attempt to come over and take it from her, Rachel dropped the magazine in her lap and drove the wheelchair forward, stopping directly in front of her sister and cutting off any hope for a clean getaway.

"It wouldn't hurt you to read one of these magazines once in a while, you know."

With a sigh, K.C. looked at the magazine. "'Married by the Millennium,'" she read the feature article title out loud. "These kinds of articles are only good for one thing. Making confetti out of them."

Rachel was not about to give up. "Let me summarize the part that applies to you, since you won't read it. The second method they mention is to find a Single Daddy Club—like the one we have here," she said pointedly, "and find a way to mingle with the men. You know how helpless men can be with kids."

Rolling her eyes, K.C. took the magazine from her and dropped it on the table. "No, thanks. I've no desire to say 'I do' to anyone—before the millennium or after."

And that, Rachel thought, was just the trouble. But she'd be damned if she stood by and watched her sister become a cloistered nun. K.C. had too much to offer to shut herself away like this.

"Just because Eric left you—"

K.C. looked at her sister sharply, a stab of pain mingled with indignation going through her. You'd think it wouldn't hurt so much anymore. "Eric didn't leave me. We left each other."

Which was just something her sister told herself to assuage her hurt feelings, Rachel thought. "Sorry, I guess Eric just left a little faster than you did." Her mouth twisted in a sarcastic smile. K.C. was better off without that loser. "It's the track star in him."

K.C. had no intention of continuing this discussion. Dropping the latest collection of toys she'd just picked up, she placed a hand on either side of Rachel's wheelchair and leaned her face in close to her sister's.

"Look, I might be your younger sister, but for the duration, and because your husband insisted on paying my agency, I am also your private duty nurse, O Pampered One, and as your nurse I highly recommend some bed rest." Her eyes narrowed slightly as she ended her suggestion with a command. "Immediately."

Rachel wasn't about to give up so easily, not when this seemed like the perfect opportunity to spark something. "I—"

Straightening, K.C. had no intention of being outmaneuvered. "That means resting all of you, including your mouth."

Her mind in overdrive, Rachel reconnoitered. Sighing dramatically, she nodded. "All right, I am tired." And then a sly smile curved her mouth. "But I can't rest if there's noise."

Turning Rachel's chair in the general direction of the back room, K.C. retreated back to Gracie. She dropped to her knees, and began to color with the little girl. "We'll be quiet."

This wasn't what Rachel had had in mind.

"You'll be quieter if you take Gracie out to play. You know how she loves being outdoors."

The town house Rachel and her husband had moved into last autumn, nestled amid several others, was designed to resemble homes along the Italian Riviera. The European flavor abounded in the small development, but what had been sacrificed was any hope of a backyard. To make up for the lack, an aesthetically appealing public park, equipped with several play areas for the very young and two gazebos as well as a picnic area and a barbecue pit for adults, had been placed in the center of a long, serpentine street and was in the middle of four developments, two of which were comprised solely of two-story garden apartments.

K.C. remained where she was on the floor beside her niece. She raised her eyes stubbornly toward Rachel. "I know where you're going with this."

She'd won. Rachel congratulated herself. She could tell by K.C.'s tone. K.C. had never been able to refuse Gracie anything. "That's why Dad always called you the smart one."

Carefully, Rachel maneuvered the wheelchair over the threshold. Because the house was built on four different, narrow levels, she found herself restricted to the ground floor, at least until such time that she felt equal to negotiating the stairs with crutches. Right now, it was nicer talking Bryan into carrying her up the stairs to their bedroom.

"And why he called me the clever one," Rachel murmured under her breath.

"I heard that," K.C. called after her.

Sitting back on her knees, K.C. looked at her niece. Wavering. It really *was* a beautiful day and there was no reason to keep Gracie cooped up inside when the weather was so perfect. The weather was why, back in the fifties, her grandfather had transplanted his small family from the snow-laden terrain of North Dakota to the land of sunshine and endless beaches.

And of would-be actors who were fickle and heartless.

The sentiment sneaked up on her unexpectedly. K.C. frowned, thinking of Eric. She'd fully expected to be ringing in the New Year—the new century—with him at her side. Toasting it and each other at the stroke of midnight.

But Eric, unbeknownst to her, had had other plans. The undying love he had pledged to her died a premature, swift and unexpected death after he'd played a few minor love scenes off-screen with the makeup girl who had worked on the one movie that was legitimately entered on his résumé.

That had been at the beginning of the year. You would have figured that she would have gotten over him by now. But she'd loved Eric, had been fully convinced that they were going to spend the rest of their lives together. To discover that she'd so completely misread the man and his intentions shook

K.C. down to her foundations and made her doubt her ability to make sound judgments where people were concerned. At least male people.

But Gracie shouldn't be deprived just because her aunt had an inability to read men, K.C. thought, fondly ruffling Gracie's hair. Getting to her feet, she took Gracie's sweater out of the closet.

"Listen to your aunt K.C." She slowly slipped one sleeve of the sweater onto Gracie's arm, careful not to bunch up the jersey sleeve underneath. "Don't trust any guy farther than you can throw him, understand?"

Silken light-blond curls only a shade lighter than her own hair bobbed up and down as the two-year-old solemnly nodded her head in agreement.

Getting the other sleeve on, K.C. hugged Gracie to her. "You're a love, honey." She laughed, though something bittersweet stirred within her as Gracie hugged back. She could have had a child of her own by now, if only Eric had been different. "I'm putting in my order for twelve of you as soon as possible."

"You'll need a man to help you fill out that requisition form," Rachel called from the back room.

Her sister had ears like a bat, K.C. thought, rising to her feet. "Haven't you heard of sperm banks?"

"Yes." Rachel's voice floated back to her. "I've also heard of satanic cults. Doesn't mean I'd have anything to do with one."

Checking her pocket for house keys, K.C. got

ready to leave. "Go to sleep, Rachel. Gracie and I will be back in an hour or so."

"Let me kiss my daughter before she goes," Rachel called to her.

Dutifully, K.C. brought Gracie into the back room. Like everything else in the house, it was decorated with an eye to make the beholder see that Rachel Collins had married money and was thrilled about it. For the time being, it had been converted to a bedroom to accommodate her convalescence.

Rachel enfolded Gracie in her arms. "Help your aunt K.C. find a man," she said in a stage whisper to the child as she kissed her.

"Huh." K.C. laughed shortly. The last thing she wanted, she thought, taking Gracie's hand in hers, was a man. They were just too hard on the heart.

It was going better than he'd expected.

They were doing all right, Bailey Quaid thought, watching his son, Bobby, play with Jeff Hamlin's boy, feeling more than a little surge of fatherly pride. Of course, Bobby's adjustment had been a foregone conclusion. He didn't remember his mother, not even slightly. The boy had only been a couple of months old when Gloria had decided that she'd made a huge mistake, both in marrying the father of her child and in having that child in the first place. Neither fit the life-style she saw for herself.

Bailey remembered the expression on his ex-wife's face when she had finally told him that she felt as if she were literally dying inside. He'd given her her freedom. What else could he do?

And he hadn't once told her how much it hurt to do so. She'd packed up his heart along with the rest of her belongings when she left.

So here he was, almost fifteen months later, still adjusting to the fact that he wasn't married anymore. Still trying to make peace with the fact that the love he'd offered had been carelessly tossed aside without so much as a backward glance.

Just because you loved someone didn't mean they had to love you back.

Except in Bobby's case, Bailey thought fondly, watching him charge through the grass, laughing as the other boy chased him. Bobby loved Bailey unconditionally. Bobby was the greatest gift Gloria could have ever given him. Even if she hadn't actually intended it that way.

"Hey, check out the new talent." Billy Stevens nudged Bailey back into Saturday afternoon with a sharp poke in his ribs. Billy had been married twice and was perpetually optimistic about the institution. He nodded toward the petite, slender blonde who had just sat down on the next bench. There was a little girl with her, but it was the woman that drew all five sets of eyes.

Nathan Calloway, the bedeviled father of twins, whistled low in appreciation. "Nice legs." In typical Southern California fashion, the crisp, cool morning had given way to a warm afternoon, and the woman was wearing denim shorts, much to everyone's viewing pleasure. He looked back at the others. "Think she's married?"

"Gotta be," Taylor Kellogg commented, dusting sand off his son. Jimmy was covered from head to toe with enough sand to fill a small sandbox. "Who'd let someone like that get away?" It was hopeless. It looked as if a shower was in order. Taylor glanced at his watch. "Wow, look at the time. I've gotta be getting back."

Billy grinned broadly. "Hot date tonight?"

"We'll see," Taylor replied enigmatically. His words signaled a general breaking up of the group as the others realized they'd already been here for longer than they'd intended. "You coming, Bailey?"

He liked the guys, but he liked sharing a little one-on-one time here with his son, as well. "No, I'm going to stick around for a while. Bobby's having too much fun on the slide." He indicated the newest structure the city had put in. "I'll see you guys here tomorrow."

The others sorted out their sons and daughters, said their goodbyes and left. It was only after Billy had driven away and Bailey had settled back on the bench that he suddenly became aware of the fact that his son was climbing on the slide.

"Dad-dee!" Bobby crowed with glee, leaning his rounded tummy against the top. Balancing himself, he waved his hands over his head to draw his father's attention. "Look!"

Bailey looked, all right. Looked at his only child tottering on the brink of disaster while his heart suddenly lodged in his throat. Bobby, part mountain goat, part squirrel, had been born absolutely fearless. Right now, Bailey had enough fear for both of them.

Knowing that the slightest jarring noise might throw his son off balance, Bailey called to him in an easy, low voice. "Wow, aren't you brave? Braver than Daddy, that's for sure. Stay right where you are, Bobby. I want to get closer to you to see you better. Put your arms down and hold on to the hand rail."

Please let me reach him in time.

Long, muscular legs cut through the city-manicured grass, praying Bobby wouldn't suddenly decide to see if he could fly.

Something about the man's voice drew K.C.'s attention away from Gracie and the game they were playing. She looked at him and then toward the object of his concern. Her heart froze when she saw the little boy at the top of the slide.

He was wiggling as he laughed.

"Oh, my God." Grabbing Gracie's hand, K.C. pulled the little girl to her and hurried quickly over to the slide.

She was almost there when the little boy decided to lean all the way over and lost his balance.

Chapter 2

Bailey was certain that his heart had stopped beating entirely as he rushed to catch Bobby. The distance between him and the slide seemed too great. A superhuman burst of adrenaline brought him to the foot of the structure just in time.

It wasn't until after the boy was clutched tightly against his chest that Bailey realized Bobby had hit his head on one of the metal rungs on his way down. And that in his haste to catch his son, he had pushed aside the woman who had gotten in his way. The woman who had come running from another direction to try to help.

Looking down now, Bailey saw that he had sent her flying, ignominiously landing on the ground.

Relieved that he had caught his son, concerned about any injuries that he didn't yet see and chagrined at his almost cavemanlike behavior, Bailey looked at the woman who was picking herself up from the grass. There was a little girl hovering beside her. Had he hit the child as well?

"Oh, God, I'm sorry. Are you hurt?" Still holding Bobby to him, Bailey grasped the woman's hand and helped her up the rest of the way. Not waiting for an answer, he tried to explain. "It's just that I—"

Gracie's high-pitched giggle assured them that no harm had come to her. Obviously Gracie thought this was some new game they were playing.

Dusting herself off, K.C. warded off his apology. "That's okay. You had other things on your mind." She rotated her shoulders, feeling just a little achy. She'd had no time to brace herself before falling. Tomorrow this was going to hurt like the devil. A grin curved her mouth as she met his eyes. "You ever play tackle for the Chargers?"

"No." Bailey flushed, excruciatingly embarrassed. "Just some track and field."

That would explain the burst of speed, she thought. "Lucky for your son."

Bailey's eyes appreciatively swept over her even as his son continued to wail. "You're sure you're not hurt?"

"No, I'm fine, really."

Just a little rattled, she added silently. She was

more concerned about the man's son. Though the child was screaming, there were no tears steaming down the boy's face. She suspected that it was probably just a matter of being badly frightened himself at the last moment, but it never hurt to be sure.

"That's a fearless little boy you have there. Great set of lungs, too." Concern creased the man's forehead as he looked at the boy, not that she blamed him. "Here." K.C. transferred Gracie's hand into the stranger's. "You hold on to Gracie while I take a look at Mr. Daredevil, here."

Not waiting for his consent, K.C. took the boy from him, slipping the child easily onto her hip. Accustomed to taking charge, she only realized belatedly that the man had no idea of her training.

"I'm a nurse." She looked at the boy's eyes. The pupils weren't dilated. Very carefully, she examined his scalp. K.C. frowned at the bump that was even now forming on the little boy's forehead.

"He's not bleeding." Bailey offered his son an encouraging smile. Bobby's screams had turned into whimpers as he looked at the woman ministering to him with wide, curious eyes.

"No," she agreed, "he's not." She couldn't help thinking that the boy looked like a miniature version of his father. "He probably just had the wind knocked out of him and got frightened."

"*He* got frightened?" Bailey laughed. "His whole life passed before my eyes."

"A featured short, huh?" Sliding her finger down

the little boy's nose affectionately, she handed him back to his father. Suddenly shy, Gracie slipped her hand into hers and watched the man from behind K.C.'s legs.

"What's his name?"

"Bobby"

"Well, I think Bobby's going to be just fine. Kids bump their heads all the time." Still, she knew it didn't hurt to be cautious. "But if you want to play it safe, you might think about having him checked out at the walk-in clinic down the road."

"Walk-in clinic?" Bailey tried to recall if he ever remembered seeing it, but his mind was still unfocused, his thoughts scattering about like so many beads escaping a newly broken string.

K.C. picked up Gracie, although it seemed that the little girl would have liked nothing better than to wander off while her back was turned. "Yes, just down the road on Baldwin." She nodded in the general direction.

Finishing up the project on his drawing board could wait. He fully intended to take the woman's suggestion to heart. This way, he wouldn't sit up all night, worried that he'd been too lax about something serious.

"Would you happen to know the address offhand? I'm fairly new around here. I just moved from Malibu about five months ago." He tightened his arms around Bobby as the boy shifted, squirming.

"Afraid I haven't had the need to visit an emergency clinic until now."

K.C. raised a dubious brow as she looked at Bobby. "I find that hard to believe." She looked back toward the houses in the development. "I'll tell you what, I'm staying right over there." She pointed out the blue-and-gray town house. "Let me just drop Gracie off and I'll drive you over."

Relief flooded through Bailey, along with more than a sizable amount of gratitude. Accustomed to being on his own with Bobby, it was really nice to have a little help once in a while. "I'd really appreciate it—if it's not too much trouble..."

K.C. was already quickening her pace. "No trouble at all. You wait right here." She kept the little girl perched on her hip as she hurried back across the street.

"You know something, Tiger?" Bailey murmured to his son, "I think we've just run into an angel of mercy. And that had better be the only kind of angel you run into for a very long time," he ordered just before he pressed a kiss to the top of the boy's head.

His arms around his father's neck, Bobby nestled in closer.

Watching the whole scene from her window, Rachel thought this one looked like a keeper.

The next moment, K.C.'s voice startled her as she called out, "Rachel, I'm leaving Gracie here. I have to go out for a while—"

Turning, Rachel was in time to see her sister running by the doorway to the back room. "I'm in here," Rachel called, stopping K.C. in midrun. "Where are you going with him?"

"Him?" K.C. echoed as she entered the family room.

"Him," Rachel repeated. "The him with shoulders you could land a small two engine plane on. The one you were talking to." She moved so far forward on her seat, it looked as if she were going to fall off. "Good job. I saw everything from the window."

"Then you saw the little boy tumble off the slide. He hit his head and I'm showing his father the way to the walk-in clinic."

"Good for you!" Leaning over, she took Gracie's hand, waving her sister off. "Don't worry about a thing, I can handle things here for a while. Just go."

K.C. couldn't leave without at least saying something. "What are you doing at the window, anyway? I left you lying down in the other room."

"I got bored." Rachel shrugged innocently. "A woman has to do something to entertain herself and I've seen all the movies on the cable channels."

K.C. sighed. Rachel was incorrigible. With a shake of her head, K.C. grabbed her purse. "I'll be back as soon as I can."

"No hurry. Take your time," Rachel called after her. "Men like to have their hands held during times of strife. By the way, you picked the best one of the litter."

"I didn't pick him," K.C. declared firmly.

Best one of the litter. K.C. hurried out of the house. Rachel made it sound as if she were picking out a puppy. Her sister sorely needed a hobby. As soon as Rachel got back on her feet again, she was going to enroll her in some kind of extension classes or something, K.C. promised herself.

Because the garage only accommodated Rachel and Bryan's cars, K.C. kept her own parked in the guest area, even though Bryan was away for the day at a meeting upstate. She got in quickly and started the vehicle up. Moving carefully along the narrow street within the enclosed development, imported gravel crunching beneath her tires, K.C. made her way out to the serpentine path that went past the park.

The man was waiting for her at the curb. It occurred to her that she still didn't even know his name. And that he didn't know hers.

At least he wasn't an operator, using this as an opportunity to hit on her, she thought, pulling up to the curb.

Bailey bent slightly so that he could look in and see her face. "I'm going to need a car seat—"

K.C. grinned. "Way ahead of you." She indicated the seat in the back. "You can put your son into Gracie's seat."

Opening the rear passenger door, he gently lowered his son into the car seat, then strapped him in. "You seem to be one jump ahead of me."

Bobby protested his confinement and began whimpering again as his father got in beside him.

"Comes with the territory. I was raised with three brothers and a sister. When you're the runt of the litter, you have to think fast if you want to survive." She realized that she'd used her sister's terminology. Rachel was definitely having too much influence over her lately, she mused.

"That must have been some litter," he murmured.

Looking in her rearview mirror to check out the road, her eyes met his. The quiet compliment warmed her. "By the way, I'm K. C. Haley."

"Casey?" he repeated. "As in the engineer in the children's song?"

He really was into kids, wasn't he, she thought. Most men wouldn't have been acquainted with the tune. She caught herself grinning. "No, as in Katherine Colleen. My mother's name was Katherine and so was my grandmother's. Grandma lived with us. Calling me K.C. just made things a little easier."

Making a left-hand turn at the light, K.C. made her way to Baldwin. The clinic was less than two miles away, but Saturday afternoon traffic was going to double the length of time it took to reach it.

"My name's Bailey Quaid," he told her. "And you've already met Bobby."

Waiting for a break in traffic to make a right turn,

K.C. glanced over her shoulder at the boy. "Hi, again, Bobby." Her eyes shifted to Bailey before she turned around again. "Tell me, does he often try to fly?"

"No, thank God. This was his maiden—and only—flight. I think he learned his lesson." Bailey turned his eyes appreciatively toward K.C. "And I certainly learned mine."

Her interest was piqued. "And that is?"

"Never take your eyes off your son for a minute."

K.C. turned the car into a square lot just adjacent to a busy bank. "Not until they at least turn twenty," she said, grinning.

Finding a spot just in front of the three-story building that housed the clinic, she parked her car and shut off the engine. Getting out, she opened the rear passenger door and began to unbuckle Bobby. The boy flashed her a broad grin as she picked him up and then set him on the ground.

In fifteen years, that same grin was going to be outrageously flirtatious, she thought fondly.

"Well, here it is." She gestured toward the building. "The clinic's located on the first floor, just to the right of the front doors." He could see it if he looked in, she thought. The rest of the suites were taken up by laboratories and doctors' offices. "I'm sure everything will be fine. Do you want me to wait and give you a ride home?"

"No, we'll just take a taxi home. But thank you

for all you've done." He took her hand, shaking it. Something warm and pleasant surprised her. Caught off guard, K.C. took a step back before letting go of his hand.

"Don't mention it," she murmured.

"Maybe I'll see you around." But as Bailey began to walk away from her, Bobby suddenly sent up a fresh howl, his hand outstretched toward K.C. Bailey took one more step before stopping. "I think he's taken a definite shine to you."

"I have that effect on short people." Knowing she should get going, she lingered a moment longer. "I was a pediatric nurse for a couple of years."

"And now?"

"Private duty. The hours are better." She'd taken the position to spend more time with Eric, but that had quickly fallen by the wayside. Still, she liked working for the agency and had decided to remain. Reaching up, Bobby grasped her sleeve and held on, tugging. She made no attempt to break the hold. "It looks like I'll be going in with you."

Bailey took his son's hand, trying to gently pry Bobby's fingers away from K.C.'s sleeve. Bobby hung on like an astronaut tethered to the mother ship. "He's not usually this forceful."

K.C. smiled. "I guess a few more minutes won't hurt." She led the way through the electronic doors, her sleeve still in Bobby's hand. "I'll watch Bobby for you. That'll give you a chance to call your wife and tell her not to worry. My guess is that she's probably out looking for you right now."

"No chance of that."

K.C. looked at him quizzically. He'd said it with such finality. "She's away?"

"You might say that." Finally managing to separate her sleeve from his son's hand, Bailey picked Bobby up into his arms. He took a step back. "Permanently," he added. He raised his eyes to hers. "I'm divorced. Not even a card for Christmas."

"Oh, I'm sorry." Is that what one said to someone who said they were divorced? She didn't know. It wasn't as if she had a whole lot of experience in this field. She was far better with people when they were flat on their backs and slightly out of their heads. Friendly, warm and giving, personal socializing just wasn't something K.C. was well versed in. The breakup with Eric was enough to tell her that. "I didn't mean to sound as if I were prying."

"You weren't. I was volunteering."

The chairs lining the walls of the small waiting area were all filled. Bailey shifted Bobby to his other arm just as the woman behind the sliding glass door asked for his name and why he was here. Bailey gave her the particulars and then retreated to find a space for himself.

Still at the reception desk, K.C. quickly scanned the room. Bailey would be here all day. There were only adults waiting to see the doctors on call. She hoped no one would mind if she pulled a few strings to get Bobby in first.

"Is Linda here today?" she asked the woman at the desk. "Linda Madison?"

Mentioning the nurse's name broke the ice a little. The receptionist's face softened. "Yes. Do you want me to get her?"

"Please." She glanced toward Bailey. He was looking at her quizzically. "Tell her K. C. Haley is in the waiting room." The woman disappeared.

Bailey crossed back to stand beside her again. "What are you—?"

K.C. waved for him to hold onto his question. The receptionist was returning. "Linda said to come in."

K.C. smiled her appreciation. It paid to be friendly with people. She and Linda had attended the same nursing school together and had run into one another when K.C. had brought Gracie in after a tricycle versus curb incident.

"Thank you." The next moment, the buzzer was sounding to admit them to the examining area. "I believe they're playing your song," she told Bailey.

Bailey smiled. "You're a good woman to know."

"That's what they all say," she laughed, holding the door open for them. "Until I have to irrigate their wounds."

Chapter 3

"And then what happened?" Rachel asked eagerly.

K.C. sighed. Rachel had pounced on her the moment she'd entered the house, demanding to know every single detail of what had gone on between the time she'd left the town house and now. In response, K.C. had given her a thumbnail summary, and to add to Rachel's growing frustration, dwelling more on the doctor's examination and Bobby's revived spirits than on Bailey Quaid.

On crutches now, Rachel hobbled quickly after her, giving K.C. no peace no matter where she went on the ground floor.

"And then I dropped him off at his house," K.C.

concluded with finality, hoping that was the end of it. She might have known better.

Rachel, K.C. discovered, could move very fast on crutches when she wanted to. "Did he invite you in?" she pressed.

K.C. stopped straightening the mess that had been made in the short time she'd been absent. Gracie was like a human whirlwind.

"Yes, as a matter of fact, he did. But I told him I had a pain-in-the-neck patient to get back to, so we said goodbye at the curb and I drove off. End of story, Rachel."

Rachel sighed in despair. "Well, at least you know where he lives."

Puzzled, K.C. stared at her sister. "And what do you propose I do, stalk him?"

Rachel looked at K.C. with furrowed brows. "No, just maybe pass by there a few times, be visible—"

"While whistling Lerner and Loewe's 'On The Street Where You Live?'" K.C. suggested with a short laugh. Even if she had the time for that kind of nonsense, she wouldn't do it. Handsome though Bailey Quaid was, she had absolutely no interest in getting into another relationship right now. Not until she was able to get the last one out of her system. Maybe not even then.

Growing tired from the workout she was getting by following K.C. around, Rachel slowly lowered herself onto a straight-back chair. She kept her crutches beside her. She knew if she went off to the other room to get her wheelchair, K.C. would use the opportunity to go upstairs and out of her range. Brooding, she eyed K.C. "You're not taking this seriously."

"There's nothing to *take* seriously."

Well-shaped brows rose incredulously on a smooth forehead. "A golden opportunity to meet a gorgeous man—"

"Did that," K.C. announced. "I met him. I rode with him in a car and everything. Okay?"

Her sister's pigheaded refusal to capitalize on this opportunity was beginning to irritate Rachel. This was a case of not only having to point out the watering hole to the horse, but having to force the horse to drink the water, as well.

"No, it's not okay. You're not going to tell me that you didn't find this Greek god attractive in a teeth-numbing way."

K.C. lifted a shoulder in casual disregard and then let it drop again. "I didn't notice."

Exasperation vibrated in the breath Rachel exhaled dramatically. Gracie stopped coloring and stared at her. "Then, since you're blind, you shouldn't be a nurse." She pressed her lips together, a wave of sympathy washing over her. Leaning forward, she caught K.C.'s hand. "I know Eric hurt you, but not everyone is Eric. You have to move on with your life, Kase."

K.C. extricated her hand from Rachel's. She didn't need this. "If you're not careful, I'm going to start charging your husband hardship pay.'' She heard the doorbell ringing and silently blessed providence. ''Saved by the bell.''

''I'm not finished, K.C.'' Rachel warned.

She was afraid of that, K.C. thought, opening the front door. Once she got started, Rachel had been known to go on for hours.

There was a delivery man standing on the stoop, holding a colorful profusion of flowers arranged in a large basket.

''Who was it?'' Rachel asked, finally reaching the door just as K.C. closed it.

''Someone sending you get-well flowers.''

Turning, she showed the basket to Rachel, hoping the flowers would distract her. K.C. plucked the card out and tucked it into Rachel's hand. Without another word, she went to place the basket on the section of coffee table that wasn't freshly littered with Gracie's toys.

A smile spread over Rachel's generous mouth as she read the outside of the envelope. ''If they're sending it to me, they got my name wrong. These are for you.''

Stunned, K.C. looked at Rachel and then at the basket that was still in her hands. ''Me? Who'd be sending flowers to me?''

Rachel balanced precariously on the crutches as she opened the envelope. A wide, triumphant smile creased her mouth as she read the message. She raised her eyes to K.C.'s.

"Apparently Mr. Gorgeous." Holding the card between two fingers she offered it back to her sister. "It says this is his way of saying thank you." Her grin turned smug. "Want to know what I think?"

Taking the card from Rachel, K.C. shoved it into her breast pocket even though she had to admit she wanted to read it for herself. But to show the slightest bit of interest would only be giving her sister more ammunition and Rachel was already firing wildly as it was.

"Not particularly."

Undeterred by the negative response, Rachel told her. "I think you should thank him for his thank you." Her eyes sparkled as her imagination took off. "Do it right and you could be at it for a long time."

"I'm not even going to dignify that inference by asking what the hell you're talking about." Turning on her heel, K.C. went into the back room.

"If I have to explain it, you've been without a man too long."

Struggling, she hobbled into the back room after K.C. "He does know you're single, doesn't he?"

K.C. snapped her fingers as if the thought had never occurred to her. "I forgot to wear my I'm Single banner and for some reason, the subject never came up."

Rachel frowned. "You are hopeless, you know that?"

K.C.'s smile was broad. "Good. Then give up."

Rachel had never been a quitter and apparently

had decided now was no time to start. "Aren't you going to call him back? He gave you his number." Balancing herself again, she reached for the card that was sticking out of K.C.'s pocket. "See, right there in the left-hand corner." She pointed awkwardly, calling K.C.'s attention to the pertinent line. "He said to call him if you ever—"

"Needed anything," K.C. read the end of the sentence. She drew the card out of her sister's fingers, returning it to her pocket. "Well, I don't." And then she looked at Rachel. "Except maybe to find a way to get my sister to stop pestering me."

"Want me to stop pestering you...?"

It didn't take a mind reader to know what Rachel was thinking. K.C. decided that the only way she was going to get any peace from her was to put a whole floor between them. Moving past Rachel, K.C. went back into the family room and picked up the basket of flowers.

"I'll call him later, when I have time," she told Rachel. "Right now I've got lunch to make for you and Gracie."

"You're stalling."

"And doing a fine job of it, too," K.C. answered, leaving.

She *was* stalling, K.C. thought as she gathered together the ingredients for a light meal for her sister and niece. There was no denying that she found Bailey Quaid attractive, almost to a fault. He *was* gorgeous, just as her sister said, but that didn't mean she was about to get involved with him—or any man for that matter. It was just too soon to go that route again, to lay herself open for hurt and heartache. Once this year was more than enough.

Still, she thought, sneaking a look at the card that was propped up against the flower basket, it would be rude not to call and at least thank him for the flowers. They were lovely and she didn't want to be rude....

Wiping her hands on her shorts, K.C. sneaked a look to see if perhaps in her quest to further this imaginary liaison, Rachel had decided to struggle up the stairs and was now lurking somewhere within earshot.

But she wasn't. Relieved that she wasn't going to be overheard and possibly be coached on the sidelines, K.C. went to the kitchen wall phone and dialed the number on the card.

He answered on the second ring, giving her just enough time to have her heart lodge in her throat.

For a brief second, K.C. thought of hanging up again. But that was the coward's way out and she hated admitting to being a coward. "Mr. Quaid? This is K. C. Haley. The florist just delivered your flowers. I wanted to say thank you. They're really very lovely."

"That was fast. Glad you like them. And please, the name's Bailey. Hope I didn't offend your husband."

If he wasn't as good-looking as he was, she would have said he was fishing to discover her status. But a man who looked like Bailey Quaid didn't have to go fishing for women. If anything, he needed a security system to protect himself from them.

"I'm not married."

"Then would you like to have dinner?" Before she could answer, he said, "Unless you're involved...?"

It was on the tip of her tongue to say that she was, putting an end to this. But in her whole life, K.C. had never managed to lie without stuttering. This wasn't the right time to see if she had outgrown this one holdover of her childhood affliction.

"No, I'm not involved."

"Great." There was a pause. "I mean, I'd really like to take you out to dinner so that I can thank you properly. Are you free tonight?"

"I'm—"

K.C. started to make an excuse, but since she'd managed to get herself into this, the sooner she put it behind her, the better. This way, it didn't hang over her head, making her nervous—and it didn't give Rachel time to harp on the event.

"—free," she concluded.

"Wonderful."

She wasn't sure if *wonderful* was quite the right word. She could hear Bailey's smile over the phone and felt her stomach flutter unaccountably. Something else she had no intentions of sharing with Rachel. If she did, her sister would be sending out wedding invitations in the morning mail.

"I'll pick you up at eight," he told her.

K.C. hung up, the tingling sensations traveling up and down her spine telling her that she'd made a mistake.

The clothes she'd brought with her to Rachel's house were all casual, earmarked for comfort, not for going to a restaurant that served its meals on plates instead of in paper containers. But when K.C. mentioned canceling rather than making the trek to her house to get something more appropriate to wear, Rachel had ridden to her rescue—or perversely destroyed her alibi, depending on the point of view taken. The sisters had been the same size since their midteens and everything Rachel owned could easily be worn by K.C. as well.

Rachel was in her glory as she threw open her vast closets, picking through rows of dresses she declared suitable for the outing.

Rachel's tastes were far more glamorous than K.C.'s and each dress that Rachel held up for her, K.C. vetoed. Each one that appealed to K.C. earned her sister's frown. They finally agreed on a sleek navy sheath with white trim at the neck and armholes.

At a quarter to eight, the telephone rang.

K.C., ready in body if not spirit for the last half hour, jumped at the sound.

"That's him. He's calling to cancel," she announced, feeling a wave of relief contrasted by just a drop of regret that she quickly shrugged off.

"How did you get to be so pessimistic?" Rachel chided, shaking her head. "It's probably just a credit card salesperson trying to get me to buy travel insurance." Rachel held out her hand expectantly.

But it was Bailey on the other end.

"K.C., I'm running a little behind," he apologized. "If it wouldn't be too much of an inconvenience, would you mind very much coming by here first?" In case she'd forgotten, he gave her his address again.

Hesitating, she debated postponing. But the words never came out of her mouth. No sense in wasting a pretty dress, she told herself. "All right. I can be there in a few minutes." She hung up, feeling Rachel's eyes boring into her. "He wants me to stop by first."

"I figured that part out for myself."

K.C. blew out a breath, wondering if she was doing the right thing. "I have a bad feeling about this," she murmured.

Rachel was all smiles. "I don't."

The statement didn't make K.C. feel any better.

Chapter 4

There was no doubt about it. Murphy's Law had a terrible way of rearing its head at the worst possible time, Bailey thought.

Finally retiring his small, worn phone book, he decided to give up. Every sitter he had ever used since Bobby was born was booked tonight.

Well, why not? he thought in frustrated resignation. It was Saturday night. If the girls weren't sitting for someone, they were out themselves, enjoying the evening. The way he wanted to. The smart thing to do, Bailey knew, was to call K.C. back and reschedule. But he had this uneasy feeling that if he did, he might never get the opportunity to go out with her again.

And he wanted to.

Something had clicked between them from the moment he'd stopped worrying about Bobby and began to focus on the woman his son's aviating attempt had brought into his life. For the most part, Bailey didn't believe in chemistry, other than what could be found between the pages of a hard-bound textbook. But he could have sworn that there had been something, that he'd felt something, when they had sat there in the walk-in clinic examination room, talking. There was something about K.C., a light, a spark, he wasn't sure just what to call it. He only knew he wanted the opportunity to examine it more closely. To examine her more closely.

It had come as a complete surprise to him. He hadn't really taken notice of any woman since Gloria had walked out on him. But any way he looked at it, K. C. Haley was a hard woman *not* to notice.

Quicksilver—that was what she reminded him of, he suddenly realized as an idea came to him. He hurried to put it in motion. Quicksilver, something that could easily slide through his fingers if he didn't make an effort to hold on to it.

Something told Bailey that he wanted to make that effort. Besides, there was no harm in spending the evening in the company of a bright, witty female who didn't get rattled by the antics of an overenergetic eighteen-month-old boy.

She was the perfect woman for man and boy, he

thought with a smile, at least for the space of an evening. After that...

They'd see.

The doorbell rang as eight-fifteen came much too soon. Bailey hadn't really intended on bringing her back to his house tonight, so there'd been no effort to make the place presentable. Looking around him now, he figured labeling the surroundings as early chaos would have been extremely charitable.

"Hope she brought her sense of humor with her," he murmured, crossing to the front door.

As K.C. pressed the doorbell, nerves swiftly traveled up and down her body, ending up knotting themselves in her stomach.

He wasn't answering. Good. Now if she could just—

The door opened, aborting her escape before it even began. Bailey was standing in the doorway, wearing gray slacks and a blue shirt rolled up at the sleeves.

She was overdressed, K.C. thought. She knew she should have stuck to her guns and gone with the casual.

His smile was warm, inviting. Her stomach tightened a little more. "Hi."

"Hi." K.C. managed a smile in response. Maybe the date was a threesome and they were taking Bobby with them. That would explain why he wasn't wearing a suit. "Emergency all squared away?"

"It wasn't exactly an emergency..." When in doubt, go with the truth. It was usually less complicated that way. At least it was easier to keep track of. Stepping back, he held open the door for her, momentarily forgetting the state of his living room. "There's just been a little change in plans. My sitter was already booked and no one else was free."

Better this way. K.C. inclined her head, ready to have him bow out of the evening. "We can make it for some other time...."

But Bailey didn't want it to be some other time. "Do you like lasagna?"

They weren't going anywhere. Why was he asking? "I love lasagna."

His smile became more hopeful. "If you don't mind one-day leftovers, I have some in the refrigerator."

"Take home?" K.C. guessed. She recalled that there was a fairly good Italian restaurant not far from where they were.

"Make home," he corrected.

"Excuse me?"

"I made it."

She still wasn't following him. "You mean the kind you get from the frozen food section in the supermarket and put in the microwave?"

None of the men in her family cooked. Eric had barely been able to make a sandwich on his own without a diagram. For that matter, Rachel couldn't cook, either. To her, the stove was just another piece of decorative furniture. Rachel, Bryan and Gracie ate most of their meals in restaurants, or ordered in.

"No, I mean I made it. From scratch," he elaborated. "After my ex-wife left, I found that I like to cook. Actually, it's kind of therapeutic. It helps me think."

"About what?"

"About those." He waved his hand around, indicating all the toys. No matter how polite she was trying to be, she couldn't have possibly missed the turmoil in the room.

Well, now that he mentioned it, she didn't have to pretend she didn't notice. K.C.'s eyes swept over the room. There were toys piled one on top of another everywhere she looked.

She turned toward him. "Speaking of which, did someone die and leave you a toy store or did one just explode in here?"

She'd never seen so many toys in one place outside of stores in a mall. The variety was astounding. Bobby had to be one eclectic little boy, not to mention exceedingly lucky. Bailey was obviously a very doting father who brought new meaning to the term *spoiling*.

"I'd thought Gracie had too many toys, but this makes her look almost underprivileged."

Amazed, K.C. went from one cluster of toys to another. All were toys geared for the very young child. No action figures, no mind-bending electronics. Just old-fashioned toys that needed love and imagination. She found that rather sweet.

"I've never seen so many different kinds of toys for one child." She glanced over her shoulder at Bailey. There was an amused expression on his face she couldn't quite read. Was he laughing at her? "Does he play with all of them?"

"Pretty much." And that pleased him to no end. Ever since he'd been born, Bobby had been his personal test market. "When he gets older, I'll move on to more elaborate toys."

She was trying to understand the connection. "Then they're your toys?"

"In a manner of speaking." He couldn't help the pride that came into his voice. "I designed them."

K.C. looked at the toys with more interest and not a little amazement. "You *make* toys?"

"Yes, why?"

She laughed at her own preconceived notions. "I'm sorry. I always thought of a toy maker as someone who looked, well, more like Santa Claus. Half glasses on the tip of his nose, round belly, that sort of thing." She couldn't help looking at Bailey's physique. Even in casual clothing it was obvious that the man was very fit. Slim hips, wide shoulders and, judging by what she saw thanks to his rolled-up sleeves, forearms that could have doubled as rock formations. "You certainly don't fit that description."

"Thank you—I think. So—" Bailey looked at her hopefully. "Now that you know that I'm not Santa Claus, just his able apprentice, does this mean you'll stay for leftovers?"

"Well, I—" Still uncertain about the wisdom of remaining, K.C. spotted a familiar stuffed animal on top of the bookcase. Crossing to it, she picked up the sweetly grinning creature and held it up. There was disbelief in her eyes as she looked at him. "You didn't design this, too, did you?"

He couldn't read her expression. "If I say yes, will that get me into trouble?"

It was as good as an admission. "You designed Mr. Fuzzy-Foo?"

Bailey winced at the name. Though he limited his participation to creation, this particular name was a sore spot for him. "I designed it, but I didn't name it. That blame belongs to the PR firm that MacAffee Toys employs." He took the blue-maned figure from her and looked at it. It still made him smile every time he saw it, which had been his intention when he designed it. "Personally, I liked Gilroy myself."

She grinned, looking at the beige face surrounded by a blue mane stuffed under a baseball cap. Multicolored short pants completed the ensemble. As close as she could see, the fifteen-inch stuffed animal resembled a comical lion that had fallen into a vat of rainbow paint.

"Oh, I don't know. Mr. Fuzzy-Foo has a certain ring to it." There was new respect in her eyes when she looked at him. A man who could design toys like this had to have a very sensitive side to him. "I want you to know that this is Gracie's very favorite stuffed animal."

It always pleased him to discover that one of his toys brought a child pleasure. He'd been creating toys ever since he could remember, dating back to the elaborate city he'd created out of discarded shoe boxes he'd enterprisingly gathered from around the neighborhood on garbage day. The city, large enough to accommodate a small doll, had been a birthday gift for his younger cousin.

"Gracie has good taste," he acknowledged.

K.C. laughed. "Don't let it go to your head. She tends to be rather fickle."

"Women her age usually are." He nodded at the creature in her hands. "That's yours, if you'd like it."

She had to admit she was tempted. There was something incredibly comforting about the way the painted-on eyes seemed to look at her. "Won't Bobby notice it's missing?"

Her protest drew a laugh as Bailey gestured around the cluttered room. He'd gone through two housekeepers just since he'd moved in here. He still hadn't found one who would just dust the toys without rearranging them. "Look around. Anyway, there are at least six Mr. Fuzzy-Foos in residence right now."

Bailey seemed to be embarrassed by the state of

the room, but K.C. could see what he didn't. She could see into the mind and heart of a small child. "I take it you're still learning about kids, aren't you?" The expression on his face told her that he didn't comprehend her meaning. "You can pack up two thousand toys with you when you go on a trip, but it's the one you left behind that they want. Children have an uncanny way of remembering everything that's theirs." She held the stuffed animal out to him. "Darling though he is, I'd better give this little guy back to you." She set Mr. Fuzzy-Foo back where he'd been sitting.

But what his offer had accomplished was to clear away her hesitation. "But you can talk me into the lasagna if you'd like. I'm kind of curious to find out how well someone who can dream this sort of thing up can actually cook."

Bailey slipped his arm around her shoulders, escorting her past the debris into his dining room. The kitchen was just beyond. If their luck held for just a few hours, Bobby would remain asleep long enough for them to have a peaceful dinner. It was something to shoot for.

"Well, I haven't poisoned Bobby yet, but then his requirements are rather simple."

Someone else might have tried to impress her with a list of dishes they could whip up. She liked the fact that he was low-key. "You don't go in for the hard sell, do you?"

Bailey thought of his wife, of how his brother had

told him he should have fought to keep her from leaving. Because he loved her, he'd been tempted, but even if he had managed to talk her into staying, it wouldn't have been the same. He wanted Gloria to remain with him and Bobby because she wanted to, not because of any arm-twisting or bribery on his part.

"I never talk anyone into anything."

Though he said it so solemnly, she realized later that it was at that exact moment that she began to relax in his company.

K.C. peered into the kitchen. Like the living room, there were toys scattered here and there, but here their function was more decorative than things that had been left behind as reminders of games that were quickly forgotten.

She looked at Bailey. "Is there anything I can do to help?"

He wasn't accustomed to having help in the kitchen. "You're doing it now." He took two dinner plates from the cupboard. "You're being a good sport about this."

"Good sport nothing. I intend to be very judgmental about the meal. I have very high lasagna standards." She took the plates from him. "I'll set the table."

Watching her walk away into the next room, he nearly caught his fingers in the refrigerator door as it slipped closed.

No doubt about it, he mused. The woman looked just as good going as she did coming.

Chapter 5

Setting down her knife and fork, K.C. moved her empty plate back. She was pleasantly full.

"That was surprisingly very good." Prepared to be polite and endure what was placed in front of her no matter how foul it tasted, K.C. had been amazed to discover that not only was the lasagna edible, it was actually delicious. The man had hidden talents.

Bailey released the breath he'd been subconsciously holding, relieved. Leaning over, he topped off her glass of wine. Disturbed, the liquid shimmered and sparkled, catching the reflection from the single candle he had managed to find at the last minute.

Sitting back, he looked at her as he took a sip

from his own glass. "I'm not sure if I should take exception to the way you phrased that or not. Are you surprised because you didn't think I was capable of cooking, or is it that you just have very low expectations in general where men's abilities in the kitchen are concerned?"

Acutely aware of warm feelings filtering through her, feelings that had their origin in his eyes, she raised her glass to her lips. The wine only added to the sensation. She toyed with the stem.

"The latter. Besides Rachel, I grew up with three brothers and a father who couldn't find the kitchen without a road map." She thought her comment over. "Not that Rachel is all that much better."

"Rachel?" Bailey echoed. Discovering himself more and more intrigued by the woman across from him as the minutes of the evening fed into one another, questions about her began to surface. He wanted to find out all there was to know.

She nodded, taking another sip, her eyes never leaving his. Was it her, or was it suddenly growing really hot in here? "My sister. I'm staying with her right now to help her with Gracie until her leg's better. She broke it skiing," she added as an afterthought. "Taking advantage of the first early snow of the season didn't exactly turn out for her."

Why did she feel as if she were fumbling inside? This was just a pleasant evening—being shared with a drop-dead, gorgeous male. But he hadn't made a move on her and that was a good sign.

Wasn't it?

She took another sip of wine.

Bailey thought of the animated little girl he'd seen with K.C. this afternoon. They'd looked so much alike, he would have never questioned that they were mother and daughter. Surprise. "Then Gracie isn't yours?"

She rolled the words over in her mind. She'd been there at Gracie's birth. Rachel had gone into hard labor so quickly, there hadn't been time to get her to a doctor. K.C. had delivered her niece in the back seat of her car. She'd been the first one to hold Gracie, wrinkled and screaming, in her arms.

"Well, I wouldn't quite put it that way." She saw his eyes narrow in a silent query. K.C. decided not to launch into a lengthy story. "She is in spirit. I think I spend more time playing with her than her parents do. Not that Rachel isn't a good mother," she interjected quickly, afraid he'd misunderstand. Mothering wasn't exactly Rachel's long suit, although there was no question that she dearly loved Gracie. She just did better with people old enough to gossip. "She's just not a very creative mother." It was up to her to create imaginary adventures and partake in long, involved picnics with invisible guests. "The games Rachel likes to play are on a slightly more adult level." Like trying to trick her into accepting an endless parade of blind dates. So far, Rachel was zero for twelve and the streak was not about to be broken any time soon if K.C. had anything to say about it.

Bailey wasn't sure he followed her, but he was willing to go on listening to K.C. for as long as she was willing to talk. She had a soft, melodic voice and a way of curving her mouth that reminded him that it had been a very long time since he'd kissed a woman. "Such as?"

"Never mind."

She'd talked too much, she realized. There was no way she was going to add to that by telling him about Rachel's matchmaking tendencies—or that her sister referred to him and his friends as The Single Daddy Club.

She set her glass aside, telling herself it was the wine that was making her so fidgety, and not the way his green eyes seemed to draw her right in. "So tell me, how did you get into designing toys?"

Some people spent years trying one thing and then another before they found their true avocation—if ever. He had been one of the lucky ones. "It just seemed to evolve naturally." He smiled, remembering. "My roommate in college was the son of a toy manufacturer. MacAffee Toys."

She was well acquainted with the name. "Gracie has a lot of their products. Their company's over a hundred years old."

K.C. thought of the slogan they'd adopted: Never A Harmful Toy. K.C. made a point of looking for the tag whenever she bought anything for Gracie.

"More like a hundred and thirty," he corrected. "Anyway, Chris, my roommate, was looking for a way to impress this girl he was seeing and I designed this sleepy-eyed squirrel for him that said silly things like, 'I'm nuts about you—' Don't laugh," he warned, so of course she did.

Like a man who'd just had a net thrown over him, Bailey found himself ensnared by the sound. It curled all around him like a warm, perfumed summer breeze. For a moment, he lost his train of thought and found himself just looking into her eyes, his mind a blank except for the single thought of how nice it would be to kiss this woman. To hold her to him and feel that soft laughter ripple against his skin.

Trying to shake himself free of the mesmerizing sensation, he murmured, "The rest is history," ending his story abruptly.

But the moment's hold and the thoughts it was generating were not very easy to disentangle. He found himself wanting her more than just a little.

Leaning forward over the small table, he brushed a strand of her hair away from her cheek, lightly skimming his fingertips along her skin. He'd been watching it sway for most of the meal. "You're lucky that didn't get any sauce on it."

The battle was lost and so was he.

His feelings had been asleep for over fifteen months. Funny, he would have thought that when their time came, they would have unfurled slowly, as if they and he were waking up from a long hibernation. Instead, they jerked up, wide-awake and at attention, as if in response to an alarm that had been sounded.

An alarm named K.C.

Hardly realizing what he was doing until a moment after he was already doing it, Bailey inclined his head toward K.C.'s and brushed his lips against hers.

Just like in the movies, K.C. thought, her heart hammering wildly.

And, just like in the movies, credits would be rolling across the screen all too soon, signaling an ending to the film. If she kept that in mind, she told herself, desperately trying to hang on to reality, then she couldn't get carried away by the fact that the man's mouth tasted of dark, forbidden things that made her head swirl and something deep inside her cry out for more.

In theory, her thoughts were sound, but in practice they held up like a tissue in raging flood waters. It broke apart and disappeared an instant into the kiss.

K.C. was only marginally aware of dropping the fork she'd been holding. Or maybe the fork had been on the table all along and she'd knocked it off as she leaned into this rhapsody disguised as a kiss that was playing along her lips.

She wasn't sure.

Wasn't sure of anything right now. Certain only that whatever was happening was drawing her in until everything else around her was being reduced to a minuscule pinprick. A little like the one and only time she'd fainted as a teenager. But that had been caused by the flu and had been a frightening experience.

This was no flu.

Awestruck, K.C. felt absolutely wonderful and on the verge of bursting into song, possibly even in another language.

It felt as if there were exotic wine being pumped through his veins instead of blood. The thought came to Bailey from nowhere, disappearing just as quickly. Leaving behind an indelible mark. Just like she was.

Threading his fingers through her hair, curving them around the back of her head, Bailey brought her mouth even closer to his. He deepened the kiss, losing himself in it even before he did so. He'd never liked not knowing his way.

This time, it didn't matter.

All that mattered was kissing her. And feeling alive again for the first time in a century.

"Dad-dee! Come!"

The small, high-pitched command burst upon them with the suddenness of a squall. Like drowning victims drawn from the water at the last moment before the sea claimed them, K.C. and Bailey gasped as they sprang apart. Dazed with touches of bewildered guilt, they looked at the child they had both momentarily forgotten.

Clad in one-piece turquoise pajamas complete with feet and dragging a matching turquoise Mr. Fuzzy-Foo with him, Bobby was standing in the dining room doorway, a wide, triumphant grin splitting his round little face.

K.C. stifled a laugh. The boy looked so very proud of himself. "Looks like we're not alone."

Bailey was already on his feet, crossing to his son. He'd left him sound asleep in his bed. In any event, Bobby had been safe in his crib.

Apparently the word *safe* no longer applied. "How did you get out of your crib?"

In reply, Bobby laughed gleefully, utterly delighted with himself. Raising his chin up, he patted his chest emulating, K.C. surmised, a cartoon character he'd witnessed. "Bobb-bee beeg boy."

"You may have to change that to Bobby Houdini," K.C. observed, tongue-in-cheek. By the surprised look on Bailey's face, she guessed that this was the first time Bobby had executed his escape trick. "How high do you have the railings?"

"They're up all the way." Worried that Bobby might fall out, Bailey had made certain that he'd extended the bars on either side to their maximum length. Obviously that was no longer enough.

Time marches on, K.C. mused. She ruffled Bobby's hair. Dark, like his father's, she couldn't help wondering if Bailey's felt just as silken to the touch. "My guess is that somebody should be in the market for a junior bed right about now."

"I thought I had a few months' grace before that happened." Holding him, Bailey nuzzled his son. "You're growing up too fast, kid." His accomplishment a thing of the past, Bobby was already reaching for K.C. with a determined expression on his face. "Too fast," Bailey repeated with a laugh.

Unable to resist, and a little shaken by what had just happened at the table with Bobby's father, K.C. took Bobby from Bailey's arms. She pretended to look at him sternly, but couldn't quite pull it off. "Isn't it past your bedtime, big guy?"

Bobby firmly shook his head, the wide smile now turned down into a frown. "No bed."

She laughed at the reply, glancing toward Bailey. "I see he's going to segue into the terrible twos very smoothly."

Bailey winced at the suggestion. He was having enough trouble just holding his own as it was. He didn't want to think about it getting any worse. "I thought that was just a myth."

Balancing the boy on her hip, K.C. feathered her fingers through his thick hair as she smiled at him. He responded by wrapping his arms around her neck. K.C. felt herself losing her heart. Was that twice in one evening? The question echoed in her mind before she firmly pushed it aside.

"Myths always have at least a germ of truth to them—" She glanced at Bailey. "Like Santa Claus."

"Santa Claus is a myth?" Bailey pretended to look so aghast, she had to laugh.

"No." She struggled to keep a straight face. "Actually, only Mrs. Claus is. They had to invent her because, what with Santa living with all those elves up there at the North Pole, people were beginning to talk." Inclining her head toward him, she confided, "I mean, how long does it really take to build a doll house anyway?"

The scent of her hair came to him just then, scrambling his brain just enough to make Bailey pause before answering, trying to collect his thoughts. "You would be surprised."

He liked her, he thought. Liked the easy way she returned his banter, liked the way she held his son as if the boy were something precious and not just a burden to transfer from one place to another.

Liked too, the way she threatened to permanently singe his socks when she kissed him.

Looking at her, Bailey made his decision. The hell with once burnt, twice leery. This was a woman worth taking a risk on. A woman he really wanted to get to know better.

Very gently, he took Bobby back into his arms. Bobby looked somewhat disgruntled about giving up his new playmate. "If you'll excuse me, I'll just put my escape artist to bed."

Wriggling, Bobby loudly declared his terms for surrender. "Sto-wee, sto-wee."

Bailey suppressed a sigh. It looked as if it were

going to be a very long night and not shaping up exactly as he'd hoped.

K.C. laid a hand on Bailey's shoulder, stopping him before he left the room. Bobby took the opportunity to wrap his arms around her arm and hold on for dear life. "I can read a story to him if you like."

Bailey looked down at the near-death grip his son had on his date.

"It looks as if you might not have a choice," he quipped. "But really, you don't have to—if you don't mind waiting until I read one to him." He had visions of her leaving before he was finished.

"I don't mind, but I hate being inactive." She gestured at the room behind her. "The alternative to my reading to Bobby is for me to start organizing your toys."

He didn't doubt that she'd make good on her threat, he thought, looking into her eyes. Though it didn't look it, he actually had a system as far as knowing where the toys were.

Bailey picked the more attractive proposition. "You can read a story."

This way, he figured, everyone won.

Chapter 6

"And they lived happily ever after."

Closing the book softly, K.C. looked over toward Bobby.

Success!

Closing one hand into a fist, she pulled it down quickly in a universal sign of silent victory. It appeared that Bobby had finally lost the ongoing battle he'd been waging with his eyelids. They didn't pop open the way they had at the end of the other three stories she had read to him.

The tireless child was finally tired and asleep.

Engulfed in a sense of triumph, K.C. shifted her eyes over toward Bailey. Since she'd offered him a reprieve, she'd fully expected Bailey to have taken the opportunity to leave his son's bedroom once she had begun reading the first story. To her surprise, and maybe, yes, just a touch of pleasure, he had remained, listening almost as attentively as Bobby had while she read one Hans Christian Andersen tale after another until her audience had finally drifted away.

Most men would have been nodding out by now. Her brother-in-law usually fell asleep by the third page when he was reading to Gracie. Bailey really was a rare man, she mused.

With a suppressed sigh, K.C. slowly rose to her feet and glanced at her watch. It had taken the better part of an hour and a half to get Bobby back to where he'd been when she'd arrived tonight. It was getting late, she thought. Maybe it was time she called it a night herself—before she was tempted to do something she might regret all too soon. Bailey had far too tempting a mouth to ignore indefinitely.

It seemed that Bailey had begun to despair that Bobby was never going to fall asleep. Having K.C. around seemed to wire the boy even more than usual. Bailey knew the feeling.

Crossing to her now from the window seat, he took the oversize book from her and placed it back on the crowded bookshelf. Toys weren't the only thing in abundance within Bobby's room. Apparently Bailey made frequent trips to the bookstore which resulted in more books for Bobby's growing library.

With his finger to his lips, he took K.C.'s hand and led her quietly from the room. Very softly, he eased Bobby's door shut behind him.

"Home free," he whispered, then smiled, still holding her hand. "Thanks for doing that."

With very little effort, she could be coaxed into leaving her hand in his indefinitely. Which was why she made a point of dropping it. There was no sense in letting herself get carried away to places that didn't exist except in fairy tales and the recesses of her mind.

Striving to be casual while strange little eruptions were going on inside her, K.C. shrugged. "I love reading fairy tales." Because looking at him in the dim hallway was suddenly generating far too intimate an atmosphere for her to successfully handle, she turned on her heel and walked back to the dining room. "Too bad life can't imitate them."

Without asking, she began clearing the table. She needed to do something with her hands.

"Actually, it probably does. At least the ones that were written by the Brothers Grimm and Hans Christian Andersen." Following her lead, he began picking up empty plates. "Have you ever read the originals?"

Looking around, she found the dishwasher. But when she opened it to place the plates inside, she discovered that it was full of clean dishes Bailey had neglected to put away.

"Those aren't them?" Stacking her plates in the sink, she began unloading the dishwasher.

"Those aren't them. The real stories they wrote were more like science fiction of the time, written with an eye for an adult audience." He thought of the couple he'd read. "They would have scared someone like Bobby into six months of insomnia."

Not knowing where the glasses belonged, K.C. lined them up on the counter. "So, even fairy tales don't have fairy tale endings?"

She hadn't been kidding about not being able to remain inactive for long. The need for activity brought other thoughts to his mind that he knew were far too premature at the moment. He began to wonder if he made her nervous. The thought amused him. The last time he had made a woman nervous, he'd stuck a frog in front of Alice Meyers.

"Those don't, but that doesn't mean you can't keep on looking until you find the right kind of story, the right kind of ending."

She began opening cupboards, looking for the right spaces to stack the dishes. "Spoken like a man who's a child at heart."

Still watching, Bailey leaned a hip against the edge of the counter. Was she going to wash the floor next? "Nothing wrong with that. Children see life through the eyes of innocence and simplicity. Nothing is hopeless and everything is possible."

It must have seemed like an incredible amount of optimism coming from someone over the age of fourteen, because she stopped stacking and looked at him over her shoulder. "You're divorced, right?"

Bailey knew what she was thinking. Divorce brought with it dual suitcases stuffed with cynicism and pessimism. He carried no such baggage with him. What his divorce had cost him was the loss of a certain amount of enthusiasm and hope.

Nothing that wasn't being replenished even as he stood here with her.

"Divorced, yes, but I'm far from emotionally terminated." Enough was enough, he thought, closing the last cupboard in front of her. "I didn't ask you over to audition for the part of housekeeper." Weaving his hand through hers, he led her into the living room, then turned to face her. "So, where were we?"

He was standing close to her. She could feel that same unsettled feeling beginning all over again. The one that warned her she was about to go over the falls in a barrel made out of spun sugar.

She wet her lips, unconsciously, he was sure. "Being interrupted by the youngest stunt man on record."

His eyes were on her lips as her tongue flicked over them again. Maybe she doing that to drive him crazy. If she was, she was succeeding. "And before then?"

How could her heart have stopped and her pulse points all be throbbing at the same time? "I was commenting on your culinary skills." The words came out in a bare whisper.

She *was* nervous, he thought, charmed. Here she was, reducing him to the consistency of Jell-O left out in the sun and he was making *her* nervous.

It gave him hope.

He lightly feathered his fingers through her hair, exciting himself. "Seems to me that there was something in between."

She swallowed. Survivalist humor glinted in her eyes while she appeared blasé. "You mean the part where you were burning off my lips?"

He wouldn't have given himself that kind of credit. If anyone was burning anyone, it was her burning him. Making him burn *for* her. "That was probably the seasoning in the lasagna."

"I don't think seasoning had anything to do with it—unless you're being metaphorical."

Oh, how he wanted her. Bailey wondered what the chances were that Bobby would sleep through the rest of the night.

"Right about now," he whispered against her mouth, "I can hardly think straight enough to be coherent, but I can be anything you like—"

With effort, she drew her head back, though she wanted nothing else but to kiss him again. But that would be a mistake. Opening her up to others.

"How about patient?"

He blinked, trying to focus. "All right," he amended, beginning to follow her. "Almost anything." But he saw that she was serious. The last thing he wanted to do was force himself on her. He blew out a breath. "Am I going too fast?"

K.C. pressed her lips together, shaking her head slowly. Her eyes never left his. "Maybe I'm just too slow."

He laughed softly, playing with the same wayward strand of her hair before tucking it behind her ear.

"Lady, there is nothing slow about you." Since he knew that if he kept on touching her, he'd want more, Bailey shoved his hands into his front pockets and took a step back. "I'll be honest with you, K.C. Bobby and I don't get out very much. We keep each other pretty busy—and then there're the toys." He nodded behind him. "Not much space for socializing." He smiled at her. "But Bobby seems to have taken a real shine to you."

This was her chance to back away. To say goodnight and retreat. Why was she staying put? And why did she hear herself asking, "And his father?"

A smile spread across his face.

"His father knows better than to question his son's judgment. After all, Bobby was the one who picked Gilroy out above the rest."

Confused, she shook her head. "Gilroy?"

"Mr. Fuzzy-Foo." He pointed to the toy. Bailey's eyes washed over her slowly. "The boy knows a winner when he sees one."

K.C. could almost feel his eyes touching her.

Warming her. She tried to steel herself off. There were places she didn't want to revisit, no matter how inviting. "You're putting a lot of responsibility on a little boy."

The truth of the matter was, even at eighteen months, Bobby was showing signs that his tastes were similar to his own, Bailey thought. He was looking forward to a long, full relationship with the boy.

And wasn't Bobby the one who had reached for K.C. first? "If you can't have faith in your own flesh and blood, who can you trust?"

"Maybe I had better call it a night." She flushed slightly. "All that 'heavy' reading has worn me out more than I thought."

Bailey saw through the quip easily. "You don't have to explain."

"It's not that I didn't enjoy tonight, I did. *All* of it," she emphasized. K.C. heard herself admitting more than she'd intended on giving away about herself to a man who inexplicably felt too intimately close to be the stranger he was. "It's just that I'm learning to take baby steps again."

She had a past. And wounds. Who didn't? "Want to talk about it? I'm a great listener." He pointed to the array of talking dolls he had designed. "It would be nice to hear a feminine voice without having to pull a string or press an elbow first."

He made her laugh again. "Not much to say. We

fell in love, he fell out." Shrugging, she said, "Wouldn't even make a decent T-shirt slogan."

So she had a gift for understatement. "But he hurt you and you're leery."

K.C. looked off, avoiding his eyes. They were far too kind. And far too sexy. No swimming lessons in the world would have kept her from drowning in them eventually. "Something like that."

Maybe it would help her if he shared a little of his own story with her. "You're not alone, you know. About being hurt, or leery. Or being the last one to fall out of love with someone."

Something in his tone pulled at her. K.C. looked at Bailey.

"I married Bobby's mother not because she was carrying Bobby but because I was in love with her and I thought that if I did all the right things, I could make her happy." A smile that was more philosophical than humorous curved his mouth. "But you can't make someone happy. They have to be happy to begin with. And our life together didn't make Gloria happy. One day, she decided to just call it quits." Though he was talking about it, he tried to keep the memory at arm's length. Fifteen months later, it still hurt. "I came home early to find her leaving a note with the sitter." Just like that, after all their time together, she left both of them with only a note in her wake. Without realizing it, Bailey set his mouth hard. "I made her read it to me, just so I could get it into my head that it was over."

Forcing the tentacles of the memory back before it ensnared him, Bailey looked at K.C. "But just because Gloria and I didn't work out doesn't mean that someday, there won't be someone who does." He paused, flushing slightly. "Sorry, didn't mean to sound as if I were preaching."

"You weren't. I appreciate your sharing that with me."

But she still wanted to run, he thought. Taking her hands into his, he looked into her eyes. Holding himself fast. "I'd really like to take you home, K.C., but—" He glanced over his shoulder toward the rear of the house and Bobby's bedroom.

"I understand."

More than anything, he wanted to ask her to stay, but he knew it was too soon. All he could do was look to the future. "And I'd really like to see you again."

She tried to sound blasé again. "I'll be in the park."

He held her hands a moment longer. "You know what I mean."

Her heart began to hammer. Oh no, she wasn't going to go there again. Once was more than enough. Visions of Eric popped into her head.

Drawing her hands away, she began to move back. "And you know where I live—"

Yes, he thought, he certainly did. "Oh, K.C., wait," he called to her before she could run off.

She turned.

Bailey handed her the beige-and-blue stuffed animal she had held earlier. She stared at him, bemused and puzzled.

"Think of it as a souvenir—or a bribe." And something to make her think fondly of him. "You can give it to Gracie if you like."

She smiled at the toy, then up at him. "Gracie has one. This one's mine."

She held it against her much the way Bobby did, he noticed.

Suddenly, she brushed her lips against his. "Thank you," she said before she left abruptly.

Best trade he ever made, Bailey thought to himself as he traced the imprint of her lips against his, watching her walk to her car through his window.

Chapter 7

Nathan Calloway's voice broke Bailey's reverie. "Is there anything particularly strange going on across the street that I can't see?"

It took a second for the question to sink in. Bailey was aware that the other men all turned to look at him with open interest. Discussion of that afternoon's football game had abruptly ceased. "What do you mean?"

Nathan waved his hand at the Mediterranean-style town houses facing the park. "Whenever you're not watching Bobby, you're looking over your shoulder at those town houses. I've been talking to the back of your head half the time I've been sitting here."

Bailey thought of covering, but that would make

the situation out to be more than it was. "Sorry, just wondering if K.C. was coming out today."

Taylor stopped tossing the football to his five-year-old. "A new playmate for Bobby?"

Jeff Hamlin laughed. He'd noticed that something was up himself. Bailey had been far too preoccupied today. "More like one for Bobby's father, from the kinds of the looks he's been shooting that way."

Bailey wasn't in the mood for ribbing. At least, not the kind these men could give. A shoulder rose and fell in studied nonchalance as he brushed off the observation. "Just someone I met."

The admission brought hoots of appreciation. Billy Stevens clapped his large hands together. "Hey, let's hear it for the Toyman." He raised and lowered his eyebrows in an age-old lecherous gesture. "Does this 'someone' have a sister?"

Bailey laughed. "You don't even know what she looks like."

Joining in, Nathan waved his hand at the protest. "Doesn't matter." His eyes wandered over toward his twins, three-year-old boys guaranteed to wreak havoc on any army. "Right about now I'd settle for any sort of female companionship. A woman who doesn't run for cover as soon as she knows that twins run in the family."

"Emphasis on *run,*" Billy interjected with a booming laugh.

Bailey knew that Billy was only half kidding. A single man with a child might be initially appealing, but the reality of the responsibilities had a way of throwing cold water on any budding relationship after a short while. Sitting back, he wondered how much to admit to the men. How much there *was* to admit to the men. He hadn't had an opportunity to explore his feelings any further because the object of his interest had been conspicuously absent since Saturday.

"Her sister's married," Bailey muttered.

Billy sighed soulfully. "Everybody's sister's married." But then his grin took over, widening encouragingly. "So, are you two going out or what?"

"Right now, 'or what' pretty much describes it." Bailey was beginning to wonder if he'd misread the signs. Saturday evening, it had seemed as if there had been a great deal of promise. But he hadn't seen her since. She hadn't even come to the park with Gracie the way she'd inferred she would. Was there a message in that? Was he to think that she was intentionally avoiding him?

Because there was a silent demand for details, Bailey gave them a quick summary of Saturday's events after they'd left. "She helped me out with Bobby," he concluded, "and I had her over for dinner that night to say thank you."

The men all looked at him expectantly, clearly not content to leave the matter hanging.

"And?" Nathan finally coaxed.

Bailey blew out a breath. "And now I haven't seen her since."

"Did you try calling?" Jeff suggested as he tied his son's laces for the third time that afternoon.

Bailey had thought about it and had even picked up the telephone once or twice. But Gloria's rejection had left scars in its wake and he wasn't entirely sold on the idea of leaving himself wide-open to enduring the same experience again so soon.

"I don't want to be pushy." His excuse, he knew, didn't exactly go over well with the others. But it wasn't the others he was thinking of. "I thought if she came out with her niece, maybe we could pick up where we left off. Start a conversation."

Nathan shook his head. "If that's where you left it off, maybe you went about Saturday night all wrong. Women like romance."

"Nothing wrong with that," Billy commented.

Nathan turned toward him. "I never said there was. I could use a little myself right now."

"Awww," Billy teased.

Taylor looked at Bailey, as if a bell suddenly went off in his head. "Hey, she wouldn't be the one that we saw last Saturday, would she?"

"The one with legs up to here?" Jeff slid into the seat beside Bailey, holding his hand up to his chin. When Bailey acknowledged the description with a nod, Jeff hooted his delight and jabbed him with an elbow. "You old dog, you." And then he realized Bailey's dilemma. "That kind isn't just going to throw herself at you, Bailey, good-looking though you might be."

Nathan drew his head back, pretending to scrutinize Bailey closely. His eyes shifted toward Jeff. "You think he's good-looking?"

Jeff spread out his hands. "Yeah. In a clean-cut sort of way."

Billy ran his hand though his blond hair, tossing it back in an exaggerated motion the way a model might. "How about me?"

Jeff snorted. "You, you're lucky your dog doesn't bury you in the backyard along with his ugly bones."

"Guys," Nathan summoned their attention back to the initial conversation. "We're working on his problem, not yours."

Bailey frowned at Nathan. How had this gotten so out of hand? "I don't have a problem."

It was obvious the others didn't see it that way. Nathan looked at him. "You want to see her again, don't you?"

He did, but this wasn't anything he was about to undertake through committee advisement. This was his to handle. No way was this supposed to be a team effort. Bailey looked off, watching Bobby playing. "Sorry I mentioned it."

But it was too late for that. Nathan was all set to give Bailey his full backing.

"No, this is good, this is good," he assured Bailey enthusiastically. Jeff and Taylor nodded their heads in agreement. "We've all been out since our divorces—however infrequently—" he added, thinking of his own experiences. "You, however, have hung back, bringing the group's average seriously down." He clamped an arm around Bailey's shoulders. "Time you started pulling your load."

Bailey had a different slant on it. "Time I stopped sharing things with you," he corrected.

But there was a germ of truth in what they'd said, he thought. If he wanted to see K.C. again, he was going to have to do something and not wait for fate to step in a second time. Fate had other paths to take and other people to move along. He'd gotten his one free get-out-of-jail card. Now it was time he did something about it—before it was too late.

If it wasn't already.

Bailey stood, his mind made up. "I'll see you guys later."

Nathan saw the look in Bailey's eyes and read it correctly. "That's my boy."

Bailey ignored him. Moving at a good pace, he cut through the grass and took Bobby down from the shiny gray whale he'd just crawled onto.

Instead of protesting, Bobby turned bright-green eyes up at him and asked, "Where?"

Bailey took a firm hold of the small hand and retraced his steps back to the bench, and to the sidewalk just beyond. "We're going to go see your favorite person—after me, I hope."

He figured it was his tone rather than his words that evoked the wide smile from Bobby, but who knew? Maybe Bobby understood more than he gave him credit for.

Bailey turned a deaf ear to the calls his departure generated from the other single fathers. He was only thankful that although some of K.C.'s windows faced the street, the entrance to her town house faced east, away from the park. At least he wouldn't be under close scrutiny as he stood on her doorstep, ringing her bell.

Crossing the street, he fervently hoped he wasn't about to make a colossal fool of himself.

K.C. set the thermometer aside. "Almost normal, kiddo," she told Gracie. The little girl popped up like toast from the bed. The few seconds it had taken to sit still while K.C. took her temperature had seemed endless to Gracie. "That means you still can't break the sound barrier.

"Too late," she murmured to herself as Gracie scrambled off the bed and ran to the other room. It never ceased to amaze her how children could be so sick one minute and then so full of energy the next, their temperatures fluctuating like waves in a choppy sea.

For her part, K.C. was relieved. Gracie had been cooped up in the house too long and had a raging case of cabin fever, fairly bouncing off the walls after almost a week. But at least tending to her and Rachel had left little time for her to think about Bailey. And wonder what he was doing.

If he even noticed she wasn't there.

Of course he hadn't. He was a man. All men had attention spans the size of dying gnats.

The doorbell rang just as she left Gracie's room.

"Get that, will you?" Rachel called.

As if Rachel would, K.C. thought, a smile twisting her lips as she glanced toward her sister in the family room. They had had the same upbringing, but Rachel had always behaved as if she had been born a princess, waiting for her coronation ceremony to begin.

"Yes, milady," K.C. called over her shoulder, unlocking the front door. "May I help y—?"

Her voice died away as she looked at Bailey and Bobby standing on her doorstep.

To say that she was surprised to see him was to give new meaning to the word *understatement.*

What was he doing here?

It took her a moment to collect herself. "Is something wrong?" Habit had her quickly looking Bobby over. She half expected Bailey to tell her that the boy had fallen again.

"No, we just want to know if you and Gracie would like to come out and play."

Come out and play. Like a child. It nudged at old, fond memories, long lost. "Well, I—"

It seemed that he didn't want to give her the opportunity to brush him off. "We haven't seen you since Saturday night and I was wondering if maybe

Bobby and I frightened you away from using the park.''

She could see how he might get that idea. ''No, Gracie had a cold. She's just getting over it.''

''Oh, I'm glad—I mean, not that she had a cold, but that it wasn't anything we—that I—'' He stopped. ''Can I start over?''

Leaning her head against the doorjamb, she smiled at Bailey. He was really very sweet. ''No need.''

''Oh, but there is,'' he assured her. ''A very big need.''

Suddenly a sultry voice called out from inside, ''Who is it, K.C.?''

K.C. closed her eyes involuntarily. *Here it comes,* she thought. ''Just a man Gracie and I met in the park, Rachel.''

The next moment, her sister was hobbling into the foyer on her crutches, eager to see if this was *the* man. The look in her eyes was very appreciative as she took measure of him at close quarters.

Balancing herself as best she could, Rachel regally extended her hand to Bailey. His handshake was firm and warm.

''Hello, I'm Rachel Collins.'' She flashed a quick smile in Bobby's direction, but it was the senior edition of the Quaid model that held her attention. ''Would you and your son like to come in?''

He appeared reluctant. ''No, we just stopped by

because we hadn't seen K.C. and Gracie for a few days and wondered—"

Her hand still in his, Rachel was already coaxing him into the house. "No need to explain. Please, I feel like a shut-in. A little conversation would do me a world of good. I've already heard everything K.C. has to say. K.C.—" she turned toward her sister "—show Mr. Quaid to the family room."

Gracie, never hanging back in the shadows for long, came running out to see who the newest visitors were. When she saw Bobby, she gleefully ran forward and took possession of his arm, ushering him into her domain with the air of a young Queen Elizabeth, showing off her newly acquired kingdom.

"I show toys!" she announced.

Gracie, her father was given to saying, had more toys than any three children put together. But she had met her match today, K.C. thought.

"Out of luck there, Gracie. This is one young man you're not going to impress with your cache of things." She looked at Rachel who seemed content to devour Bailey with her eyes. "Bailey makes toys."

"I know, you mentioned that." Only after she had all but crawled down her sister's throat and pulled the words out, Rachel added silently. But even then, it was evident to Rachel that Bailey Quaid had made one hell of an impression on her sister. Not that, after one look, she had to wonder why.

There was a match here, she just had to find how to make them see that. Rachel's mind went into overdrive as she drew her guest into the family room.

Chapter 8

"I am really sorry you had to go through that." K.C. searched for the right words to frame her mortified apology as she walked Bailey and Bobby to the door. Nothing seemed really equal to the job.

For the past two hours, while K.C. alternately cringed and flung back terse quips, Rachel had subjected Bailey to a barrage of questions while smiling fetchingly. She interspersed her modern-day version of the Spanish Inquisition with tales meant to showcase K.C.'s virtues. As far as K.C. was concerned, her sister had all but put her on the auction block, hung a sign around her neck and started the bidding with her eyes on a very limited market.

Bailey had to admit that it was an unusual afternoon, but he had walked into it on his own. And he found the flush of embarrassment on K.C.'s cheeks incredibly appealing.

Slipping a jacket on Bobby, he made light of her apology. "Your sister means well."

Not in her book, K.C. thought, struggling with a temper that usually lay dormant. Rachel had dragged out stories from their past that even she had forgotten about. She'd begun to feel as if she'd fallen headlong into a very bad English drawing room comedy entitled *Marrying off Katherine.*

"My sister is lucky I didn't toss her through the window and break her other leg."

He tried to envision that. After listening to Rachel, he'd come away with the feeling that K.C. could tackle absolutely anything she set her mind to.

He began to wish that it were him.

"I love a physical woman," he said, laughing. And then the laughter died away as he shrugged into his own windbreaker. "I was serious the other night." His eyes held hers. "About wanting to see you again."

"After what you just had to put up with, I feel as if I owe you something."

He pretended to roll her words over. "Guilt. I like it." His eyes teased hers playfully. "When all else fails, I'm not above using guilt." He knew he had to make his pitch quickly, while the advantage was still his. In some ways, this was not unlike pitching toy ideas to the board, he thought. "So, when are you free?"

Saying that all her evenings were pretty much open didn't seem like the right thing to admit. She knew that Rachel would highly disapprove if she were listening. But K.C. had never believed in playing games. Besides, she reminded herself, she wasn't looking to get involved. Even with a man who seemed so nice.

She shrugged, deliberately trying to seem careless. "Why don't you pick an evening and I'll tell you if I can make it?"

He grinned. "Honest and physical. What more could I ask for? How's Wednesday night sound to you?"

Wednesday night. Far away enough for her to feel safe, close enough for her to be able to appease Rachel. She glanced over her shoulder to make sure that Rachel wasn't around somewhere, listening. "Sounds fine. Your place again?"

Bailey wanted to take her to a play. He had a friend who worked behind the scenes at the nearby Performing Arts Center. A little bartering might score him two tickets third row center for the current play. He knew for a fact that the theater kept a certain amount of choice tickets on reserve for celebrities, critics and special occasions. But he didn't want to say anything to her until he was sure.

"No, this time I'll get a sitter even if I have to pay her off in rare toys—"

"Now there's a bribe." She wondered if he was referring to certain discontinued action figures her brothers used to collect, benign now by modern standards. "You have rare toys?"

He gave her a deliberately mysterious look. "Rare comes about if the supply is suddenly dried up—or cut off." He twirled an imaginary mustache. "I'll do what I have to, to secure a little time with you."

No matter how hard she tried not to, she kept warming to him. "Put that way, how can I refuse?"

He winked at her, sending a sudden, unexpected and delicious flutter spiraling through the center of her stomach.

Knowing he could make better time if he had physical custody of Bobby's body, Bailey picked him up. "That's the idea." Impulse had him brushing a kiss against her lips at the last moment before he turned away.

The taste of her mouth lasted with him long after he and Bobby left.

K.C. groaned as she sank down onto the sofa in Bailey's living room. Soft, oversized pillows threatened to swallow her up whole without leaving a trace. She didn't care. "I am so exhausted, I don't think I could move off this sofa even if it was on fire."

He smiled down at her. "We won't put that to the test."

Bailey's eyes swept over her as he thought how

good K.C. looked on his sofa. And how good she might look in his bed.

They'd been seeing one another now with a fair amount of regularity for the past six weeks. His busy season was finally behind him. Beginning in the spring and exploding in the summer, it invariably leaked over into the fall. During that period, he worked hard to produce new designs for the toys that would hit the stores in time for Christmas. With the holiday season getting into full swing, he felt he'd more than earned his time off.

And he wanted nothing more than to spend it with K.C.

She seemed to enjoy his company and unless he completely misread all the signs, she enjoyed kissing him as much as he enjoyed kissing her. But like planes circling the landing field, unable to get clearance to touch down, they'd been locked in a holding pattern for a while now. Bailey had no idea how to break it without pushing.

He didn't want to push.

But he did want her.

Badly.

"All your own fault," he said, taking a seat next to her. Bobby had been sound asleep by the time they came home. They had put him to bed together, something else Bailey knew he could get used to easily. "You were the one who insisted on going to Knott's Berry Farm for the day."

It had been her suggestion and her treat. To pay

Bailey back for all the times he'd taken her out. They'd taken Gracie with them, as well. K.C. had thought there was safety in numbers.

But no matter how many people there were, it didn't erase the effect being with Bailey had on her. She would have been drawn to him in a crowd. And she knew the danger in that.

K.C. could barely turn her head to look at him. "I thought Bobby would enjoy it."

"Enjoy it? He loved it. And I have to admit that this is the first time to my recollection that he fell asleep on the ride home since I first brought him home from the hospital when he was three days old." He moved a little closer to her. "Indications are, he's going to sleep like a rock. All through the night."

K.C. let out a deep breath. With very little prodding, she could fall asleep right here. It occurred to her that maybe it hadn't been the wisest thing to drop Gracie off first before they came to Bailey's house. But like Bobby, Gracie had fallen asleep on the way home and K.C. hadn't wanted the evening to end.

So they had stopped at the town house first, leaving Gracie for Rachel to put to bed. And now her doubts, so silent before, were inching their way forward, telling her she'd made an error. And was in line to make an even bigger one.

As it was, she knew that in these past six weeks she'd been getting closer to Bailey than she knew it was safe to be. Resisting and losing a battle she knew she had to win.

"You could stay here if you'd like." His voice wound seductively around her.

Exhaustion vanished, driven away by a salvo of adrenaline. She knew what he was inferring. Something that was on her own mind more and more, even though it shouldn't be.

Yes, I'd like, but that's beside the point, K.C. thought.

She slanted her eyes toward him. "That would be complicated."

He slipped his arm around her. "No, it wouldn't." Remembering his promise to himself, he put her needs ahead of his own, although it was becoming increasingly more difficult to behave like an eagle scout when every fiber of his being yearned to make love with her. "I have a spare toothbrush, spare pajamas and," he added the pièce d'résistance, "a spare bedroom."

"You don't want me in the spare bedroom," she said quietly.

"No, I don't." Very slowly, he slid the back of his hand along her cheek. He couldn't remember when he'd wanted someone so much. "But I'm not going to pressure you, either. The decision where you sleep is yours."

She caught her lip between her teeth, her eyes never leaving his. "No, it's not. Not when you look at me like that."

He couldn't help smiling. So the ache was visible, was it? "Like what?"

"Like you want me."

"I do."

The words vibrated within her chest, making her ache for him. But she knew that being with him would lead to expectations on her part, which would lead to disappointment. Better never to know than to know and then do without.

She touched his face. "Bailey..."

Turning her hand over, he pressed a kiss to her palm. Much as he wanted her, he didn't want to put her through this. He could see the turmoil in her eyes. "Okay, the discussion is tabled for now. I'd better see you home before my evil twin takes over."

She laughed at the idea. "You don't have an evil twin."

Bailey snapped his fingers as if he were being foiled again. "Just my luck."

He rose from the seat, then took her hand and helped her to her feet, bringing her up so that her body brushed against his. He knew by the look in her eyes that she felt the same sizzle between them that he did. If his scruples were just a little less finely tuned...

"Of course, I can be talked out of this long, arduous journey—"

She laughed at the exaggeration. For some reason, it reminded her of some of the toys he created. The endearingly fuzzy Friends in the Forest creatures that talked when you hugged them.

K.C. pointed out the obvious. "I'm staying less than two miles away, remember?"

Now that he had her in his arms, he was reluctant to let her go, chivalrous principles or no chivalrous principles. "Hey, *long* is an arbitrary word. If I were an inchworm, the trip would take two years."

K.C. grinned. "What about if the inchworm is driving a car?"

"Even longer." Bailey deadpanned. "He'd have to make his way back and forth across the pedals, not to mention the steering wheel. Given that method, it might take him years to reach your place."

Her heart warming, she attempted to mimic his expression and had no luck. "Lucky for me you're not an inchworm."

"In more ways than one." He kissed one corner of her mouth, then the other. She groaned as she melted against him.

K.C. looked at him accusingly. "You're not playing fair, Bailey."

"That's because I'm not playing."

If only she were braver. Or hadn't already lost her heart once. If only she could believe that things could really have a happy ending. "Yes, you are. Playing with fire."

His eyes caressed her face, fanning the flames that were already inside her. "Are you lit up yet?"

She couldn't lie if she wanted to. He'd know. "Can't you tell?"

Yes, Bailey thought, he could. If only because she had lit him up inside like a night sky exploding with fireworks. Framing her face with his hands, he kissed her eyes, her temples, her nose, working his way to her mouth. By the time he reached it, his heart was racing.

As was hers. He could feel it against him. Feel her against him. And ache for her with every fiber of his being all over again.

But her protest still echoed in his head. If she gave in to him now, it would only be because he'd broken down her resistance. He knew it wasn't right, wasn't fair. Maybe it was old-fashioned, maybe it was because he'd steeped himself in the innocence of children for too long, but he wanted K.C. to be with him because she wanted to be there, not because he'd seduced her into being there.

Still framing her face, he looked at it as he drew away. He was doing the right thing, no matter how awful it felt.

"C'mon, I'd better get you home before I come to my senses." Turning, he started for Bobby's room. Though the boy was sound asleep and would remain that way, he didn't want to leave him home alone, even for the short duration it would take to drive to the town house and back. "I'll strap Bobby back in and then you strap me down," he quipped dryly. "Don't let me up no matter how much I beg."

Following him, K.C. shook her head behind his back. Bailey made her feel guilty and grateful all at the same time.

"You're one in a million, Bailey."

He opened Bobby's door. "Yeah, which is probably why I'm going to wind up being extinct," he muttered to himself.

Chapter 9

When K.C. raised her head, she saw Rachel's reflection in her bureau mirror. Hurrying to get ready for her date with Bailey, K.C. had accidentally left her bedroom door ajar. Rachel didn't need more of an invitation than that.

Belatedly, K.C. realized she was humming. She stopped, knowing the damage had been done. It didn't take much to get Rachel started.

"And what are you so happy about?" There was a smug smile on Rachel's facc as she asked the question. "As if I didn't know."

Yup, it didn't take much. K.C. avoided her sister's eyes in the mirror. An evasive answer sprang to her lips, rescuing her. "Just happy that you're finally better and that after the holidays, I can go back to my own life, not to mention my own bed."

"Or someone else's," Rachel muttered. Out loud she said, "And that's why you're humming?"

Satisfied that she'd done as good a job as she could on her makeup, K.C. turned around to face Rachel. "That's why I'm humming."

"Liar." The taller of the two by two inches, Rachel bent over and kissed K.C. on top of her head. "I'm thrilled for you."

K.C. raised her eyes to Rachel's. "Thrilled I'm going back to my own life?"

How long did her sister intend to play this ridiculous game? How long was she going to pretend that she wasn't in love with Bailey?

Because Rachel loved her sister, she elaborated. "Thrilled that you finally are going to *have* a life."

The prediction, meant to be a comfort, instead sent a cold shiver of fear down K.C.'s spine. Fear of what was to come. Fear of the inevitable.

There was no denying that she'd enjoyed going out with Bailey and his son, enjoyed being with them doing absolutely nothing. But she was getting too comfortable with this. She was feeling things for Bailey. Things she didn't want to feel.

Throughout her day, when she wasn't with him, K.C. found herself thinking of him. Humming. Remembering little things he'd said to her, how he looked when he laughed. How it felt when he kissed her.

The realization that she'd been down this path before, only to find herself suddenly alone, seized K.C. in an iron grip that hurt as it tightened around her. She didn't want to feel anything for Bailey because to feel meant to open herself up to the emptiness that went hand in hand with the joy. The emptiness that was so overwhelming, it washed away all memory of the happiness that came before, leaving only hollow ashes in its wake.

K.C. straightened slightly, squaring her shoulders. "I don't know what you're talking about, Rachel."

Something in K.C.'s body language warned Rachel not to push it no matter how much she wanted to. "Okay, have it your way." She began backing away, leaving K.C. to finish getting ready.

"I intend to." She said it with such finality, Rachel stopped to look at her.

Biting back a comment that would only start an argument, Rachel glanced at the floor. "You'd better put your shoes on. He'll be here any minute."

The shoes weren't the important thing, K.C. thought, reaching for them. What she needed to put on was Bailey-proof armor.

Bailey came for her at seven. Came with flowers and looking so good, she had to throw bars up around her heart just to keep it from leaping out of her chest.

"They're beautiful." The fragrance swirled around her even as she took them from him.

"Roses, how lovely." From out of nowhere, Rachel materialized to take the flowers from K.C. and put them in a vase. "They're K.C.'s favorites."

"Yes, I know," Bailey acknowledged, his eyes never leaving K.C.

He knew a lot about K.C. It hadn't been easy, drawing information out of her little by little these past two months, but he had slowly managed to construct a whole picture out of the bits and pieces he'd husbanded and felt he knew as much about Katherine Colleen Haley as she would allow anyone to know. And maybe a little more.

Knew enough to know he wanted to spend the rest of his life with her.

"Ready?" He put his hand out to her.

She slipped her hand easily into his and said, "Ready," but knew she wasn't.

Restless, the small box burning a hole in his pocket, Bailey tried to broach the subject all evening. During the drive over to the restaurant, and then over dinner. But each time he began, K.C. would curtail his words with a counter movement of her own, changing the subject or making light of it, taking the conversation in directions that veered away from where he wanted it to go.

He was not unaware of what she was doing and wondered if perhaps she knew what he was trying to lead up to, or if he was reading too much into it.

The main course had come and gone. There were

now half-eaten servings of dessert at their table and he was no closer to taking the box out of his pocket than he had been when he'd driven over to her sister's town house.

Now or never, he thought.

A slow song was beginning to play, setting the scene for him. "Would you like to dance?"

She smiled her answer.

Bailey rose, rounding to her side of the table. "C'mon, I want an excuse to hold you in my arms."

He keeps saying things like that, she thought. Sweet, lovely, romantic things that turned her head and upheaved her heart. But how long could that last? How long before all that was followed with "Goodbye?"

Taking her hand, he led her onto the moderately populated dance floor.

"You know," he murmured, holding her close as the music surrounded them, "you've been acting skittish all evening. I thought we'd worked our way passed that."

Nothing got by him, she thought. The fact that he could pick up on her moods still managed to surprise her, although she was beginning to learn that he was very in tune to her. As she was to him. And she had the uneasy feeling that something was up.

"'Worked?'" The choice of words amused her. She knew he hadn't actually meant anything by it. "Has it been work for you, being with me?"

Bailey felt her smile against his chest. Warm feelings enveloped him.

"At times," he admitted. She raised her head to look at him quizzically. "You're not the easiest woman to get to know."

K.C. had always had two faces, one she turned toward the world, and one she wore in private, for those she loved. It unsettled her a little that he could see through her so easily. "Sure I am. Ask any of my patients."

"I know all about you being witty and outgoing and kind. A stranger could figure that out after a few minutes in your company." But he didn't want to be lumped in with her patients or to be just another peripheral person in her life, someone just passing through. Not anymore. "I'm talking about the real you. The K.C. who worked so hard to overcome a stutter in first grade. The one who always felt she had to take charge of things, even though she was the youngest. The one who can't watch a greeting card commercial without feeling a tug on her heart. The one who always wanted a puppy as a little girl, even though her father said no and made up for it by playing with the neighbor's dog, secretly pretending it was hers and naming it Conrad."

The recitation astonished her. He seemed to have absorbed every slip she'd made, every peek into her private life she'd given him. "Do you have one of those photographic memories?"

"No, it's selective, actually. I just remember what

I want to remember.'' He crooked his finger and used it to raise her chin until their eyes met. ''And what I want to remember is you.''

Remember. A word to recall something from the past. K.C. braced herself. Here it came. The breakup. He was going to tell her that he couldn't see her anymore.

She raised her chin even higher, her eyes meeting his. ''Why, are you going somewhere?''

He thought about that for a moment, rolling the phrase she used over in his mind. Maybe he was at that. ''In a way.''

She was right, she thought. But triumph eluded her even though she was trying to congratulate herself for not getting involved with Bailey. Eluded her because it was a bald-faced lie.

''In a way?'' she echoed.

He didn't want to confuse her, or to play word games. But he didn't want to frighten her away, either. He saw something in her eyes, a wariness he hadn't seen for the past few weeks. Bailey tried again, feeling his way around cautiously. ''Maybe I should have put it in a figurative way. I'd like to go to the next level.''

The music had stopped. Standing still on the dance floor, K.C. stared at him, her eyes wide, her heart hammering. Her emotions suddenly scrambling, running for high ground even as they wanted to gravitate toward what he was about to say to her.

Her throat felt incredibly dry as she made her guess. "You want to sleep with me."

What else could he be talking about? Even as she said it, K.C. felt an ache seep into her body. There was no denying that she wanted him, wanted to be with him in every possible way. But that would only complicate matters and make everything worse when he finally left—as he inevitably would.

"More than anything in this world." The confession had just slipped out. It wasn't what he was preparing to say. This wasn't the way he wanted her to remember things. "Come on, let's get off the floor." Taking her hand, he led her back to their table.

As she followed him, K.C. framed words saying yes, she framed words saying no. Bailey had been wonderful and patient with her and she wanted to be with him in every sense of the word, but that would just make it so much harder. She'd just prepared herself for a break up and now her emotions were springing back up. She couldn't take this kind of roller-coaster ride.

He'd made up his mind, just after they had started to dance, that perhaps he'd tell her as they walked along the beach. There was nothing like a moonlit night to aid a proposal. But he changed his mind again. They had their whole lives together to take romantic walks on the beach. He wanted to give her the ring now.

To hear her say yes now.

Helping her with her chair, Bailey slid into his

own. He put his hand into his pocket, covering the small velvet box housed there.

Okay, here we go.

"Close your eyes," he instructed.

Her eyes remained open as she stared at him, looking as if uneasiness was weaving a web around her. "What?"

"Close your eyes."

K.C. ran the tip of her tongue over her lips, as if she were fighting nerves. "Okay."

She exhaled the word, closing her eyes. Her nerves wouldn't settle down. She felt Bailey picked up her hand. Nerves jumped up another notch.

"Is this going to be some kind of marketing test?"

He flipped the lid on the box with his thumb while holding her hand. "Not exactly. This is only going public on a very limited scale. Ownership—one." His hand was steady, even though it felt as if it were trembling, as he slipped the ring on her finger.

The moment she felt the metal sliding along her skin, K.C.'s eyes flew open. The light from the candle on their table seeped into the diamond. Tiny rainbows of colors leaped out, dazzling her.

Her heart leaped and sank as the moment brought another moment back to her. Eric slipping a piece of costume jewelry on her finger, saying someday he would get a real ring for her. She'd worn it even after it had turned her finger green.

Oh, no, no, please don't have him say it. Don't have him ask me.

But Bailey was already saying the words. Taking her hand in his again, his eyes captured hers.

"K.C. sometimes a person just knows when something feels right. And this feels right to me." He took a deep breath, telling himself those were tears of happiness filling her eyes. "K.C., will you marry me?"

One tear spilled out as she pulled her hand back. "No."

Chapter 10

Feeling as if he'd just walked headlong into a sucker punch, Bailey tried to rally. He couldn't have misread the signs so badly. Could he? "Is that a 'forever' no, or a 'no, not this minute'?"

With hands that were shaking, K.C. pulled the ring off her finger and held it out to him. "I just can't marry you."

Something dark and burning twisted inside him, creating a wound that made the one that had scarred over seem inconsequential. "I'm sorry. I guess I got my signals crossed. I thought that you and I had something special. That you cared about me—"

Since he wasn't taking the ring, she placed in on the table in front of him. More tears spilled down her cheeks. "I do care about you. That's just the trouble."

He wanted to hold her to him and comfort her. He wanted to shake her and ask what was wrong, why she was doing this to both of them.

For both their sakes, he tried to find refuge in humor. "So, you're only willing to marry people you don't care about?"

There was no way she could make him understand. She'd already ventured out farther than was safe. To go any farther than that terrified her. "I'm not willing to open myself up to be hurt again, all right?"

At least she had the luxury of closing herself off. Being with her had taken that away from him. He hadn't wanted a relationship either, yet here it was, all around him. All around them.

Couldn't she see that?

"You're not the only one who's ridden that bus," he said, reminding her of something he'd said the first time they'd gone out together. "What makes us grow is going past things like that."

Feeling shaky inside, struggling to maintain a shred of composure, she raised her chin. "Maybe I'm not interested in growing. Maybe I'm just interested in keeping things the way they are."

His eyes held hers, loving her. Hating what she was putting them both through. Refusing to believe that it could end this way. "Nothing stands still, K.C. It either grows, or it dies."

She rose so fast, her chair almost fell backward behind her. K.C. caught it with one hand, steadying it at the last moment. "Then I won't stay to watch it die."

Apprehensive, Bailey shot to his feet with her. "Where are you going?"

Her mind ran about like a mouse lost in a tangle of passageways. K.C. didn't know where she was going. Away from here. To hide. And cry.

A single word came to her. "Home."

Turning on her heel, she raced off before he could catch her wrist to stop her. A couple got in his way as he started to go after K.C. He was halfway to the door when he remembered that the ring was still on the table. Hurrying back, he grabbed it.

By the time he reached the street, K.C. was nowhere in sight.

His fingers tightened around the ring in his hand. The ring she wouldn't wear.

"Merry Christmas," he murmured bitterly to himself.

"So, you're running away."

Looking up, K.C. knew the look she would find in her sister's eyes before she saw it. To her surprise, it wasn't annoyance in Rachel's eyes, it was compassion. That almost made it worse.

K.C. pressed her lips together and continued packing. There wasn't much to put into the suitcase, but it seemed as if it were taking forever. Somehow, her fingers kept getting tangled as she worked and it felt as if there were molasses in her veins.

She tossed in a sweater that defied folding. "I'm not running. The cast came off, you're getting around, you don't need me anymore. And I'm way overdue for a vacation."

Rachel eyed her. K.C. thrived on doing, not relaxing. "You don't take vacations."

No, K.C. thought, she didn't. But maybe it was time she did. Maybe it was time she tried something different. She needed time to get away and sort out her thoughts. It had been five days since she'd run out of the restaurant, leaving Bailey and his proposal behind. She thought she'd feel better by now. She didn't.

Five days and he hadn't even tried to see her or even called. She'd been right. There was no future for them. Her refusal had just precipitated the inevitable.

K.C. reached for a makeup bag and realized it was empty. Her makeup was still on the bureau. "I'm going to Cancun. Lay around on the beach for a while."

As if that were possible. A sense of urgency had Rachel getting into K.C.'s face. She had to be made to see reason. "I know you. You'll wind up organizing the seashells according to size half an hour after you arrive."

K.C. swung around, catching the side of the suitcase with her hip and sending it sliding off the bed.

Clothes that had taken her forever to pack tumbled out. She blinked back tears. This was stupid. She wasn't going to cry again, she wasn't.

Stooping, she began tossing things haphazardly into the suitcase. "I have to get away."

Rachel was on the floor beside her, gently placing her hands on the suitcase. Trying to commandeer it away from K.C. "But not until Christmas Day, all right? It's already dark and it's Christmas Eve. You have to stay until tomorrow."

She could remember when Christmas Eve had been special to her. Her mother would cook a big meal for dinner and then her parents allowed her, Rachel and their brothers to open one present apiece just before they went to bed.

But it had been a long time since she'd been a little girl. "Why?"

Drawing the suitcase away from her, Rachel rose and placed it on the bed. "Because I won't deprive Gracie of her favorite playmate just because she's turned out to have feathers instead of skin."

"Feathers?"

Rachel turned to face her. There was an affectionate smile on her lips. "As in chicken." She slipped an arm around her younger sister's shoulders, coaxing her away from her packing. "C'mon, for Gracie." Her eyes searched K.C.'s to see if she was getting through. "And for me. I worked hard on this dinner."

What would it hurt? Maybe it might even help

make her feel a little better. She loved watching Gracie open presents, giggling amid a flurry of wrapping paper and toys. K.C. allowed herself to be led out of her room.

"You called takeout," she pointed out.

Rachel held up one well-manicured hand, waving three-quarter-inch-long nails in the air. "What, you think dialing isn't hard work with these nails?" Then, with a laugh, she hugged K.C. to her. "C'mon, it'll be like the old days. Remember the year you wanted nothing more than a skateboard?"

"Broke my leg in three places." That was the summer she decided to become a nurse, because of the one that she'd had. The woman had gone the extra distance, staying behind and reading to a frightened little girl long after she should have gone home herself.

K.C. stopped short when she entered the dining room. The table was festively decorated for the holiday. It was also set for six.

Suspicion brought uneasiness. K.C. turned toward her sister. "I thought you said this was going to be just like the old days. I assumed they were our 'old days.'" She gestured at the table with its bright-red cloth and tiny snowmen at each setting. "There're extra places set. Who's coming?"

Rachel's smile never wavered. "A new version of the old days. The millennium is only a week away. I thought we'd make a fresh start a little early."

Her sister was hedging. K.C. looked toward her brother-in-law for help. Bryan was a good guy, one of the last. He could be counted on to side with her. "Who else is coming, Bryan?"

Bryan's eyes indicated something directly behind her. The next minute, she had her answer even before she turned around.

"Us."

Swinging around, her heart doubling its rhythm, K.C. saw that Bailey and Bobby were standing at the holly-decorated entrance of the room. Suddenly the overwhelming extent to which she had missed him these past five days came home to her.

But it didn't change the fact that embarrassment flooded her. He hadn't called her on his own. Had her sister begged him to come?

"I'll get you for this, Rachel," K.C. promised between barely moving lips.

"I'm sure you will," Rachel returned, whispering against K.C.'s ear. She was entirely unfazed by the fact that she had taken it upon herself to butt in and find out what had caused her sister's sudden edgy behavior. That was what sisters were for.

Rachel kept a firm grip on K.C.'s arm to keep her from suddenly bolting from the room. "Just behave, okay? Bryan still doesn't know he married into a crazy family."

"Living with you, I'm sure he suspects." Uncoupling herself from Rachel, she bent down to greet the little boy first. She had missed his adorable face. "Hello, Bobby." Straightening, she looked at Bailey. She wasn't sure what to expect, but he smiled at her as if nothing had happened between them. Her nerves settled a little, but a spot of hurt took over the space. "Hello, Bailey."

"Hello, K.C. Merry Christmas."

If she didn't know any better, Rachel thought, she would have said they both looked like prize fighters just before the bell to round one sounded. "All right, everyone," she announced, ushering Gracie toward the table, "let's eat before dinner gets cold."

"How have you been?"

Dinner had gone surprisingly well. Bryan and Rachel had kept the conversation moving at a fast pace and Bailey had joined in. K.C. had even managed a few interjections of her own once she'd gotten over her surprise. But now Rachel had somehow managed to get them seated together on the family room sofa, while she and Bryan were keeping the children occupied on the other side of the room by the tree.

She concentrated on her mug of hot buttered rum, staring into the contents. "Fine."

"Too bad." His answer had her looking at him in surprise. "I was hoping to hear you say that you were as miserable as I was." He still nursed hopes in that department. "Rachel said you've been impossible to live with."

It was on the tip of her tongue to say that it was Rachel who was impossible to live with, but she found that the lie wouldn't emerge. Not without her stuttering, which they both knew was a dead give-away, thanks to her sharing that bit of information with him.

It occurred to her that she had shared a great deal with a man she hadn't intended on sharing her life with.

She shrugged, trying to seem nonchalant. "I guess maybe I have."

Bailey drew a shade closer to her. "Any particular reason?"

Trapped, she had no choice in her answer. "You know I can't lie without stuttering." She shivered, a warm sensation shimmying up her spine. He was outlining the shell of her ear with the tip of his finger.

"I'm counting on it."

She knew she should just get up and walk away, leaving his question unanswered. She remained sitting. Absorbing the feel of having him close. "All right, I've missed you."

His smile heated her. "Nice to hear."

Nice. The word vibrated in her head. So, he was just satisfied that she'd missed him and nothing more. Well, what had she expected? This was what she had wanted, wasn't it?

No, damn it, she thought suddenly, no longer able to lie to herself. It wasn't what she wanted. She wanted him. Wanted the whole package. Wanted Bailey and Bobby and a life together. She'd wanted it all along and the fierceness with which she wanted it had frightened her so badly, she'd frozen.

But now she was finally thawing out at the worst possible time. Thawing out to the knowledge that she'd ruined the one opportunity she'd had to find happiness by refusing his proposal.

It took everything he had not to kiss her then. To kiss away the unhappiness he saw suddenly take root in her eyes. But he held on to his self-restraint for just a moment longer.

"By the way, I brought you something." From the floor next to the sofa, he picked up a metal, rectangular box with sprigs of holly painted on its sides. Rather than being wrapped, there was a red bow taped to the top. He held it out to her.

Taking it, she could only stare. It looked more like a gift for Gracie. "A jack-in-the-box?"

"New version of an old toy. Go on, turn the crank." He held his breath.

She did as he instructed. It took her less than a second to realize that the toy was playing the song they had danced to that night she'd run off.

The night he'd proposed.

K.C. stopped turning the handle and looked at him quizzically.

His expression never changed. "Keep cranking."

Uncertain, she resumed turning the small green handle. She almost jumped when the lid flew open and the figure popped up. Her eyes widened. Instead of the gaily dressed clown figure she'd expected, she was looking at a figure that more than passingly resembled him.

A smile playing on her lips, she raised her eyes to his. "A Bailey-in-a-box?"

He had pulled a lot of strings and done his share of pleading to get this made on time. "As close as they could get."

It warmed her heart just to look at it. And then she realized that there was something tied between the figure's hands. "What's he holding?"

By now, his breath had come to a complete standstill in his lungs. "Why don't you open it and see?"

Hoping, and being afraid to hope, K.C. untied the string and took the small tissue-wrapped item from between the figure's hands. She was unaware that Rachel and Bryan were looking her way. All she was aware of was that her heart was hammering wildly just before it got caught in her throat.

It was the diamond she'd left behind in the restaurant.

He wanted to slip it on her hand again, but this time, he was gun-shy. "Be interested in a slightly used engagement ring? Only been on one other finger for a couple of seconds."

Tears obstructing her vision, she raised her eyes to his. "Then you still want to marry me?"

He took that as a yes. "I never stopped wanting it." With relief, he took the ring from her hand and put it on her finger. Where it had belonged all the time. "Lady, maybe you haven't learned this yet, but I'm not the fickle type.'' He kissed her softly, sealing both their fates. ''I love you, Katherine Colleen Haley, and I'm here for the duration.''

And this time, she believed him.

Epilogue

As Nathan took three more sheets from the dwindling stack of pages that represented copies of a single article from the August issue of *Prominence,* he looked at Jeff. "Tell me why we're doing this again?"

They were sitting in Rachel's living room, part of the guests who had gathered together to see K.C. and Bailey married by the last moment in 1999. Shredding pages into tiny squares of confetti. Their task had come about thanks to an offhanded remark K.C. had made about the article that Rachel somehow thought responsible for at least indirectly bringing them together.

"I'm not sure," Blake confessed, shredding the

last of his page. All the pieces were going into bowls and were to be tossed at the bride and groom as soon as the vows were exchanged. "But it has something to do with the bride's wishes."

One eye on his twins, who were being entertained by the sitters Rachel had provided for the occasion, Nathan looked a little uncertain at the explanation. "She wants to be pelted by confetti made out of some woman's-magazine article?"

Jeff laughed, glad to see that Bailey had finally found someone to share his life with that didn't spring off a drawing board first. "Hey, whatever it takes. The main thing is that they're both happy."

Looking regal and triumphant, Rachel swept into the living room and looked around. After exchanging a few words with the minister, she made her way to the men she had put to work.

Her smile was beatific. "It's almost time. Are you ready?"

Jeff indicated the overflowing bowls. They'd been shredding pages for the last half hour. "Got enough here even if they run in slow motion."

Pleased, Rachel nodded. "Wonderful." She glanced at her watch out of habit, though there was no need. She knew exactly what time it was. There was a little less than half an hour until midnight of the last night of the last year of the century. "Then let's get this wedding moving before the bride gets cold feet."

But she was worrying needlessly, she thought, as

she reentered the bedroom where her sister was getting ready. If the bride's face was any indication of what the rest of her was like, her feet were warmer than freshly baked bread.

Rachel closed the door behind her. Her wedding dress, with a few modifications, looked wonderful on K.C. "I've never seen you look happier."

K.C. gave her veil a last adjustment. "That's because I've never been happier." She hugged Rachel impulsively. "Thanks for butting in—and if you ever tell anyone I said that, I'll deny it."

"You're welcome." Rachel beamed, in her element. "But I just nudged things along." She adjusted the train. "Bailey wasn't about to let you get away."

In her heart, K.C. knew Rachel was right and she was glad. Glad Bailey had loved her enough to keep trying. Because she loved him so much it hurt. But it was a good hurt.

Rachel looked at her watch again. They were running out of time. "Hey, if you want to get married before the next century," she cracked, "you'd better move this along."

Butterflies flapping madly in her stomach, K.C. took a deep breath to try to calm them down a little. She had marginal success as she pressed her hand against her abdomen. "I'm ready."

"Just a second," Rachel ordered, holding up her hand.

The strains of the wedding march began a moment after Rachel popped back into the room. K.C. looked quizzically at her sister.

"Stereo system," Rachel explained. She held the door open for K.C., one eye on the train to make sure it didn't get caught. "I'm trying to keep this as official as possible."

Gracie was in the hall where she'd left her. Deftly, Rachel took her daughter's hands and placed them at the edge of the train.

"Okay, honey, try to keep up with Aunt K.C., and whatever you do, don't pull on this." Her eyes met K.C.'s. "We'll count ourselves ahead of the game if you don't arrive before the minister naked."

"I'll do my best," K.C. promised.

They were lucky to find a minister on such short notice. A lot of other couples had the same idea as K.C. and Bailey had. But the Reverend Simmons was a friend of the family and he had agreed to perform the ceremony at what had amounted to almost a moment's notice.

Slowly moving into the living room, which Rachel with her unerring eye had managed to transform into the perfect setting for a millennium wedding, K.C. tried to find Bailey. Her heart swelled when she saw him. He was so handsome, it made her ache just to look at him.

When he smiled at her, the last of the tiniest doubts disappeared.

She was getting a wonderful man. And a fantastic little boy as an added prize for making the right choice. She saw Bobby, all dressed up, nestled in the corner of the sofa, his little head drooping. On his lap was a satin pillow, a ribbon with two wedding rings tied to it. They'd wanted him to be part of their wedding, just as he was so very much a part of their lives.

In the background, a big-screen television set was turned on. A popular television host was on, every unswaddled part of his body freezing as he stood in Times Square, waiting for the official end of the old century and the beginning of the new. K.C. could just barely make it out above the din in the room even though she was concentrating on the words the kindly faced minister was saying to Bailey and her.

"Do you, Katherine Colleen Haley, take this man, Bailey Quaid..."

As the minister began saying the words that would forever seal her to the most wonderful man in the world, they intertwined with the words from the big-screen droning on in the background.

"Ten—"

"I do," K.C. promised.

"And do you, Bailey Quaid, take this woman—"

"Seven—"

"—As long as you both shall live?

Bailey looked at her, love in his eyes. "I do."

"The ring, please."

"Four—"

"—Then by the powers vested in me by the state of California—"

"Three—"

"I now pronounce you—"

"Two—"

"Husband and wife."

"One!" the man on the television set cried as the world on the screen seemed to explode in a volley of sounds and colors. Laughter filled the air. "Happy New Century, everybody!"

In Rachel and Bryan's living room, cheers aimed at K.C. and Bailey were coming from all directions. Someone switched the lights off and on in the time-honored tradition of ushering in the New Year as others threw confetti at them wildly.

K.C. inclined her head toward Bailey. "We made it," she cried, laughing breathlessly.

"We certainly did," Bailey agreed just before he kissed her. The first kiss of the century. The first of many.

* * * * *

Dear Readers,

I confess to being a romantic and to truly believing in the power of love. I consider love, marriage and family the most special gift life has to offer a man and a woman. I'm one of those fortunate women who, after over thirty years of marriage, is still deeply in love with her husband. We've weathered many storms, but what kept us afloat is the fact that we faced our problems together, hand in hand. Even when we occasionally didn't like each other very much, we always loved each other. We're fortunate that, although we married very young, we have grown together and not apart. And our dedication to each other and our children has created a strong and lasting bond.

When asked to write a short story for this anthology, I had to come up with a good reason why an intelligent woman would advertise for a husband. Deciding that she would aim her ad at one specific man—a man she already loved, but who thought of her only as a friend—made perfect sense to me. Since I enjoy writing about protagonists who come from very different backgrounds, I chose a self-made man from the wrong side of the tracks as my hero and a wealthy Southern belle heroine who is determined to make it on her own without her family's millions. Taking Bennie and Holt on the journey of love, marriage and happily-ever-after reminded me once again of life's greatest joy and of how blessed I am to be married to my own special hero.

Sincerely,

Beverly Barton

Getting Personal
Beverly Barton

To Norma Koons,
a dear and lovely lady, who possesses a marvelous positive attitude and a truly kind heart.

Chapter 1

Stop thinking about it! Just do it! Marianne Bennett's gaze darted back and forth from the August issue of *Prominence Magazine* lying open on her desk to the telephone. *How many more years of your life are you going to waste waiting for Holt to notice that you're a woman? If he hasn't shown any personal interest in you in all this time, what makes you think he ever will?*

Lifting her hand, she reached for the telephone. Her fingers hovered over the receiver. *You want to get married and have children, don't you?* she asked herself. Yes, of course she did. But it had been so long since she'd had a date that she couldn't even remember the last guy's name. *So, make that call. You've got to start somewhere!*

Her lack of a love life was all Holt Jackson's fault—the big jackass! Why couldn't he just open his eyes and see that the perfect woman for him was right under his nose and had been there for the past five years?

It wasn't as if Holt was stupid. Far from it. The man had built his own business, from the ground up. Bennie laughed. No pun intended, of course. Holt was a building contractor who had started out with nothing and was now a millionaire. But when he'd hired her as his secretary, he had just landed his first contract and was trying to acquire a bank loan. That had been five long, unrequited-love years ago.

"What's so funny this early on a Monday morning?" Rene Lowe bounded energetically into Bennie's office. Holt's present secretary held two cups of coffee in her hands. She offered one to Bennie, who clasped the yellow mug like a lifeline.

"Thanks, I need another jolt of caffeine. I didn't get much rest last night thinking about this article. The one you showed me Friday." Bennie tapped her index finger on the magazine. "And as far as my morning chuckles— Well, let's just say that I was amusing myself by thinking about actually giving one of the suggestions a shot."

Plopping her skinny behind down on the edge of Bennie's desk, Rene giggled as she focused her gaze on the magazine. "Ah, the 'Married by the Millennium' article that listed all the ways to snare a husband by the end of 1999. So, which tried and true method have you chosen to capture a mate?"

"I'm going to place an ad in the personals section of the *Herald Daily.* I was trying to work up enough courage to make a phone call to the newspaper before Holt storms in for the day."

"It would serve that man right if some fabulous Prince Charming stole you right out from underneath his nose. I swear the man has to be blind not to see how hog-wild crazy you are about him."

"Thanks for reminding me what a fool I am." Bennie's lips curved into a mockingly sad smile. "Everyone in the whole world—at least here in Fairmount—knows how I feel about Holt. And they all know how he feels about me. He thinks I'm the best damn personal assistant a guy could ask for."

With a bright-red mug in one hand, Rene slid farther onto the desk, then reached over and laid her other hand on Bennie's shoulder. "I'm afraid the boss man is a lost cause. We've tried making him jealous by sending you flowers at work and dropping hints that you were having an affair. We've put you in a tight sweater to show off those great boobs of yours. We've let your hair down from that bun and even gave contact lenses a try. The man is blind. I'm telling you, he's blind!"

"You're one hundred percent right! I've wasted five of the best years of my life mooning over that man, hoping and praying he'd fall in love with me. Now, I'm beginning to think Holt has no idea what love is. He goes through women like a chain smoker goes through a pack of cigarettes."

"So what are you waiting for?" Rene asked. "Pick up that phone and call the *Herald Daily.*"

Slightly hesitant, but nevertheless determined, Bennie lifted the receiver. "I just hope this doesn't turn out to be a mistake."

"Dial, woman. Dial!"

Bennie punched in the number she had looked up in the directory when she'd first arrived at the office this morning. But now the voice of the *Herald Daily*'s receptionist created uncertainty in her mind. She almost hung up. But one look at Rene's frown and she cleared her throat.

"Yes, I'd like to place an ad in the personals section of your newspaper."

"Drop by the office here on Courtland Street anytime between nine and five, Monday through Friday, pick up one of our forms for the personal ad, fill it out and return it with your payment."

"Oh, all right. Thank you." Bennie's stomach churned. Her hand quivered as she replaced the telephone receiver.

"So?" Rene peered directly into Bennie's face.

"So, I have to pick up a form and fill it out."

"I'll pick the form up for you on my lunch hour today and I'll help you fill it out. If you word it yourself, you'll be too modest. After all, you're not likely to say that you're beautiful, brilliant and filthy rich."

"Shh!" Bennie glanced through the open doorway leading from the office into the reception area. "What if Holt had heard you say that?"

"So? He's got to know that you're beautiful and brilliant—"

"Brilliant? Maybe. Beautiful?" Bennie glanced down at her round, hourglass figure. "Not by today's standards. But the comment that I didn't want Holt to hear is about my being filthy rich. You know he doesn't have any idea that I'm independently wealthy, that I have money other than the salary he pays me. Sometimes I regret I ever told you about my trust fund."

"How could you not tell me? We've been best friends for the past four years."

Bennie remembered the day she'd hired Rene as a part-time gofer around the office, back when Rene had still been in college. The two had hit it off immediately and gradually become best friends. Her good buddy had picked up on her obsession with Holt almost immediately and begun devising methods for Bennie to gain his attention. They had tried everything short of Bennie sashaying around the office stark naked.

Rene sipped on her coffee as she stood and sauntered toward the door. Glancing back over her shoulder, she grinned. "Even if you hadn't told me the truth about your family, I would have figured it out after that day your mother came by your place. If the Mercedes she was driving hadn't given me a clue, then the million dollars worth of diamonds she was wearing would have given it away."

Bennie chuckled. "If there's one thing that Mary Bennett isn't, it's subtle. All Mother has to do is walk into a room and everyone immediately assumes she's wealthy. As much as I love my mother, I don't want to be a carbon copy of her. I want to be liked for me—not my money. You know that's one of the reasons I moved from Montgomery and built a life of my own here in Fairmount. Mother will never know who her true friends are or if any of the men she's dated since Daddy died like her for herself or her millions."

"Okay, so we won't include anything in the ad about your being the heir to a multimillion-dollar fortune." Rene traced her jawline with the tip of her hot-pink fingernail. "Let me see...we could put in something about your being from a prestigious old Southern family. There are plenty of women around from those kinds of families who don't have a lot of money, but are welcomed into all the *right* circles. After all, if you can't snag Holt, then you might as well go for a man like dear old dad, right?"

"Wrong! I don't want a man like my father. Someone born with a silver spoon in his mouth. If that's the kind of man I wanted, I could have married Grayson Stafford IV five years ago. I broke off my engagement and left home so that I could find a man like... Well, like Holt. A man who had nothing and built his fortune himself, with his own two hands. And I want a man who will love me for me—not my family's wealth. Not because I'm his social equal and we can produce another generation of inbred blue bloods."

"So, if you place the ad and some wonderful guy shows up, are you going to be able to forget about Holt?"

"I don't know," Bennie admitted. "If I thought for one minute that I had a chance with Holt, I'd—"

"Morning, all!" A deep baritone voice rumbled as the big boss man blew into the outer office like a March whirlwind.

Bennie's heart skipped a beat at the sound, then when she glanced past Rene and saw Holt, a hundred untamed butterflies did a wicked Saint Vitus's dance in her belly. From the first day she met him, Bennie had thought Holt Jackson was the sexiest man alive. His features were a little too rugged to be classically handsome, but there was a chiseled strength to his face, as if an artist had painstakingly sculpted the high cheekbones, the square jaw and the aquiline nose.

And that body! All six feet two inches of Holt Jackson was lean and mean and powerful. Broad shoulders tapered to a long, slim waist, narrow hips and taut buttocks that had inspired more than one erotic fantasy. Masculinity oozed from his pores like syrup from a tapped maple tree.

These days he kept his straw-blond hair short and neat. But when she'd first come to work for him, he'd always been in need of a haircut. And sometimes a shave. She had been the one who had pointed out to him that, even in his business, first impressions were often made as much by a man's appearance as by his business acumen. And over the years, Holt had taken her advice more times than not. However, even she hadn't been able to persuade him to wear a traditional business suit. Today, as most days, he stubbornly stuck with his jeans and plaid shirt. However, after years of coercing, he had finally conceded to wear a tie and sport coat. The coat, more often than not, ended up hung over the back of his chair, with the tie stuffed into a pocket.

But that was one of the things she loved about Holt. His nonconformity. He was, first and foremost, his own man. She had grown up around soft, cultured gentlemen who knew more about their Civil War ancestors than they did their own children. She'd even been engaged to one—a man handpicked by her family.

"Well, aren't we in a good mood this Monday morning?" Rene said. "You and what's-her-name—the six-foot-tall redhead—must have had a hot and sweaty weekend."

Another thing Bennie loved about Holt was that he didn't stand on ceremony. He treated all his employees as equals. He even got a kick out of Rene's teasing jibes. But that didn't mean he couldn't be a hard taskmaster when the occasion required it.

"Her name is Carmel and I haven't dated her in

over a month.'' Holt slapped his briefcase down on Bennie's desk. ''I spent the weekend with Bo and Patsy Reynolds. Bo's chairman of the committee that will chose a contractor for the new golf and country club.''

''Hobnobbing with the big dogs, huh?'' Rene shook her head, bouncing the tips of her silky blond bob. ''I'm curious. What are they really like? They're part of the snob set that's run this town since it was founded, so tell me—just how different are they from average folks like us?'' Rene cast Bennie a meaningful glance.

''Well, actually, Bo's all right.'' Holt grinned. ''For a guy who doesn't have to work for a living. However, Patsy's a different matter. What I needed this weekend was a wife who spoke that woman's language. Someone from the same type of social background.''

''You're certainly not going to find that kind of wife dating women like Carmel,'' Rene said. ''Actually, the person you needed to shmooze Mrs. Reynolds this weekend was Bennie.''

Directing his sky-blue eyes at Bennie, he settled his gaze on her face. ''You know, Rene's right. You're always good with our hoity-toity clients. But I can't impose on your weekends for the rest of your life.''

''I don't mind helping you,'' Bennie said. ''After all, it's my job to assist you, isn't it?'' She tried to keep her tone light, to not allow Holt a glimpse of the real Marianne Bennett, who had been pining away for him all these years.

"I've imposed on your personal time too often," Holt told her. "I know this business couldn't get along without you, but you can't be at my beck and call twenty-four hours a day."

Oh, God, Bennie thought, there was nothing she wanted more than to be at Holt's beck and call twenty-four hours a day. Days in the office working at his side. Nights in his bed, making passionate love with him.

Just as Bennie opened her mouth to respond, Rene injected a well-chosen comment of her own. "You're so right. Bennie needs to concentrate more on her personal life and not so much on Jackson Construction. And you, *Mr.* Jackson, should start looking for a wife with the kind of breeding and family connections that could get you in good with all the really important people in Alabama and in the whole southeast."

"For a smart-mouthed kid, she gives pretty good advice, doesn't she, Bennie?"

"I don't know how good her advice is," Bennie said, "but she's got plenty of it."

"The Lawson contracts are in my briefcase," Holt said. "Take a look at them and then come into my office and we'll discuss details." He turned to Rene. "Bring me some coffee, will you, kiddo?"

"Sure thing, boss." Rene salaamed Holt, her actions a mocking display of homage.

"If I didn't find you so damn entertaining, Lowe, I'd fire you." Holt winked at Rene, then marched out of Bennie's office.

Both women watched Holt as he exited. The minute he was out of earshot, Rene closed the door. Swirling around, she smiled broadly, showing her perfect teeth.

"Holt said that he needs a wife with certain credentials. And you, my dear Marianne Colburn Bennett, fit his requirements to a tee. Why don't you tell the man that you're the girl of his dreams?"

"I do not want the man I marry to marry me because of my blue-blooded background and my sizable inheritance." Bennie sighed. "Besides, I've given up on Holt, remember? I'm placing a personal ad in the paper in order to acquire a husband by the new millennium."

"I thought you might want to give Holt one last chance." Rene grinned impishly.

"What are you talking about?"

"Wake up and smell the coffee, honey. Holt wants a wife with certain qualities. So in your personal ad, you should list those specific attributes. Then suggest to Holt that he might find a qualified bride-to-be in the personals."

"You, Rene Lowe, have a very devious mind." Bennie bit down on her bottom lip as she contemplated the suggestion. "It wouldn't work. Holt would never look for a socially refined wife in the personal ads."

"Nothing ventured, nothing gained. What have you got to lose by giving it a try?"

"More of my precious time," Bennie said. "I'm already twenty-nine and not getting any younger."

"So what's one more week in the grand scheme of things? Besides, if you can't talk Holt into checking out the ads, then you can always respond to the dozens of other guys who are bound to put in a bid for a date."

"Oh, all right. What difference will a few more days make, after I've already wasted five years!"

Holt downed half a cup of black coffee as he sat behind his massive oak desk. He wanted the country club project. Wanted it enough to have spent the weekend with a good ole boy who had more money than sense and a woman who looked down her snobby nose at him the entire time they'd been together. His construction company was successful. He had become a rich man. But he had lost some of the projects that could have made a name for him in Alabama. Despite his competitive bids, he didn't always land the deals that should have been his. And nine times out of ten, his lack of the right connections played a part in his failure. He needed an entrée into Alabama's good ole boy's club.

The right wife could give him the one thing all his money couldn't buy. A well-bred lady on his arm could open doors that had been permanently shut in his face. But how the hell did a guy like him meet that kind of woman? Even with all his money, he wasn't receiving social invitations into the best homes.

People in these parts didn't let a guy forget that he'd been born on the wrong side of the tracks. They might like him, might even admire him and could, on occasion, do business with him. But they let him know, in subtle ways, that he wasn't one of their kind.

If Holt was honest with himself, he'd have to admit that his need to be accepted was as important to him as not missing out on the occasional deal. Those missed deals usually went to a competitor who'd been an old fraternity buddy or a guy who was married to the wife's sorority sister. After a stint in the army, Holt had worked his way through college and helped provide for three younger brothers by holding down two jobs. His social life back then had consisted of bar hopping with his redneck buddies.

After college, he'd been too busy building his little empire to even think about marriage. But he'd always promised himself that he'd marry and settle down to raise a family when he turned thirty-five. He had a birthday coming up in January. His thirty-fifth!

The time is now, he told himself. Choose a suitable woman, propose and get married. A simple business deal. She could give him social standing and he could give her just about anything her heart desired. There had to be women with the right pedigree whose family fortunes had dwindled. All he had to do was find one of those women and offer her a deal she couldn't refuse.

By Wednesday morning, Holt had decided he wanted Bennie's opinion of his marriage plans, but they'd both been too busy for much more than brief hellos. However, he had managed to ask her to share her break time with him.

Holt lifted his head when he heard the soft peck on his office door. "Come in."

Bennie entered his office, a pleasant smile on her face and a newspaper tucked under her arm. "Are you ready for that midmorning break?"

"Absolutely." The sooner he discussed his plans with Bennie, the sooner he could put them into action.

"Would you like me to get you some coffee? I picked up some baklava at the bakery this morning."

"Nothing for me, thanks."

He surveyed her from the top of her black hair to the tips of her sensible, two-inch heels. As always, she wore a simple suit. Today's attire consisted of dark-blue trousers and a double-breasted jacket. The only jewelry she ever wore was a watch and a pair of small gold earrings.

Bennie was more than an employee, more than a valued personal assistant. She was his friend. Probably the best friend he'd ever had. And she was a woman. So, who better to talk to about his personal plans than Bennie? She'd be the first to tell him if she thought the idea was stupid. One of the things he liked about her was her brutal honesty. She didn't cater to his ego like so many of the women he knew. Of course those women were the ones he dated, the ones who thought they might be able to put a ring through his nose.

Besides, Bennie already knew just about everything there was to know about him. Five years ago, he'd been struggling to launch his construction business when he'd hired her. She'd seen him through some pretty rough times. Always at his side. Always supportive and encouraging. She had sacrificed her own personal life, as much as he had his, to devote herself to the business.

Did a woman like Bennie, a no-nonsense professional woman, ever think about getting married and having kids? She wasn't bad-looking, in a plain sort of way. Maybe a few pounds over the currently fashionable model-thin physique, but then he liked his women with a little flesh on their bones. She'd worn her hair down a couple of times and he'd been amazed at what a mane of long, black curls she was able to confine in a neat bun at the base of her neck. And behind those little wire-frame glasses were a pair of green cat eyes that seemed capable of seeing right through him. Sometimes the way she looked at him was downright unnerving.

What the hell was he thinking? Bennie wasn't one

of his women. She was his valued assistant. And more importantly, she was his friend. Whenever any stray thoughts of her as a desirable woman crossed his mind, he dismissed them. After all, lovers came and went, but top-notch assistants and good friends were worth their weight in gold.

When she stared at him quizzically, he realized he'd been ogling her. He cleared his throat. "I need to discuss something with you."

"Certainly." She cleared off a stack of blueprints lying in the leather chair across from Holt's desk. After sitting, she crossed her legs at the ankles, placed the newspaper in her lap and then folded her hands together over the paper.

Holt rose from his chair. "I want you to be honest with me."

"I usually am," she replied, a soft smile curling her lips.

Holt came out from behind his desk. "You know my background. You're aware, probably more than anyone, that I've got some pretty rough edges." He paused to look at her face, seeking a reaction. She continued smiling, but said nothing. "What I want to know is do you think a guy like me has a snowball's chance in hell of persuading some socialite to marry him?"

"Some socialite?"

"You know the type—someone who was a debutante, a member of the DAR, whose family either has money or a family lineage that includes Robert

E. Lee or Benjamin Franklin. Preferably both." His gaze met Bennie's and they both laughed.

"I'd say if the lady loves you, you've got a very good chance. She's not going to care what your background is if all she wants is you."

Holt shook his head. "No, no, no! None of that love stuff. I'm talking about a business deal here. An exchange of services, so to speak. We'd both know up front what we're getting."

"Gee whiz, it all sounds so romantic. Just what any woman would want."

"Cut the sarcasm, Bennie. I'm serious here. I'm going to be thirty-five in January. It's time I got married and settled down and—"

"And you want your marriage to be a business deal instead of wedded bliss, huh? The whole thing seems a little too calculated to suit me. I can't imagine any woman in her right mind settling for such an arrangement." *Especially not with a man like you Holt Jackson.*

"Well, it's the best I can do." Holt paced the floor. "You've known me long enough to know that I'm not the romantic type. And as far as love goes, I've seen too many poor fools ruin their lives by falling in love with women who destroy them. A couple of my brothers are prime examples."

Bennie glanced down at the newspaper in her lap, then nervously flipped the edges with her thumb. "Have you ever considered advertising for a wife? Or checking the ads to see if—"

Holt abruptly halted his agitated pacing and glared at her. "Are you talking about those stupid personal ads people put in the newspaper?"

"Yes, that's what I'm talking about. And they aren't stupid. I've heard of several people who'd met the love of their lives that way."

"A guy would have to be pretty desperate to resort to taking out an ad. Or to answer one, for that matter!"

"You seem pretty desperate to me. You want a specific type of woman who is willing to enter into a business deal marriage with a man who's from a totally different background. And you want to achieve that goal in less than six months."

Grasping the Wednesday edition of the *Herald Daily* in her hand, Bennie stood, walked across the room and smacked the paper down on Holt's desk.

"Why don't you look over the personal ads and see if you find something you like—someone who meets your criteria." Echoing Rene's words to her, Bennie said, "What have you got to lose?"

Holt glanced at the newspaper on his desk, then looked directly at Bennie. "I think the whole idea is ridiculous. But—" he paused for dramatic effect "—since you usually don't steer me wrong, I'll think about it."

"You might not want to waste too much time thinking," Bennie said. "After all, the woman of your dreams could get snapped up by someone else—while you're thinking about it."

Chapter 2

Holt wolfed down his second bowl of cornflakes, then scooted back his chair as he picked up the empty bowl. After placing the bowl and spoon in the sink, he poured himself a cup of coffee. The Thursday morning edition of the *Herald Daily* lay on the kitchen counter. Still folded and encased in a plastic wrapper, the paper challenged him.

Go ahead and open the damn thing, he told himself. You'd better at least glance over the personal ads. After all, he had promised Bennie that he'd give her less-than-brilliant suggestion a try. Last night, he'd decided that finding a suitable wife in the personal ads was out of the question. Even if Bennie's advice was usually sound, this time she'd gone off in left field. He had tossed the newspaper she'd given him into the trash and dismissed the whole idea. But upon second thought this morning, he'd realized she was bound to ask him if he'd looked through the ads. He didn't want to lie to her.

While standing at the kitchen counter, he slipped the newspaper from its wrap, spread it open and flipped through the pages. He hesitated at the personal ads, then forced himself to glance over them. What sort of people advertised for dates? Desperate people? Lonely people? People seeking the thrill of the unknown?

> SWF, 25, great body, good dancer, loves having fun. Wants young, attractive man who can afford her desire for the good life. Seeking man between 25-35, with good job and no kids.
>
> WWF, 30, tall, slender, college degree, animal lover, seeking a sensitive, well-educated man with a good job who could be seriously interested in a woman with a six-year-old son and two cocker spaniels.
>
> DWF, 33, 5'6'', 110 lbs, loves sports, likes hiking, jogging and guys over six feet tall. Have lots to offer the right man. Good cook, experienced lover, not seeking permanent relationship. Has no children and no pets.

Shaking his head, Holt chuckled as he scanned the page of personal ads. There were plenty of women looking for the right man, but from what he'd read, not one of those females—single, divorced or widowed—was a suitable candidate for becoming Mrs Holt Jackson. He'd known this was a stupid idea, but at least now he'd be able to tell Bennie that he'd given her suggestion a try.

As he continued scanning the page, he finishing off his coffee. Just as he started to set his mug on the counter, an ad caught his attention.

> SWF, 29, intelligent, attractive professional, DAR member, prestigious family lineage, seeking a gentleman who appreciates a lady of good breeding and refinement. Prefer a man 30-35, self-made and successful, who is seeking marriage.

He read the ad twice. It wasn't possible, was it? The lady sounded too good to be true. Why would a woman with her credentials have resorted to placing an ad in the local newspaper? Wouldn't a woman like that have her pick of men?

Maybe she wasn't all that attractive, Holt told himself. Maybe she's built like a stick and is ugly as a mud fence. Or maybe she's fat as a butterball and has no personality.

At face value, the woman sounded perfect. Everything he wanted in a wife. But there had to be a catch to it. Ms. Right wasn't going to just fall into his lap this easily. Every instinct Holt possessed warned him against answering the ad. But how could he get out of responding? Bennie was sure to have seen the ad. She'd probably be waiting to ambush him the minute he went into the office this morning.

Okay, so the worst case scenario would be that he'd have one date with the woman, she wouldn't be what he wanted and after suffering through dinner with her, he'd never have to see her again. And he'd be off the hook with Bennie.

There had to be a better way to find a wife—one who met his needs. Maybe Bennie could come up with another idea. She seemed to always find solutions to his problems. What would she do, he wondered, if he asked her to find him a wife? Knowing how capable she was, he didn't doubt for a minute that she'd produce a suitable candidate. But did handpicking a wife fall under the job description for a personal assistant?

"What difference does that make?" he questioned himself aloud. From the very beginning, his relationship with Bennie had been more like partners than employer and employee. As a matter of fact, he had already talked to his lawyer about giving Bennie a piece of the business. After all, she deserved it.

He thought it would make a nice Christmas present.

Of course, he'd have to go through with responding to this personal ad, just to show Bennie he respected her suggestion. Then, if the lady wasn't suitable, he'd turn Operation Wife Search over to Bennie while he dealt with more important matters.

The minute Holt entered the office, Bennie prepared his morning coffee. With mug in hand and the day's agenda on her mind, she nudged open his door with her hip. She handed him the coffee, then leaned over his shoulder and punched in a file name on his computer.

Holt liked the way Bennie always smelled—like the roses that had grown in his grandmother's yard when he was a kid. Tilting his head slightly, he brushed the side of her face with his nose. She jerked away from him as if an electrical current had passed from his body to hers.

"Here's the list of suppliers you wanted to see." She nodded to the computer, then eased around the side of his desk and took a seat across from him. "You have a ten o'clock appointment with Mr. Sandler. Then I've scheduled you for a haircut and a manicure at eleven-thirty."

"I don't need a haircut!"

"Yes, you do. You don't want to look like a bum for your brother's wedding tomorrow." She glanced at his hair. If she didn't remind him to get haircuts, he'd let his hair grow out shaggy again. It had taken her years of cajoling to persuade him to have an occasional manicure. And even now, he often balked. "Your round-trip ticket to Louisville is on

Rene's desk. Your flight leaves at two-thirty this afternoon and your return flight will get you back to Fairmount around ten tomorrow night. Your hotel reservations are at the Kentucky Inn."

"Don't forget to cover for me with Randy Johnson this afternoon."

"I've already scheduled Randy for cocktails and I E-mailed him the new specifications for the bowling alley."

"Sometimes I think you could run this business without me." Holt smiled at Bennie, but she didn't return his smile. He noticed that she was staring at the folded newspaper lying on top of his briefcase. "Oh, yeah, I need you to do something for me while I'm gone."

"What?" Had she forgotten something? she wondered. She was sure she'd thought of everything. She prided herself on keeping things around the office running smoothly.

Holt lifted the newspaper off his briefcase, opened it to the personal ads section and folded the page in half. "Set things up with this woman, will you?" He handed Bennie today's issue of the *Herald Daily.*

When she stared at him, a puzzled expression on her face, he pointed to the ad he'd circled in red ink. "Interview her for me and see what you think. She sounds too good to be true. You're a pretty good judge of character, so after you talk to her, decide whether or not it would be worth my time to ask her for a date. I'd prefer it if you could get her to come by the office so you could get a good look at her."

"You want me to handle this for you?" Bennie forced herself to remain calm, to grasp the newspaper without trembling. Had he chosen her ad? Was he asking her to set him up on a date with "SWF, 29, intelligent, attractive professional, DAR member, prestigious family lineage?"

"Absolutely. Contact the paper today and explain the situation—that you're my assistant, etcetera—then interview this perfect woman, and when I call you tonight, you can give me a report. If she passes muster with you, then you can set up a date for us."

Bennie glanced down at the newspaper. Her heart caught in her throat when she read the ad Holt had chosen. Her ad. Oh, God, now what?

"Are you sure?" she asked.

"You're not having second thoughts about this, are you? After all, my checking the personal ads was your idea." He noted the odd way Bennie was staring at him, as if she were concerned about him. "What are you so worried about? She sounds like a woman who knows exactly what she wants. She's looking for a man who'll offer marriage. She didn't mention anything about love."

"I think most women consider the two a package deal."

"Well, you tell her up front that I want a woman who's interested in a business deal. I'm not going to waste time romancing someone."

"What if she wants to be romanced?" Bennie asked.

"Then she's the wrong woman for me."

"And if she's interested in a business deal, is there anything in particular that you don't want in a woman? If her background checks out, then she's obviously what you're looking for, but I'm sure you have specific—"

"If her background checks out and she's not a real dog, then I don't care if she's blonde or brunette or if she's tall and slim or short and plump. All I ask is that she be reasonably attractive."

"Reasonably attractive," Bennie said. *Am I reasonably attractive? Does Holt think I am?*

And as the day wore on, she found herself repeating those questions again and again. She must have been temporarily insane to have suggested to Holt that he pick a wife from the personal ads. Even more so, had she completely lost her mind by allowing Rene to tailor her ad for his specific needs?

"So, what are you going to do?" Rene asked, then bit into her cheeseburger.

Friday night, when most single women had dates, Bennie found herself at a local restaurant with Rene, who had recently broken up with her steady fellow.

"I don't know. I suppose when Holt calls tonight, I'll tell him that the lady's background checks out okay and that she's reasonably attractive, although a little on the plump side."

"And what are you going to say when he asks if

she'd be interested in a business deal arrangement instead of a love match?'' Rene squirted ketchup on her French fries.

''I might have to fudge the truth on that one,'' Bennie admitted. ''Be honest with me. Do you think I'd be nuts to go through with it, to actually set myself up on a date with Holt?''

''What have you got—''

''To lose. Yeah, yeah, I know.''

''There's one thing you haven't thought of,'' Rene said. ''What if, after your date, Holt offers you marriage on a strictly business basis? After all, you really are the girl of his dreams.''

''This isn't going to work,'' Bennie said. ''I was nuts to have thought it would. I won't marry Holt or any man without love. And you're right—once Holt realizes that his faithful, loyal assistant possesses all the qualities he wants in a wife, then he'll probably make me an offer.''

''I fixed up your personal ad too good, didn't I?'' Rene slurped on her cola.

''I told you not to put in the bit about a prestigious lineage or my being a member of the DAR. I'm sure those are the very things that caught Holt's eye and maybe the very things that would turn off any other guy.''

''So, if you don't want Holt to know the complete truth about you, tell him that I filled out the ad for you and I embellished it a little.''

"When he calls tonight, maybe I should tell him that the woman was a fraud."

Running her index finger up and down the moist plastic cup, Rene smiled coyly. "Why is it that every time Holt is out of town, he calls you?"

"I'm his assistant. Why wouldn't he call me?"

"He calls you at night, at your house. That doesn't sound too businesslike to me. What do y'all talk about when he calls?"

"Just what are you getting at?" Bennie asked.

"I'll bet you two don't talk about business, do you?"

"Of course we— Sometimes we discuss business. But usually he just tells me about his day. And occasionally we wind up talking about a book we've read or a movie we've seen or even what's happening politically in this country."

"Friend talk."

"Yes, of course. What else did you expect?"

"Nothing, I suppose. I just find it odd that he doesn't call whatever woman he happens to be dating at the time. Or better yet, why is he always alone in his hotel room calling you instead of bonking some willing bimbo? We both know Holt doesn't have any problem attracting women."

"I don't know why Holt calls me, other than the fact that we're friends." Bennie had wondered, more than once, why Holt often kept her on the phone for an hour or longer, not only when he was out of town, but often when he was home alone. She tried not to question his motives, but she couldn't stop herself from hoping that he turned to her as a confidante because he cared for her.

Maybe he didn't realize himself how much she meant to him. Maybe going out on a real date with him would force him to open his eyes and see her as a desirable woman. Setting up this date with Holt could very well be her one big chance—her last chance—with the man she loved.

Bennie stepped out of the shower and wrapped a towel around her wet hair. Just as she began drying off, the phone rang. Holt! She had given up on his calling and decided to bathe and go to bed. After all, it was past midnight.

With moisture dripping from her body, she raced into the bedroom. After checking her caller ID, she grabbed the phone.

"Hello."

"Bennie?"

"Yes."

"You sound out of breath. Are you okay?"

"Fine. I was just getting out of the shower."

An image of Bennie standing naked under a warm shower spray flashed through Holt's mind. What the hell was wrong with him? He was having lascivious thoughts about his best friend. And this wasn't the first time! Damn, he should have taken up the offer the stripper at Jason's party had made to spend the night with him. Instead of tormenting himself with thoughts of what Bennie looked like naked, he could be frolicking with a bleached blonde who probably knew every trick in the book.

"Holt, are you there?" The silence at the other end of the line made her wonder if they'd been disconnected.

"Yeah, I'm here."

"I thought you'd call me before the bachelor party instead of afterward."

"To be honest, I wasn't going to call at all," he admitted. "I'd pretty much changed my mind about the date with the lady from the personal ad."

"Oh. I see. So, you want me to call her tomorrow and—"

"What was she like?" he asked. "Did you just talk to her or did you meet her?"

"I—I met her," Bennie said. "She's nice."

"Did you check her out? Is she what she claims to be?"

"Uh, I'm not sure. I'm still checking. I think she might have exaggerated the part about her family lineage, but I don't think she out-and-out lied. She could be what you're looking for, if...if you're willing to settle for—"

"Is she butt ugly?"

Bennie gasped, then laughed. "No, she is not! She has dark hair and is very neat. Medium height. Slightly plump. Pretty, in an ordinary way."

"Do you think I should set up a date with her or

not?" he asked, hoping Bennie would tell him the woman wasn't worth wasting his time.

"Well, I...uh..." Tell him no and end this farce right now, she told herself. You're never going to make Holt Jackson love you. He isn't capable of falling in love with anyone.

"Sounds as if you've got some doubts about this lady being the right woman for me," he said, seeming relieved.

"Actually, I think this lady *is* the right woman for you," Bennie heard herself saying as if the voice were coming from someone else.

"Oh. So, you think I should have dinner with her and see for myself if she's—"

"Yes, I think you should meet her and judge for yourself."

"Well, all right, if you think so."

"Is next Saturday night too soon?" Bennie lifted her robe from the foot of the bed, eased her arms into the sleeves, then sat on the bed and stuffed her feet and legs under the covers.

"No, Saturday night's fine."

"I'll make arrangements for you. I assume you want me to make dinner reservations."

"Yeah. You know her type. Set up something you think she'd like."

"Should I have Rene order flowers for the lady?"

"Sure. Tell her to send the usual dozen red roses."

''This lady doesn't like red roses,'' Bennie told Holt. ''She prefers white roses.''

''Yeah, she would. They're more expensive, aren't they?''

''Yes, they are. So, do you or do you not want Rene to order white roses for her?''

''Yeah. And make it two dozen. We want her to know just how loaded I am, don't we? Two dozen roses should impress her.''

''All right. I'll have everything set up when you get back. Just give me a call Saturday morning and I'll let you know the time and place you're to meet her.''

''Sure thing. By the way, what's her name?''

''Her name?'' Oh, God, what could she say? She could hardly tell him the woman's name was Marianne Bennett, could she? ''The lady asked to remain anonymous until the night you meet. I'm afraid she's a bit of a romantic.''

''Damn, Bennie, I told you—''

''She knows how you feel about love,'' Bennie said. ''I explained that, if things work out between the two of you, you're interested in marriage, but not in love.''

''And she agreed to that?''

''She's willing to meet you and see what happens.''

As Bennie clutched the phone to her ear, she yawned loudly. She lay down on the bed, then curled up against her pillow.

"Are you sleepy?" Holt asked. "I thought I heard you yawn."

"Just tired. It's been a long day."

"I'm sorry I called so late. I should have waited until morning."

"That's all right." She didn't care when he called—day or night. Just listening to his voice was a pleasure.

"Why do you put up with me, Bennie? I'm so inconsiderate and I'm always taking advantage of you. I'm surprised you're still my friend, after all the times I've imposed on you."

Why do I put up with you? Oh, Holt, you idiot. I love you. I love you so much it hurts. Why is it that everyone else can see how I feel, but you're totally blind? "You'd be there for me, if I needed you, wouldn't you, Holt?"

"You know I would," he assured her. "I'd do just about anything for you."

Love me, she wanted to scream. Love me the way I love you. "Did you have fun at the bachelor party tonight?"

"I guess," he said. "I can't believe my brother's getting married again. This makes wife number three and the guy's only thirty-two!"

"Looks like he's going to keep trying until he gets it right."

"I intend to get it right the first time," Holt told her. "None of this falling in and out of love. Just two sensible people willing to go into a marriage based on mutual respect and reasonable expectations.''

''All marriages based on love don't end in divorce,'' Bennie said.

''No, not all, just half, according to the latest statistics.''

''So, you think a mutually beneficial business deal marriage will prevent a divorce? That *not* being in love with your wife assures you both of a long-lasting marriage?''

''You sound as if you disagree with me. Don't tell me that my sensible, levelheaded Bennie is actually looking for love.'' Holt chuckled. ''I've never thought of you as the type who'd expect romance in a relationship. I thought you were far too smart for that.''

''Just goes to show you that you don't know me as well as you think you do.''

''You don't have a secret lover stashed away that you haven't told me about, do you?'' Holt asked teasingly.

''If he's a secret lover, then I would hardly tell you about him, would I?''

''Are you saying that you actually have a secret—''

''I'm saying good night. You need to get some sleep so you'll be alert for your brother's noon wedding. And I need at least a couple hours of rest before I head back to the office and hold down the fort for you while you're gone.''

"I know a brush-off when I hear one." Holt chuckled again.

"Then say good night."

"Set up the date for me," he said. "And Bennie?"

"Yes?"

"I hope this secret lover of yours deserves you. I wouldn't let just any man have you, you know."

Chapter 3

Holt read over the directions to Wildwood Lodge, a restaurant and inn about fifteen miles outside Fairmount. He didn't like the idea of meeting this woman at such a romantic place and he'd told Bennie so. But she had assured him that this kind of fancy restaurant would be just what his mystery lady expected.

"I've been to the Wildwood Lodge," Bennie had said. "It's the kind of place I adore. And since this lady and I seem to have a great deal in common, I'm sure she'll love it, too."

He had grumbled about Wildwood Lodge giving his mystery lady the wrong idea, but he now realised the real reason he'd been so out of sorts with Bennie. The minute she'd mentioned having been to the Wildwood Lodge, he'd wondered with whom she'd shared a romantic evening. He hadn't realized there was a special man in her life.

Even now, hours after their conversation, he couldn't get the thought out of his mind. Bennie with a secret lover. Sharing a cosy dinner for two. Spending the night together. Making passionate love.

Cursing a few heated obscenities, Holt beat one big fist into the palm of his other hand. Who was this guy, this secret lover? And why keep him a secret? Was she seriously involved with this man?

If Bennie got married, she might leave Jackson Construction—she might leave him. No, Bennie would never give up her job. She liked working for him, liked running his life and keeping him in line. But if she had children someday, she'd want to stay home with them, wouldn't she?

The image of a very pregnant Bennie flashed through his mind. She'd be beautiful pregnant. She had the kind of body made for— Dammit, Jackson, what the hell do you think you're doing, fantasizing about Bennie again? And this time, you've got her pregnant.

Okay, so he found Bennie attractive. He always had. But he'd never acted on that attraction. And maybe that was what was wrong with him now, the reason why he kept daydreaming about her. Usually when he wanted a woman, he had sex with her and got her out of his system. But Bennie was his assistant and his best friend. Sex with her could ruin their working relationship and end their friendship.

But dammit all, he couldn't help being concerned about her lover. Bennie deserved only the best and something told Holt this guy wasn't the best. If he were, why would she keep her affair with him secret? He knew one thing for sure and certain—if this man hurt Bennie, if the guy broke her heart, he would break him in two.

Rummaging through his closet, Holt pulled out a clean pair of jeans and a dark-green button-down shirt. Bennie had tried for years to put him in a suit, but she'd finally given up and settled for his wearing a sport coat and tie. Would his mystery lady dislike his casual attire? Was she looking for someone who was more of a gentleman in appearance and personality? If so, why had she specified a self-made man? Most self-made men weren't Southern gentlemen. Most were, as he was, rednecks who had clawed their way up from the bottom of the heap.

Checking his watch, Holt saw that he had more than enough time for a workout before he showered and shaved. In the four years he had lived in this one-bedroom apartment he had made few changes. Although he could afford the best, he remained in this inexpensive apartment and all his furniture was still secondhand. Bennie had helped him convert the small storage room off the kitchen into a minigym.

How many times had she sat on the floor, blueprints spread out before her, a cola in one hand, and discussed a new project with him while he exercised? How many times had she stayed with him until the wee hours of the morning, the two of them laughing and talking and enjoying being together?

When he married, what would happen to those special times they often shared? Even in a marriage of convenience, he doubted his wife would approve of his spending so much of his free time with Bennie. And what about Bennie's husband, if she married her secret lover? He'd want all Bennie's attention when she wasn't at work.

Holt didn't especially like the idea of losing those fun times with Bennie. But that was exactly what would happen when they each married someone else.

Forget marriage. Forget the mystery lady. Forget the secret lover. And forget Bennie! What he needed right now was a good workout—something to clear the cobwebs from his brain and burn up some of the frustration he felt. Holt stripped down to his briefs, then headed for the minigym, intent on vanquishing all thoughts of Marianne Bennett from his mind.

Bennie laid out the dress she and Rene had chosen for her date tonight. The most important date of her life. She backed several feet from the intricate oval and floral designed iron bed that dominated her apartment bedroom. The red dress shimmered brightly in direct contrast to the pale cream damask coverlet on which it rested. The snug-fitting little knee-length dress looked great on Bennie, or so Rene had said. She supposed it did. As a child her mother had dressed her in reds and pinks and yellows—bright, warm colors that she'd been told looked good on brunettes.

The dress accentuated every curve of her body, making her full breasts look even larger and her small waist appear tiny. Remembering how round her curves looked encased in the dress made Bennie wish for the impossible. If only she were twenty pounds lighter or six inches taller. But she wasn't. She was as she'd always been—five foot three and plump.

Bennie scrambled in her jewelry box, seeking the right accessories for tonight's outfit. Finding nothing suitable, she pulled out a small velvet drawer in the box and lifted a pair of sparkling diamond earrings into her hand. The oval diamond hoops had been an eighteenth-birthday present from her father. Her dear, sweet, humble father, a man she had both loved and pitied. Robert Bennett had been mild mannered, highly intelligent and the product of a mutually beneficial marriage between third cousins. He had made a smooth transition from being dominated by his mother to being dominated by his wife, and yet he'd seemed perfectly content with the arrangement.

Poor Daddy! Bennie thought. He had died of a

heart attack, peacefully in his sleep, when she was twenty.

The earrings would be all the jewelry she'd need to enhance the simplicity of the dress. She wanted to be not only beautiful for Holt, but also elegantly sexy.

Glancing at the clock on the European luggage rack she used as a nightstand, Bennie noted that she had exactly four hours and fifteen minutes until she was to meet Holt at Wildwood Lodge. Four hours to pamper and prepare. Four hours to convince herself that she could pull this date off without making a fool of herself.

After drawing a bubble bath, she immersed herself in the water and reclined her head, resting it on the rim of the tub. Closing her eyes, she began thinking about what might happen tonight. As she allowed her body to relax, her mind created several different scenarios—everything from Holt laughing himself silly the minute he saw her to his sweeping her into his arms and carrying her off to one of the private rooms in the lodge.

Thoughts of Holt's lovemaking sent shivers through her body. A throbbing tingle began in her feminine core and slowly spread upward and outward until she ached all over.

Grabbing the rose-scented soap from the soap dish, she lathered her face, then using her washcloth, scrubbed vigorously.

Holt wasn't going to make love to her. Not tonight! Not ever! She had been living with that hopeless dream for years now and where had it gotten her? The minute he saw her tonight, he was going to be angry—once he recovered from the shock. And she could hardly blame him, could she? After all, she had perpetrated a hoax on him. He thought he was going to meet a stranger, a woman with whom he had no emotional ties. But instead he was going to get a surprise, possibly an unpleasant surprise.

Once he realized his date was good old Bennie, would he leave her sitting there alone at the restaurant?

Bennie jumped at the sound of nearby thunder. Great, just great, she thought. That's all she needed. Rain. Humidity. Her naturally wavy hair would curl in the dampness and she wouldn't be able to do a thing with it. And she had planned a sophisticated French twist, a style that would show off her long neck and highlight the diamond hoops.

Don't rain! Don't rain! she chanted silently.

She could see herself now, her hair frizzed, her shoes muddy and her clothes damp. By the time Holt saw her, she'd look like a drowned rat!

Call him and tell him the lady canceled at the last minute. Tell him she changed her mind, that she got a better offer. Tell him anything, but call him and end this farce before it goes any further.

She finished her bath hurriedly, got out, dried off and slipped into her robe. Just as she headed toward the cordless telephone she had earlier tossed onto the antique leather-and-wicker chair at the foot of her bed, the doorbell rang.

Who could it be? Probably Rene, even though she wasn't due here to fix Bennie's hair for another thirty minutes.

Bennie raced through the living room and to the front door. Peering through the viewfinder, she saw a delivery woman carrying a vase filled with two dozen cream-white roses. She had forgotten all about the roses—the ones she had insisted Holt have Rene send to his date.

Bennie opened the door, accepted the roses and thanked the delivery person. When she tried to tip the woman, she was told that the tip had been included in the payment for the order.

After placing the roses in the center of her coffee table, she gazed at the beautifully arranged bouquet. She had always loved white roses. Her father had cultivated and grown his own hybrid roses. In her honor, he had named a cream white rose, fringed with yellow gold, The Marianne.

The doorbell rang again. This time she knew it had to be Rene. And sure enough, when she opened the door, there stood her best gal pal, a carryall thrown over her shoulder.

"I know I'm a little early. But we want you to look your best tonight. I brought makeup, hot rollers, styling gel—the works." Rene unzipped the carryall as she walked into the living room. "Wow, the roses are gorgeous. I told the florist not to spare any expense, that Mr. Jackson wanted the very best."

"I suppose you know that everyone in Fairmount will know by tomorrow that Holt Jackson sent his personal assistant two dozen white roses."

"So, who cares?"

"I'll care and so will Holt, if tonight backfires on me."

Rene grabbed Bennie's shoulder, whirled her around and headed her toward the bedroom. "No more negative thoughts. I forbid it." She hurried Bennie across the room, then shoved her down on the padded stool in front of the small vanity table in the corner. "Once Holt gets a look at you tonight, he won't be able to resist you."

A loud clap of thunder shook the windowpanes. Rene gasped. Bennie huffed.

"It's going to rain and you won't be able to do anything with my hair." Bennie gazed into the mirror and saw that her hair was already beginning to curl around her face. Dammit, she'd look like an overaged, brunette Shirley Temple by the time she arrived at the restaurant.

Lifting Bennie's long wavy locks, Rene studied the dark mass. "You're right. A French twist is definitely out." She dropped the carryall on the floor, then bent over and retrieved a brush, a comb and a plastic container filled with bobby pins. "But just leave everything to me. What I have in mind will be even sexier."

"I'm having second thoughts," Bennie admitted. "Maybe I should call Holt and cancel the date."

"You'll do no such thing!" Rene brushed Bennie's hair with vigorous strokes. "You're going to meet Holt at Wildwood Lodge if I have to hog-tie you and carry you there."

Bennie drove her four-year-old Grand Am over the bridge that crossed the winding Noxubee River, a deep, narrow waterway that followed the county line and separated the Wildwood community from the rest of civilization. Booming thunder and streaks of brilliant lightning followed her path. Just as she parked her car at the lodge, raindrops began splattering onto the pavement and nearby brick walkway.

After opening the car door, she stuck out her red umbrella and lifted it above her head, then exited the car and made a mad dash to the lodge entrance. A hostess greeted her the minute she entered.

"Good evening and welcome to Wildwood Lodge." The woman held out her hand. "May I take your umbrella?"

"Thank you." Bennie handed the wet umbrella to the hostess, then glanced past her to the elegant dining room. "I'm meeting someone here. We have reservations for seven."

"In what name?" The hostess asked, as she hung Bennie's wet umbrella on a wooden coatrack.

"Jackson. Mr. Holt Jackson."

"Ah, yes. Mr. Jackson's secretary gave us very

precise orders for tonight. I'm sure you're going to be pleased.'' With a mannerly sway of her hand, the hostess invited Bennie to follow her.

She'd had lunch here six months ago during her mother's last visit and had immediately fallen in love with the place. The restaurant possessed a rich yet casual elegance, with its dark wooden floors and wainscoted walls, deep jewel-tone upholstery fabrics and antique-style lighting fixtures. Sparkling crystal, gleaming silver and delicate china comprised each inviting place setting. Crisp white linen tablecloths and matching napkins, secured with brass rings, graced each private table. Sturdy wooden chairs with cloth-covered seats were arranged in even numbers, ranging from two to ten, depending upon table size.

The hostess led Bennie to a secluded table in the corner, near a window overlooking a large patio and flower garden, illuminated by lampposts reminiscent of a bygone era. A bouquet of white roses served as a centerpiece for the table and atop one of the china plates lay a small golden box of Bennie's favorite chocolates.

Rene had thought of everything! Bennie halfway expected to see a band of gypsy violinists appear out of nowhere.

''Would you care for a drink while you wait for Mr. Jackson?'' the hostess asked.

''Water with lemon, please,'' Bennie said. She certainly didn't want anything alcoholic this early in the evening. When Holt arrived, she'd need all her senses sharp and her mind alert.

By the time Holt turned his Jaguar off the main highway and onto the two-lane road leading to Wildwood Lodge, it was raining so hard he could barely see two feet in front of him. He'd heard a flash flood warning issued when he'd been flipping through the radio stations trying to get a weather report. A September storm was brewing and this one followed two earlier gully washers that had hit the area the previous week. Creeks and rivers ran high and if more rain fell tonight, some could overflow their banks.

The storm fit Holt's mood. Dark. Gloomy. Miserable. The closer he got to Wildwood Lodge the more he dreaded the evening. If he hadn't agreed to this blind date, he could be home right now, warm and comfortable, with a beer, a pizza and Carmel curled up next to him on the sofa. No, not Carmel. They had parted, by mutual consent, over a month ago and she already had a new boyfriend. Well, maybe Lori. No, not Lori. She'd moved from Fairmount a couple of months ago, hadn't she? So what about Tiffany? He could have called and asked her to drop by after her shift at JoJo's Bar ended. They could have shared a late supper and then some enjoyable sack time.

Come on, Jackson, he said to himself. Admit it. What you'd like to be doing is spending time with

Bennie. You'd like her to be the woman sharing your beer and pizza. And the woman sleeping in your bed tonight.

Over the years, every time he'd allowed sexual thoughts about Bennie to creep into his mind, he had always run toward the nearest available female as a means of protection. So, maybe this woman—this perfect woman—he was on his way to meet could solve that problem permanently. Once he was married, he'd have no choice but to keep Bennie at arm's length. Even if he wouldn't be in love with his wife, he intended to be faithful to her. He'd seen too many marriages wrecked because of infidelity. His parents' for one. And his thrice married younger brother for another.

He and his two brothers had grown up without a father's love, financial support or presence in their lives. His mother had worked herself to death raising three boys on her own. She'd died when Holt was in the army. She'd been forty-one. As far as his old man went, Holt had no idea where he was or if he was dead or alive. Jerry Don Jackson had left town with another woman twenty-five years ago and hadn't been heard from since.

Damn! If the rain got any worse, he'd have to pull off the side of the road and wait until it slacked up a bit. If he had to do that, he'd wind up being late for his date with Ms. Mystery Woman. Maybe he should go ahead and call the lodge to let her know he'd be late. Or he could call and cancel, tell her the road conditions were terrible. No, he couldn't do that. He wasn't the type of guy who'd stand up a lady, especially on such short notice.

Fifteen minutes later, Holt parked his car. He scanned the floorboard for an umbrella. Then he remembered he'd left the thing at the office this past week. Oh, well, a little rain wouldn't kill him. He'd probably wind up a little less presentable, but what the heck. The lady might as well see him soaked to the skin, irritable and less than his usual charming self.

As he entered the building, an oil painting of the lodge that hung in the vestibule caught his attention. He realized the structure, which in fact was a huge old farmhouse, had been remodeled and turned into an inn. A one-story addition housed the restaurant.

Within two minutes after Holt sloshed his way into the dining room, he noticed two things simultaneously—the attractive young hostess heading his way and the scarcity of dinner guests. Not more than six of the two dozen tables were occupied.

"Good evening, sir," the hostess greeted him.

"I'm Holt Jackson," he said. "I'm supposed to meet a young lady for dinner."

"Yes, of course. Right this way, Mr. Jackson. Your date arrived about twenty minutes ago."

"I ran into some bad weather," he explained as he followed the hostess. "Doesn't look as if many people came out tonight."

"Business is slow. We've had numerous cancellations."

"I can understand why. I almost canceled myself."

"That would have been a shame, considering we've made all the special preparations your secretary requested to make this a perfect evening for you and your date."

All the preparations his secretary had requested? Just what sort of instructions had Rene given these people? he wondered.

The hostess paused when they reached a secluded table in the far corner. The woman waiting there faced the opposite direction. All he could see was the back of her dark head; her long slender neck and her shoulders encased in red silk. Before he could round the table, a violinist, playing some asinine romantic melody, approached. No doubt this fiddle player was one of the *special preparations* Rene had requested.

Holt slipped a couple of fingers under his collar in an effort to loosen his tie. He hated the damn things, but Bennie had convinced him that the lady would expect at least a sport coat and tie. He didn't own a suit and had no intention of buying one!

Taking a deep breath, he walked around the table and held out his hand. "Hi. I'm Holt—" The woman looked up at him and for a split second he thought he was seeing things. "Bennie?"

He wasn't seeing things. The woman sitting before him was Bennie all right. But not the Bennie he knew. This was some new version of his assistant. She was breathtakingly beautiful. Her black hair was piled atop her head, the little wire-frame glasses she usually wore were nowhere to be seen. A pair of really nice fake diamond hoops circled her earlobes. And a slinky red dress hugged every luscious inch of her body.

Holt swallowed hard. "Bennie, that is you, isn't it?"

She offered him a fragile smile. "Yes, it's me."

"What are you doing here?"

"Having dinner with you." A warm flush crept up her neck and highlighted her already pink cheeks.

"What happened to my date—the woman who was so perfect for me? Did she call and cancel at the last minute?"

"No, she—she didn't cancel."

"I don't understand. If she didn't cancel, then where is she and what are you doing here?"

"I'm your date, Holt." Bennie squared her shoulders, tilted her chin and looked him square in the eye. "It was my ad in the personals section of the *Herald Daily* that you chose."

"Your ad?" Holt stared at her, an incredulous look on his face.

"Yes. You see, I'm the woman who's perfect for you."

Chapter 4

Slumping down in the chair, Holt continued staring at Bennie. With his mouth slightly agape, he shook his head. "I don't understand any of this. You're—" he pointed his index finger at her "—my date? You're the mystery lady?"

Nodding, Bennie struggled to keep her weak smile in place. "Rene gave me a copy of *Prominence Magazine* that had an article called 'Married by the Millennium' and one of the suggestions was—"

"I should have known Rene would be involved in this somehow!" Holt grappled with the knot in his tie until he loosened it. "What on earth would possess you to listen to Rene? She's a great secretary, but she doesn't know beans about how to get and keep a man. Her love life is usually a mess. You're the one who's always giving her advice that she won't take. Why would you think she's an expert on anything involving men?"

"Rene didn't give me the advice," Bennie said. "The advice came from the magazine article."

"An article on how to get married? Are you saying you placed an ad in the personals section of the *Herald Daily* because you really are husband hunting?"

"That's right. I'll be thirty my next birthday and I'm tired of waiting—" she had been about to say *tired of waiting for you* "—and I'm ready to get married and have children."

"What about your secret lover?" Holt asked. "Isn't he the marrying kind?"

"What secret lover?"

"The one you told me about last night."

"I didn't tell you that I had a...ah...I remember now." Her tentative smile strengthened. "You just assumed I had a secret lover and I simply didn't bother to correct you."

"Are you saying there's no secret lover?" A sense of relief washed over Holt.

"That's right. I don't have a secret lover. As a matter of fact, I don't have a lover at all, secret or otherwise."

Holt pulled his tie through the knotted loop, then whipped it off and stuffed it into his pocket.

The violinist stood several feet away, but his music was obviously directed at their table. The tune he played sounded like something from an old movie, Holt thought. One of those romantic chick flicks.

"Did Rene request the violin music?" Holt nodded to the portly musician.

"Yes."

"Hmm."

The waiter delivered champagne to the table. Holt eyed the label. He didn't know a damn thing about vintages, but he'd bet his last dime that this was some of the expensive stuff.

Lifting the crystal flute, Holt examined the champagne. "I suppose Rene ordered this, too."

"Yes."

Within minutes the waiter placed their salads before them, then scurried away. Holt noted that his was a house salad with French dressing. His favorite.

"Tell me something. If your purpose in placing an ad was to find a husband, why set up this date with me? Why, when I showed you which ad I'd chosen, didn't you just tell me that the woman was you? You could have saved us from wasting our time with each other." Holt took a sip of the champagne, then set the flute on the table and picked up his salad fork.

Good question, Bennie thought. Why indeed? Now give him a good answer. A logical, reasonable answer. "The whole thing was Rene's idea." That's it, blame Rene. Well, she had to blame someone, didn't she? She could hardly tell Holt that she'd been madly in love with him for years and dreamed of being his wife.

"Why am I not surprised? What did she think—that you and I would be perfect for each other? How did she convince you to go along with such a harebrained idea?"

"I don't think it's so harebrained!" Control yourself, Bennie. Don't jump down the man's throat. If you overreact, he's bound to become suspicious. "Rene pointed out to me that since I'm looking for a husband and you're looking for a wife, the logical thing to do was for the two of us to get together."

Holt undid the top button of his shirt. "How is our getting together logical? You're not what I'm looking for in a wife and I don't figure I'm your ideal man."

When Bennie didn't respond, he speared a tomato in his salad and brought it to his mouth. Bennie sat there, staring at her Caesar salad.

"Not hungry?" he asked.

Instead of responding to his immediate question, she said, "I think our getting together is totally logical. We already know each other, like and respect each other and we work well together. In business, we're the ideal couple. So, why not—"

"Did you fill out the information for the personal ad or did Rene?"

"What?"

"I said, did you—"

"Rene filled out the ad for me."

"So, what did she do—concoct the type of ad she knew would catch my eye? She invented a history for you that would match what I was looking for in a wife, didn't she?"

"Something like that."

"Bennie, I'm really flattered that you'd even consider marrying me." Holt laid down his salad fork, then extended his hand across the table toward her. When he reached for her hand, she snatched it away. "Look, honey, if you really had the pedigree I was looking for, we might discuss terms. But we both know that what I need is a lady whose social position can help me out. An old redneck boy like me can go only so far in this business before he starts running into closed doors that only the right wife can open for him."

Bennie had to bite her tongue to keep from telling him the truth. She wanted to stand on the table and shout at the top of her lungs that she, Marianne Colburn Bennett, had blood so blue you could substitute it for ink. And a part of her longed to wipe that smug look off his face and tell him that she had already opened quite a few doors for him. Five years ago, she had used her trust fund as collateral for the bank loan that had gotten his business off the ground. Something she'd made sure he would never find out. And on several occasions, she had asked an uncle or a cousin to vouch for Holt, without his ever knowing about what she'd done.

"Jackson Construction seems to be doing all right. You're a very wealthy man and getting wealthier every day. So, you can't convince me that a society wife is essential for your success." Bennie stabbed a small chunk of lettuce, then stuffed it into her mouth.

Holt downed the remainder of his champagne, then refilled his flute. "I've always been honest with you, Bennie, so I'm going to be totally honest now. You're right about Jackson Construction. And maybe, if I hadn't been raised so damn poor, hadn't had my teeth kicked in so many times by guys like Bo Reynolds, hadn't watched my mama work herself to death cleaning rich people's houses, then marrying above me wouldn't matter so much.

"But why should I settle for less? Why can't I have it all? By marrying *class,* it'll help my business and it'll assure my kids won't ever have to go through what I did. Nobody's going to look down their nose at my son or daughter!"

Tears lodged in Bennie's throat and gathered in the corners of her eyes. Poor Holt. She'd known, of course, how very poor he'd been and how wretchedly he'd been treated by the people his mother worked for. And she understood his need to shove his success down those very same people's throats. If only she had listened to her head instead of her heart, she wouldn't be sitting here right now, feeling like a total fool.

"Love doesn't enter into it at all, does it?" Bennie swallowed the emotions that threatened to choke her.

"See, that's another reason, we aren't suited for each other. You expect love and romance and I don't."

"I'm really sorry, Holt. About tonight." She reached out and grasped his hand. "I want you to be happy. And I suppose I thought that I was the woman who could make you happy."

"Bennie—"

She squeezed his hand. "No, it's all right. Honestly. It's just that we're such good partners at work that I thought we might make good life partners, too."

She released his hand, scooted back her chair, dropped her napkin on the table and then stood. Instinctively, he got up out of the chair, dropping his napkin on the floor in the process. Bennie picked up the golden box of chocolates and her small evening bag from where she'd placed them on the table.

Garnering all her strength, she glided languidly over to Holt, who stood stiffly by the table, and kissed him on the lips. A quick, closemouth kiss that nevertheless sent shock waves through her body. Even though she had dreamed for years of kissing Holt, this was the first time.

"I'll see you at work, Monday." Bennie turned and walked away.

"Don't go!" The minute Bennie stopped and glanced over her shoulder at him, he ran toward her.

She turned and waited for him. Holt halted abruptly, then grabbed her by the shoulders. "There's no reason for you to leave. We've both weathered a storm to get here tonight and everything's all set up, thanks to Rene. So, why don't you stay? We can eat and talk and maybe even dance." He nodded to the empty dance floor and the pianist seated by the big bay window.

"Holt, are you sure about this? After all—"

He slid his arm around her waist and led her back to the table. "I'm sure. There's no reason why two good friends can't have a romantic dinner together."

His wicked smile curled her toes. Why, of all men on earth, had she fallen in love with this big lug?

"Okay, I'll stay, if you promise me something." She allowed him to seat her.

Holt sat back down across from her. "Ask away. You know I can't refuse you anything."

You've refused me what I want most, she thought. "We'll pretend, only for tonight, that this is a real date. Just a man and a woman enjoying each other's company. No past. No future."

"Sure. Why not?" His gut instincts warned him that this was a mistake, that having a "date" with Bennie was asking for trouble. Agreeing to spend the evening with her, just man to woman and not friend to friend, was enough to send his libido into overdrive. For years he had deliberately avoided putting himself in a romantic situation with her for this very reason.

He was only human. And the sight of Bennie in the sexy red dress had him fighting the urge to drag her upstairs to the nearest bed. It wasn't that he hadn't been aware that she had a luscious body, but the dress's low cleavage revealed the round, firm swell of her breasts, and the snug fit clasped her small waist and hugged her hips and fanny. His hands itched to caress her, to pull her close and press her against his arousal.

The waiter removed their salads, then returned with their entrées—medium-rare T-bone steak and loaded potato for Holt and a filet mignon and steamed veggies for Bennie.

Okay, so the ploy to capture Holt had failed, Bennie admitted to herself. But she didn't accept defeat. The night was still young, they were on a real date and Holt was looking at her as if he found her more delectable than his meal. Anything could happen. She smiled as she sliced into her filet.

Two and a half hours later, the restaurant was lit only with candlelight. The storm had progressively worsened and become so severe that the inn had lost electrical power. But the couples who occupied the six tables didn't seem to notice. Holt and Bennie were no exception.

Holt led Bennie out onto the dance floor for their fourth dance of the evening. Giddy with the pleasure of his company and the feel of his arm wrapped around her waist, she followed where he led. The pianist, who had been playing mood music for the past couple of hours, performed a duet with the violinist. A moody, almost bluesy rendition of "Summertime." Odd how every time she and Holt danced, the musicians played the same song.

Rene really had thought of everything. White roses. A violinist. The finest chocolate candy. The best champagne. Holt's favorite meal. And one of Bennie's favorite songs. She couldn't help but wonder what other surprises Rene had in store for them?

Holt brought her into his arms, but maintained a discreet three inches between their bodies, as he had done each time they'd danced. She longed to wrap her arms around him and lay her head on his chest. And from the look in his eyes, he wanted the same thing. But she wasn't going to make the first move! If Holt wanted her any closer, he'd have to take the initiative.

All evening they had talked and laughed, their comradery vanquishing any former uncertainty and hesitation. Although she and Holt had spent many evenings together in the past, none had ever been like this one. They both knew this was more than two buddies hanging out together. This was real and romantic and seductive.

"I don't think I told you how pretty you look tonight," Holt said.

"Thank you." Bennie's heart fluttered wildly. "You look pretty good yourself." Holt always looked good, even when he needed a haircut and a shave. Even when he came straight from a construction site, all hot and sweaty.

"I've never seen you wear your hair like that."

He studied the purposefully disarrayed arrangement, loose tendrils curling around her face and trailing down her back. It was all he could do not to reach up, remove the pins from her hair and watch it fall into his hands. Bennie had the most gorgeous hair!

"I had planned on a French twist, but with this horrid humidity, my hair wouldn't cooperate, so Rene just piled it all on top of my head."

"Makes you look as if you just crawled out of bed." Out of some man's bed, Holt thought. After a night of passionate lovemaking.

Bennie stroked the back of her head. "Does it look that bad? I promise you that it has been brushed."

"I like it." He ran his gaze over her shoulders, across her breasts and then back up to her face. "I like your dress, too. You look good in red."

"Guess I'll save this dress for when I have dates with the other men who answered my ad."

"Other men replied to your ad?" It had never occurred to him that other men might actually want the same thing in a woman that he did and that they might have contacted Bennie.

"*Five* other men, to be exact." She strongly emphasized the word *five.*

Unaware of what he was doing, Holt drew Bennie closer, his big hand pressing her possessively against his body.

"Have you told them that the DAR membership and the prestigious lineage parts of the ad weren't true?"

"I was completely honest with every one of them and all five want to set up dates. So you see, I've got a good chance of landing myself a husband before the end of the year."

Holt rubbed his cheek against hers as they swayed with the seductive music. "Maybe you'd better let me check these guys out to make sure they're on the up-and-up. I can't have some guy taking advantage of my best friend."

"You act as if I'm a sixteen-year-old virgin and you're my big brother. Believe me, Holt, I'm perfectly capable of choosing the right man. And I think I have enough sense to be able to separate the wheat from the chaff."

Anger rose inside Holt, like molten lava building inside a volcano. He wasn't sure exactly what had produced that anger, but he knew it had something to do with the thought of Bennie being involved with another man. Maybe with five other men!

He knew she had dated various men over the

years, knew she had an ex-fiancé somewhere, but he'd just never pictured Bennie—his Bennie—getting seriously involved with someone. And the thought of her actually having sex with some guy just didn't sit right with Holt. Maybe he did think of her as a sweet, vulnerable kid sister, someone he had to protect.

Yeah, sure, Jackson. Tell that to someone who'd believe it. You know damn well that the thought of Bennie with some other guy makes you jealous. You can't stand the idea of some other man making love to the woman you'd like to have all for yourself.

The music stopped unexpectedly. The three couples on the dance floor slowed their movements, but remained in one another's arms as they turned their attention to the hostess who stood by the patio.

"Ladies and gentleman, I have an announcement," she said. "I'm afraid the Butler Bridge across the Noxubee River is closed. The heavy rainfall has submerged the bridge and made travel across it impossible."

A low rumble of disbelief and concern rose from the customers.

The hostess cleared her throat and continued. "We will do our best to accommodate those of you who don't already have reservations for the night. If you'll speak to Mr. Perkins, the inn's manager, he can explain the situation further."

Still captured in Holt's embrace, Bennie didn't care if they were trapped at the lodge for a week.

The longer this magic night lasted, the better. "Guess we'll be sleeping on the floor tonight. Maybe the inn will provide some pillows and blankets."

"Wonder if all the rooms are booked?" Holt mused aloud.

"Probably, but I suppose we could ask."

"Come on." Holt grabbed her hand and led her off the dance floor and through the restaurant.

A pair of French doors led to the lobby of the inn. The manager, a short, stout man of about sixty, met them the moment they entered. His small gold nameplate read Mr. T. Perkins.

"Mr. Jackson." The manager offer his hand. "I hope everything has been satisfactory tonight."

Holt shook the man's hand. "Everything's been just fine, except for this bad weather."

"Yes, it is rather frightening to think that the Butler Bridge is impassable, but I'm sure that once the rain stops and the river waters subside, y'all will be able to get back to Fairmount."

"I'm sure you're right. My guess is that we should get out of here by tomorrow afternoon, unless it rains all night," Holt said. "But our main concern is tonight."

"Oh? Is there some reason you're concerned?" Mr. Perkins inquired. "I assure you that your room has been prepared exactly as your secretary instructed. If once you've seen it and find anything unsatisfactory, all you need do is let me know and I'll take care of the problem myself."

"My room?" Holt asked.

"Rene booked us a room?" Bennie's cheeks flushed. How dare Rene book them a room at the inn! What would Holt think—that she had expected to spend the night with him?

"Yes, of course," Mr. Perkins said. "Ms. Lowe reserved our finest—the Blue Room."

"I swear to you that I had no idea Rene would go this far," Bennie explained. "I wasn't expecting anything beyond dinner."

Mr. Perkins cleared his throat. Holt chuckled. Bennie cringed.

"Well, Mr. Perkins, under the circumstances, I hope you can provide us with a few items for our overnight stay." Holt grinned wickedly at Bennie.

"Is there another room available?" she asked.

"Why no, ma'am. All our rooms are booked." Mr. Perkins then turned to Holt. "Just what will y'all need, Mr. Jackson? The bathroom is fully stocked and there are robes provided. And of course, per Ms. Lowe's instructions, a fire has been lit in the fireplace, another bottle of champagne is already chilled and your breakfast will be served in your room whenever—"

"I get the idea," Holt said, then winked at Bennie. "Rene really did think of everything, didn't she?"

Chapter 5

A king-size cherry wood canopy bed, draped in endless yards of blue print fabric caught Bennie's eye the moment she stepped into the room. All the fabric, from curtains to coverlet, complimented the Blue Willow plates that were displayed in the antique bookcase. There was a vague familiarity about the room and its elegant furnishings. She had grown up surrounded by expensive things. Indeed there had been a time when she had taken her family's wealth and social position for granted.

Candles burned on the bedside tables and lined the mantel. A glass lantern burned softly in the center of the round table that held a silver ice bucket and a tray of edible delights.

"Now, this is some room," Holt said. "Take a good look around you, Bennie. This is the kind of style the right wife for me will have."

"Does this remind you of the homes your mother used to clean?"

"Yeah."

Holt strolled over to the double French doors on the far side of the room, then opened them. "Looks like the rain is slacking off." He glanced over his shoulder at Bennie. "Mind if I leave these open for a while? I kind of like listening to the rain."

"No, I don't mind. As a matter of fact, the cool night air feels pretty good." She glanced meaningfully at the brightly burning fire in the elaborately decorative fireplace. "It's really too warm for a fire tonight. But I'm sure Rene didn't take the temperature into consideration when she placed an order for it."

"Rene wasn't thinking about anything but romance." Holt turned slowly and inspected the entire room. "That must be the bath." He nodded toward the door to his left. "You want first dibs?"

"What?"

"The bathroom," he said. "I'd like to take a shower before I turn in."

Bennie eyed the enormous bed. "I suppose you've noticed that there's only one bed."

"So? It's a big bed, honey. There's room enough for both of us."

"Are you suggesting that we sleep together?"

Holt laughed, the gesture crinkling the tiny lines around his eyes. "Yeah, sleep. Nothing more. Your virtue is safe with me."

"I wasn't implying anything else," she told him. "But you must admit that this is a very awkward situation."

"Only if we make it awkward. Just think of this as a business trip and the hotel screwed up our reservations. We've had connecting rooms dozens of times and once, in Atlanta, we had to share a room. Remember?"

Remember? She'd never forget that sleepless night! "There were two double beds."

Holt sauntered across the room, dropped down on the bed and bounced several times, then patted the blue-and-white plaid coverlet. "This bed's so big we'll never even brush elbows. And it's comfortable." He bounced up and down a couple of times as if to test the bed's sturdiness.

"All right. I'll take the bathroom first." Bennie glanced down at her red dress. "May I have your shirt?"

"You want my shirt?"

'Yes!" she snapped her reply. "I assume you aren't going to sleep in it, so I'd like to borrow it for a nightshirt."

"Oh. Sure. No problem."

Bennie looked everywhere except at Holt. She scanned the hand-painted settee at the foot of the bed. A needlepoint pillow and a pale-pink cashmere shawl lay against one of the slender ebony arms. Tapping her foot nervously, she darted a glance at Holt. His unbuttoned shirt hung open, revealing a wide expanse of swirling brown chest hair. She sucked in a deep breath and looked away hurriedly. Her gaze rested on the bamboo étagère in the corner by the bathroom.

"Here we go," he said.

Bennie turned around just in time to see Holt's hunter-green shirt flying through the air toward her. She reached out, grabbed the shirt and pressed it to her chest.

"Thanks."

She tried desperately not to look at his naked chest, but she couldn't help herself. Mercy! He was beautiful. He had such broad shoulders, such big arms and such a washboard-lean belly. And his chest! Swirls of honey-brown hair spread out between his tiny nipples in a triangle shape and dissected his body from collarbone to navel…and below. His jeans fit snugly, accentuating his narrow hips and defining the oh so masculine part of his lower body.

Tiny fireworks exploded in Bennie's stomach, sending shock waves through her system. Heat suffused her body.

"Take as long as you'd like in the bathroom." Holt glanced at the champagne bottle chilling in a silver bucket on the round table in front of the French doors. "I think I'll open the champagne.

Since I'm paying for it, there's no need to let it go to waste."

"I won't be long." Bennie rushed into the bathroom, closed the door, then leaned against the door as she caught her breath.

How was she going to sleep in the same bed with Holt and keep her hands off him? But if she made the first move and Holt rejected her, she'd feel like even more of a fool than she already did.

So help me, God, when I get my hands on Rene, I'm going to choke her! She overstepped her bounds when she reserved a room for Holt and me.

Bennie took her time undressing, making sure to fold her red dress neatly. She'd have to wear it out of here tomorrow and she didn't want to leave the inn looking like a rumpled mess.

A big claw-foot tub awaited her. A variety of toiletries, including her favorite rose-scented soap and lotion, lined the vanity. A dozen candles in various-size brass-and-crystal holders filled the room—on the windowsill, on the vanity, on the floor. A separate shower enclosure nestled in the corner. And two plush, terry cloth robes hung on a brass rack.

She'd already had one long, relaxing bubble bath today, so she opted for a quick shower tonight. Trying to tuck all her hair under the shower cap proved an impossible task, so she gave up on stuffing the last few loose strands inside the cap.

Fifteen minutes later, teeth brushed, body lotion applied and damp hair hanging down around her shoulders, Bennie slipped into Holt's shirt. The cuffs hung off her fingertips. The hem hit her midthigh. She lifted her arm to her nose and sniffed the sleeve, breathing in the unique smell of Holt Jackson.

Hugging her arms around her, she closed her eyes. Why, oh, why did she love the man so damn much? You can't hide away in the bathroom all night. Holt is perfectly all right with this situation, so you should be, too. It doesn't seem to bother him the least bit that y'all are trapped together for the night.

Bennie grabbed one of the robes from the brass rack, put it on and tied the belt securely. Squaring her shoulders, she opened the door and marched into the bedroom.

Damn! She stopped dead in her tracks when she saw Holt. He had stripped down to his briefs and, with a glass of champagne in his hand, rested leisurely against the frame of the doorway that opened to the small balcony. With his back to her, his shoulders looked six feet wide! Her stomach flip-flopped madly.

He glanced over his shoulder at her and smiled. For a second there, she thought she was going to faint.

"Finished?" he asked.

"Uh...yes, all finished."

"The little chocolate mint on my pillow wasn't half bad. If you don't want yours, I'll eat it later." He held open his hand to show her the unwrapped mint, then dropped it onto the table.

As he moved toward her, Bennie heard her heartbeat drumming in her ears. Get hold of yourself, she cautioned. At this rate, you'll be jumping on him the minute he comes to bed. "It's all yours. The bathroom and the chocolate mint." She smiled nervously.

Holt paused at her side on his trek to the bathroom. "If you're tired, don't wait up for me." He caressed her cheek with his knuckles.

She held her smile in place by sheer force of will. If he touched her again, she would break into a hundred pieces and the shattered fragments of her body would fall at his feet.

"Right side or left side?" she asked, hoping the tension inside her hadn't relayed to her voice.

"Doesn't matter. I usually sleep all over the bed since I sleep alone."

She didn't move a muscle until he disappeared into the bathroom. Then she doubled over and gasped in huge gulps of air. She couldn't do this! She could not do this! No way! No how!

And what was that crack about his sleeping alone? Ha! Ha! Ha! Like anyone would believe that. Holt changed women as often as she changed the sheets on her bed. Weekly! And nobody could convince her that all of those brief relationships were nonsexual.

Bennie eyed the champagne. Maybe she should get drunk. That way she'd probably fall asleep quickly. Either that or puke her guts out. The only time she'd ever been drunk was the New Year's Eve when she'd been engaged to Grayson. The romantic evening he had planned turned sour when she spend most of the night in the bathroom throwing up. She had been so nervous at the thought of their making love, she'd drunk way too much.

Looking back on her engagement to Grayson, she wished she'd gotten drunk the night that they finally had consummated their relationship. It had been the singular most uneventful night of her life. She'd been a virgin and Grayson had been a fumbling, wham-bam-thank-you-ma'am lover. A couple of subsequent tries had been dismal failures, at least as far as she was concerned. She looked back on their breakup with relief. She shuddered whenever she thought how close she'd come to having a miserable life.

Okay, so scratch the idea of getting drunk! she decided. Just go to bed and pretend you're asleep.

Bennie slipped the robe off, laid it on the settee and then crawled into the massive king-size bed. Taking the right side, she shifted her weight until her knees touched the edge. She intended to give Holt plenty of space, otherwise he might think she was coming on to him.

What a situation! She'd be sharing a bed with the man she loved and yet she couldn't encourage him to make love to her. If anything happened between them—tonight or in the future—Holt would have to come to her. She didn't want him regretting anything later and blaming her for seducing him.

Bennie laughed. Oh, yeah, like she could seduce any man. Her only sexual experiences had been five years ago with the most disappointing lover on God's green earth.

Holt took the longest shower of his life. He had never dreaded anything as much as going back into the bedroom and getting into bed with Bennie. Lying next to her, without touching her, would be sheer torture. But Bennie wasn't the kind of woman you fooled around with and then forgot. She wanted a husband and kids, not a one-night stand. And even if she were willing to settle for less than a commitment, what would their having sex do to their business relationship?

Keep reminding yourself that you don't want to lose Bennie as your assistant or your friend.

Yeah, yeah, yeah. He'd been doing just that for the entire five years he'd known her, and with each passing year, keeping his hands off her had gotten progressively more difficult.

If anybody had told him that he'd be sharing a bed with a woman he wanted—and wanted badly—without even touching her, he'd have called them crazy. It wasn't as if he were a Don Juan or anything. He had dated a lot of different women, but all those dates hadn't ended up in the sack. He had a sixth sense when it came to women—he could easily weed out the ones who had wedding bells ringing in their ears. Those were the kind who could get a guy in big trouble. A girl like Bennie, to whom sex and commitment were synonymous, had always been strictly off-limits.

If only Bennie did have that prestigious lineage that Rene had fabricated when she'd filled out the form for the personal ad. His life would be so simple if he could ask Bennie to marry him. She was right about their being perfect work partners. And he'd never known anyone he enjoyed being with more. Of course, it wouldn't hurt being married to a woman who turned him on. Even without love and romance, the sex would be hot enough to set the sheets on fire.

Damn! Get your mind off sex! Holt stood in the middle of the bathroom, totally naked and painfully aroused. He had a feeling he wouldn't get much sleep tonight.

Grumbling to himself, he snatched the robe from the brass rack, stuffed his arms through the sleeves and loosely tied the belt. When he opened the door, he found the bedroom dark and quiet. Apparently Bennie had blown out all the candles, leaving only the kerosene lamp and the soft firelight to illuminate the room. As he crossed the area rug, he noticed that Bennie was curled up on the far right side of the bed. Humph! If she moved an inch closer to the edge, she'll fall off on the floor.

Holt removed the robe, tossed it to the foot of the

bed, then eased back the covers and slipped under them. He probably should have worn his briefs—had even considered putting them on—but he was used to sleeping naked. And what difference would it make? It wasn't as if he and Bennie would ever touch during the night.

The bed was softer than his bed at home. He liked a firmer mattress. Tossing and turning, he tried to find a comfortable position. He jerked the top pillow from under his head and threw it onto the floor. Then he punched the remaining pillow and folded it in half. Spreading out on his back, he tried to relax.

Minutes ticked by. Bennie didn't move. He begin to wonder if she was even breathing. She was playing possum, pretending to be asleep, he thought. Well, two could play at that game. Holt closed his eyes, took in a long, slow breath and released it gradually.

Try as he might, he couldn't relax. Knowing Bennie was within arm's reach played havoc with his nerves. And being able to smell that sweet, rose scent that was her signature fragrance was driving him crazy.

An hour after Holt had come to bed, Bennie felt relatively certain that he was asleep. He hadn't moved or groaned in quite some time. She was glad one of them would get some sleep tonight. But it wouldn't be her. Her body ached from lying in one position for so long. Get up and move around, she told herself. If Holt's asleep, he'll never know.

She crept out of bed, then silently padded across the room to the open French doors. The rain had stopped, leaving behind a damp fog that obscured the view. She walked out onto the balcony, allowing the dark night to envelop her. The cool breeze sent shivers up her bare legs. She hugged her arms around her body and listened to the soft wind sighing and the residue of raindrops dripping off the roof.

Suddenly, strong, warm arms enveloped her. Bennie gasped, then relaxed, leaning her body back against Holt's chest. His sex pulsated against her buttocks. As he held her close and safe, she realized that somewhere, on a subconscious level, she had known that if she left the bed, he would follow her.

"What's wrong, honey? Can't sleep?" he asked, his voice a whispered breath in her ear.

"No, I can't sleep," she replied, her own voice a hushed sigh.

"We're a fine pair, aren't we?" He nuzzled the top of her head with his chin. "We shouldn't be here together this way and we both know it."

"If I said that I didn't care about tomorrow, that tonight would be a moment out of time, then would you—"

He whirled her around to face him. Holding her securely by the shoulders, he gazed into her eyes. "Don't make me an offer like that, unless you mean it.'' Sliding one hand down her shoulder to her waist, he caressed her with gentle strength. With his other hand he cupped the back of her head. ''You have no idea how much I want you...or how long I've wanted you.''

''You—you've wanted me for a long time?'' She swayed toward him.

''Yeah. For years.''

''Oh, Holt.'' She lifted her face, offering him her mouth. ''Don't you know I feel the same way? I've wanted you since the first day I walked into that stupid little trailer you used as an office and you hired me to be your secretary without even checking my credentials.''

''You've wanted me that long, huh?'' His sex throbbed. His heartbeat roared in his ears. If he didn't take her and take her soon, he was going to die from frustration.

Bennie slipped her arms around his waist and pressed her breasts against his chest. ''It seems as if I've wanted you all my life, but you never...you always treated me like a buddy.''

He nuzzled her neck, then painted a moist trail from her earlobe to the V of the shirt she wore. His shirt! Bennie trembled.

''You are my buddy,'' he said, his lips on her throat. ''My best friend. My invaluable assistant.'' He cupped her hip with one hand, while the other hand maneuvered her head closer and closer to his. ''But tonight I want you to be my lover.''

He had doomed them both. The logical part of his brain tried to warn him, but his aching body overrode all sensible thought. Nothing mattered, not Jackson Construction, not any future socialite wife, not even the risk of losing Bennie's friendship forever. Ruled by desire and desire alone, he consumed her mouth in a kiss of total possession. And she surrendered with a whimpering cry of acceptance.

Holt worked his hand down her leg, then up and under her shirt. His fingers encountered the smooth, firm flesh of her naked behind and began a slow, sensuous massage. Bennie clung to him, shivering, as he deepened the kiss. While his tongue explored, taunted and tasted, his fingers slipped inside her. Keening softly in her throat, she closed her thighs around his hand, both capturing and encouraging his rhythmic probing.

Moisture coated his hand as she melted around him. Releasing her head, he moved his other hand down to the buttons on the shirt. With a frantic jerk, he ripped open the only garment that stood between him and the naked flesh he longed to see and touch. With her breasts exposed, he lowered his mouth to lave one tight nipple.

Bennie cried out with agonized pleasure, as pure sexual sensation flooded through her body. Like liquid fire racing through her veins, passion set her ablaze.

"Oh, Holt!" She threaded her fingers through his

hair and held his head in place at her breast, savoring the sweet torment of his talented tongue.

Pushing her ever closer to the brink with his attentive mouth and hands, Holt taught Bennie what it truly meant to be a woman—his woman. From her urgent little cries of surprise, Holt surmised that her sexual experience was limited. The realization that he wasn't competing against a horde of former lovers pleased him in a way that shocked him.

She was ready for him. Hot and wet and pliable. But she was so close to climaxing that he chose to give her release before seeking his own pleasure.

No other man had ever given Bennie an orgasm and having Holt be the first was like a precious gift. Racked with shudders of fulfillment, her body spiraled out of control.

Holt swept her up into his arms and carried her inside to the bed. With trembling fingers, he removed his shirt from her body and came down over her.

He had never wanted anything in his entire life the way he wanted Bennie.

Chapter 6

His sex brushed her intimately. Their gazes locked and held as Holt braced himself with his arms on either side of her. Bennie's mouth opened on an indrawn breath. A log in the fireplace crackled. The same breeze swirled the lace curtains that draped the open French doors. And somewhere in the faraway night, distant thunder rumbled.

Bennie reached up to touch his sex. He jerked when she caressed him. He was large and hot…and she was totally fascinated by the look and feel of the silky smooth shaft.

She placed her arms around Holt's neck, her actions a silent invitation—no man in his right mind could resist.

His sex probed, seeking entrance. She opened her thighs and lifted her hips. With one powerful, penetrating lunge, he thrust into the welcoming heat of her moist sheath. She cried out as he filled her, his size stretching her until the fit was perfect.

Clinging to him, she undulated her hips, beckoning him to embed himself completely, fully, to the very core of her body. Easing his hands under her, he lifted her hips. His sex pulsed inside her. He moved slowly, allowing the feeling to surround him. She was hot and wet and so very tight.

"It's been a long time for you, hasn't it, honey?" he whispered in her ear.

"Yes," was the only reply she could manage.

She loved the feel of him so deep within her, plunging and retreating with a throbbing rhythm. She had never felt so complete. Her lips sought his, wanting his mouth on hers. He consumed her, taking her wildly, his tongue delving to taste and entice.

Her breasts ached. Her nipples beaded. And as if understanding her hungry need, Holt suckled one breast and then the other. She arched her spine, rooted the back of her head into the pillow and joined him in the mating dance. Her body moved beneath his as if they had made love a hundred times. Perfectly matched. Each beat in unison.

With every thrust, Holt increased the tempo. The building urgency inside them coalesced at a frantic pace, whirling them into a spinning vortex that consumed them.

Perspiration coated their bodies. Mouths and tongue moved with frenzied pleasure. Hands and fingertips sought out each sensitive spot. They pawed and clawed, moaned and groaned, tossed and turned in an act of passion that neither had thought possible.

As her body tightened in agonized expectation, Holt pounded into her repeatedly. She fell apart in his arms, crying out his name, weeping with release. And while wave after wave of completion washed over her, he rode her hard, until he reached his own climax.

They lay entwined, their bodies sticky with sweat, each one's heartbeat audible to the other.

Bennie lay beneath Holt, exhausted and satisfied beyond her wildest dreams. This was what love-making was supposed to be. An all-consuming passion with a man you loved to distraction.

Holt eased off her onto the bed, then drew her up against his side. She cuddled close to him and laid her head on his shoulder. He kissed her temple, then ran his fingertips down her arm, over her waist and across her hip.

"Holt?" She wanted to tell him that she loved him and that he had made this experience the most incredible event of her entire life.

"Shh. Don't talk, honey. Not right now." He caressed her hip lovingly.

"Mm-hm." She closed her eyes and allowed the

languid, sated cloud on which she floated to carry her off into sleep.

Something tickled her neck. Something warm and moist. And now something was moving over her breasts—that same warm moisture. Bennie's eyelids fluttered. She opened her eyes and glanced down to see Holt's head, his mouth at her breast.

Oh, thank you, it hadn't been a dream! She and Holt really had made love.

"I want you again," Holt said. "And this time, we won't take any chances."

He took her hand and placed it around his sex, letting her feel the protective sheath. Startled by the realization that he was wearing a condom, Bennie grabbed his shoulder and shoved him away from her. Where had he gotten a condom?

"Where did you get that?" she asked.

"Bathroom. I found them in a basket with shave creme and a razor."

"Rene?"

"That would be my guess." Holt sat back against the headboard and opened his arms. "Come here, honey."

She hesitated momentarily, then went into his embrace. "We forgot about protection the first time, didn't we?"

"Yeah, I'm afraid we did. I'm sorry, Bennie. It was my fault. I should have—"

She placed her right index finger over his lips.

"Neither one of us was thinking straight. We both lost control."

He nuzzled her neck as he stroked her hip. "I'm fast approaching that point again."

"Oh, Holt." She couldn't resist him. Didn't want to resist him.

Their second mating was less hurried, less frantic, leaving them time to explore each other's bodies more thoroughly. After bringing her to the edge several times, without allowing her to plunge into the abyss, Holt lifted her up and on top of him.

She teased him, dangling her breasts over his mouth and rubbing her mound intimately against him. When he'd taken as much of her torment as he could endure, he clutched her hips and brought her down over his rigid sex. She tossed back her head and forked her fingers through her hair, lifting it into the air.

Holt guided her movements, lunging upward as he watched her dark, curly hair fall about her shoulders when she spread her open palms on either side of his head. Her full, round breasts demanded his attention. He lifted his head and brought one tight, begging nipple into his mouth.

She rode him at a steady pace, allowing the friction to stroke a spark in her femininity. With each passing moment the tiny flame grew hotter and brighter until it blazed out of control. As a shattering completion claimed her, Bennie drew every ounce of pleasure from her climax, then slid down on top of Holt and closed her eyes.

While fluttering aftershocks rippled through her system, Holt stirred beneath her. She opened her eyes and smiled at him. He returned her smile, then flipped her over and grabbed her ankles. As he slid across the bed, he dragged her with him. When his feet hit the floor, he lifted her legs and draped her heels over his shoulders. She lay before him, her thighs spread, her body open and totally vulnerable to whatever he intended to do to her.

"Holt?"

"I'm just going to love you some more," he assured her.

He caressed her belly, then moved lower to twine her dark curls around his fingers. She sighed. His hand opened to cup her mound. She bucked against his hand. He stroked her repeatedly until he felt her relax, then he moved closer and rammed himself to the hilt. She writhed and squirmed. She had taken all of him before, yet this time she felt more invaded, more completely impaled. He urged her hips back and forth, up and down, as he hammered into her.

When she felt the renewal of aching sensation, she urged him on, encouraging his completion with each movement of her body. They shared a simultaneous orgasm that depleted every ounce of energy they possessed. Exhausted afterward, they fell asleep in each other's arms.

* * *

Bennie woke to the sound of running water. When she opened her eyes, the bright morning sunshine prompted her to shut them again. With her eyelids closed she felt around on the other side of the big bed. Empty. That meant Holt must be in the shower. Turning her head toward the inner room and away from the windows and open French doors, she eased her aching body up enough to rest her back against the headboard of the cherry canopy bed.

Every muscle in her body had been used thoroughly during their lovemaking and she felt the aftereffects of Holt's ardent attention in every fiber of her being. The soreness was a delicious consequence of their unrestrained passion. In her heart of hearts, she had always known sex could be wonderful and Holt had proven to her just how wonderful.

She felt perfectly comfortable naked. And why shouldn't she? After their heated lovemaking sessions, Holt had not only seen every inch of her body, he was now intimately acquainted with it. As she stretched her arms over her head, she smiled with delirious happiness. Her dream had come true—Holt was her lover. Now, nothing stood between them.

With her gaze riveted to the closed bathroom door, she contemplated the look that would be on his face when she told him that she *had* been a debutante, that she *was* a member of the DAR and that she had a multimillion dollar trust fund. Of course, she'd wait and surprise him with that little bit of news, after he proposed to her.

Hugging herself tightly, Bennie giggled. Easing out of bed, she searched and found Holt's shirt. She slipped into it, then realized several of the buttons were missing. She closed her eyes to savor the memory of Holt ripping the shirt off her body last night.

Just as she began twirling around and around in a gleeful dance, the bathroom door opened and Holt emerged, shirtless, barefooted, but wearing his jeans. Their gaze met. She smiled. He smiled.

"Good morning," he said.

"A very good morning." She raced across the room and then threw her arms around him.

He clasped her waist with both hands. "We need to talk, Bennie."

She tried to kiss him, but he held her at arm's length. "What's wrong?"

"Probably nothing," he said. "But just in case there is, I want you to know that I've decided to postpone wife hunting until we find out whether or not you're pregnant."

"What?"

"I could have gotten you pregnant last night...that first time when I was so careless."

Bennie eased out of his hold. "What do you mean you're going to postpone wife hunting?"

"Well, it wouldn't be fair to a prospective wife if I had to break our engagement so I could marry you, if you turn up pregnant.'' Holt looked at her beseechingly, his hands held open in supplication.

''Oh.'' Oh! Now she understood exactly what he meant. Last night hadn't meant the same to him as it had to her. All that passionate lovemaking hadn't meant that he loved her. It had meant only that he'd wanted her. And this morning, his greatest concern seemed to be that he might have gotten her pregnant and ruined all his matrimonial plans.

Damn him! Damn him for making her believe that he loved her. Oh, no, you can't blame him for your own misguided delusions, she told herself. He doesn't know you're in love with him. He thought last night was all about good sex and nothing more. You're the fool who's in love. Not him. You're the idiot who convinced herself that he felt the same way you did.

''If I'm pregnant, you'll marry me?'' she asked.

''Bennie, honey, you know I will.''

When he took a tentative step toward her, she held up her hands in a stop gesture. He halted immediately.

''But if I'm not pregnant, you plan to follow through with your campaign to find a *suitable* wife, someone with the proper background.''

Having the good grace to look embarrassed, Holt dropped his gaze to the floor. ''You know, you were right about our being good work partners. And after last night, we found out that we're good bed partners, too.'' When she groaned loudly, he lifted his gaze in time to catch the anger in her eyes. "So, if we have to get married, it won't be that bad for either of us."

"But you don't want to marry me, do you? You think my blood's not blue enough! I'm not what you want, am I? If my family had the right connections, you'd marry me in a New York minute. I'm good enough to screw, but not good enough—"

Holt bolted toward her, grabbed her shoulders and shook her. "Shut up! Dammit, just shut up!"

She fought to free herself from his hold, but he gripped her with fierce tenacity. They glowered at each other, each intensely aware of the other.

"Bennie, honey, if anything, you're too good for me. You're beautiful and smart and I've never cared for anyone as much as I care for you. Don't you see, you deserve a guy who can love you the way you want to be loved. A guy who can promise you the moon and stars."

"You gave me the moon and stars, Holt. Last night." She dared him to deny the power of their lovemaking.

He loosened his hold about her shoulders. She eased away from him, tears gathering in her eyes.

"How soon can you take a home pregnancy test?" he asked.

"Don't worry about it. I wouldn't marry you if you were the last man on earth!"

She stomped across the area rug to the bathroom, went inside and slammed the door. Balling her hands into fists she pummeled the wall as the ache in her heart spread through her chest and tears streamed down her face.

"Bennie?" Holt called out to her from the bedroom.

Hurriedly, she locked the bathroom door.

"Honey, come out and let's talk this over like two reasonable adults."

"No!"

"I don't understand why you're acting like this," he said.

"Then you're a bigger idiot than I am!"

"Are you angry because I got so carried away that I didn't use a condom the first time?"

"No!"

"Then what? Look, I'm sorry if I hurt your feelings in any way. You know the last thing I'd ever want is to hurt you. You're my best friend."

"Well, I don't want to be your best friend," she told him. "I thought last night changed our relationship just a little. I thought we were more than friends now."

Holt knocked on the door. "Come on out here and let's talk this over face-to-face. We are more than friends," he admitted. "But you said yourself that last night would be a moment out of time, that tomorrow didn't matter."

"I lied!" she screamed. "So sue me!"

"Bennie, if you don't come out of that bathroom

and explain to me what's going on with you, I'll...I'll..."

"For your information, Holt Jackson, I love you. I've loved you for five long years. From the first moment we met, I knew you were the one and only man for me. All I've ever wanted is to be your wife!"

"My God! I had no idea."

"Well, now you know. So, please go away and leave me alone."

"I can't do that."

"Please, Holt. Let me keep a little bit of my pride, will you? Just leave me alone. I promise that I'll take a home pregnancy test."

"I don't want to leave you this way," he said.

"I'm not coming out of the bathroom until you're gone, even if I have to stay in here all weekend." And she meant every word of what she'd said. No way was she going out there to face him, now that she'd admitted she loved him.

"If I do what you ask, will you promise that you'll come to the office tomorrow morning, as usual? We'll discuss everything then and work out a solution."

"I'll be at work in the morning," she said. "You have my word. Now, will you go away and leave me alone?"

"Yeah, I'll go."

Holt stuffed his socks in his pants pocket, slipped on his shoes and gave the closed bathroom door one last glance. He'd have to see if Mr. Perkins could find him a shirt to wear home. That is, if he could get home today. Surely the Butler Bridge had been reopened by now.

He plodded down the hallway, all the while wondering what the hell had happened to his life. As fantastic as last night had been, the last thing on earth he wanted or needed was to have Bennie in love with him.

Holt had spent a miserable Sunday afternoon worrying about Bennie. And he hadn't gotten more than two hours of sleep all night for thinking about how badly he'd hurt her. How could he have been such a dope? Why hadn't he realized that Bennie was in love with him? He'd figured out that she wanted him as much as he wanted her, but he had assumed—until recently—that she was far too levelheaded to ever fall madly in love with anybody, least of all him. He'd meant it when he'd told her she was too good for him. She was. And he didn't doubt for one minute that she was a better person than any socialite he could marry.

But he didn't want a wife who loved him. He wanted a mutually beneficial marriage, without the incumbrance of a fiery, passionate love that was bound to burn itself out and wind up ruining the marriage. He didn't want his kids to end up with divorced parents the way he and his brothers had. A good solid business deal was the only way to prevent that kind of disaster.

Somehow, someway, he had to make Bennie see reason. No matter how hot the sex between them had been, they would both be better off remaining just good friends and business associates.

The minute he entered the office on Monday, he sensed something was wrong. His first clue was a missing Rene. He glanced at the closed door to Bennie's office. Rene was probably with Bennie, helping her roast him over the coals. There was no hope that Bennie hadn't shared details of their torrid night together with Little Miss Fairy Godmother Rene.

After entering his private office, he removed his sport coat, draped it over his chair and then sat down in the tufted leather chair. A pristine white business-size envelope lay atop the clutter on his desk. He eyed the envelope suspiciously. A knot of apprehension formed in his gut.

He ripped open the sealed envelope and removed the one-page letter. Scanning quickly he realized he was reading Bennie's resignation.

Dammit! She had taken this lovesick routine a little too far. How dare she resign! Didn't she know he couldn't run this business without her?

Of course she knew. That's why she was doing this—to put the fear of God into him.

He was not going to let her get away with this. She was acting like a silly fool, letting her emotions get in the way of their friendship and her career.

Hell, he had planned to give her a share of the business as a Christmas present, hadn't he? She wouldn't walk away from a deal like that.

Clutching the letter in his hand, he stormed out of his office. Without even knocking, he flung open the door to her office and barged in. She and Rene were packing her belongings in two cardboard boxes, but stopped abruptly when he interrupted them.

"Just what do you think you're doing?" he asked.

"Packing a few of my things," Bennie said. "After I've worked out my two weeks' notice, I should have everything cleared away so your new assistant will have a clean, empty office."

"You're not leaving!" He glared at Bennie, who hadn't even bothered to glance his way.

When Rene cleared her throat, he turned his heated gaze on her. "Get out, will you? I need to talk to Bennie alone."

Rene looked to Bennie, who nodded and said, "It's all right."

The minute Rene exited, Holt reached out to grab Bennie, but she sidestepped him. "Don't touch me!"

"Bennie, honey, be reasonable, will you?"

"I'm being reasonable," she said. "An unreasonable woman would have left you without giving two weeks' notice." She opened a bottom desk drawer and began clearing it out, dumping several things into the wastebasket in the process.

"I don't want you to go."

"I don't care what you want." She sorted through several files, then tossed two of them into one of the cardboard boxes.

"Are you pregnant?"

"What!" She gripped the edges of the box.

"Are you—"

"No!"

"How can you be sure?" he asked.

"Because it's...it's that time of the month," she lied to him. "And I'm on time. I'm not pregnant. Aren't you relieved?"

"I'm relieved for your sake." He took a step toward her. She backed up against the wall. "I'd make you a lousy husband."

"I think we finally agree on something."

"Don't do this, Bennie. I don't want to lose you. I don't want to lose my best friend and—"

"And the best darn assistant any man could have," she finished his sentence for him. "Well, I'm tired of being your best buddy and I'm tired of your taking me for granted around the office, too."

"I don't take you for granted," he said, then admitted to himself that he probably had taken her for granted most of the time. "Look, maybe you're right, but I want you to know something. I've already talked to Fred Sanderson about drawing up papers to give you an interest in Jackson Construction. It was going to be your Christmas present."

Bennie bit down on her bottom lip. Tears glazed

her eyes. "I devoted the past five years of my life to helping you turn this business into a huge success, not because I wanted an interest in the company, but because I loved you."

"Ah, Bennie..."

"I don't want your pity. And I don't want an interest in the company. All I want is for you to leave me alone and let me work out my two week's notice. After that, I won't ever bother you again."

He started to protest once more, but realized all his pleas were falling on deaf ears. Bennie was damned and determined to leave him and there wasn't much he could do about it, except keep trying to change her mind.

Chapter 7

Today was her last day at Jackson Construction. In less than an hour she'd walk out of her office for the final time. After over five years with Holt, helping him build his company into a thriving business, she was leaving her job *and* the man she loved. She'd had more than one "second thought" about her resignation, which she'd tendered in the heat of anger. The first week, Holt had tried every possible persuasion to convince her to stay. Once or twice she'd thought he was actually going to break down and ask her to marry him. But the more stubborn she was, the more obstinate he became, until all this past week they'd been at a Mexican standoff, neither willing to give an inch.

As much as she wanted to stay, she refused to surrender and let Holt win on his terms—with the former status quo remaining unchanged. After the night they'd shared at Wildwood Lodge, there was no way she could be only Holt's friend and assistant. And she felt certain that, if he were totally honest with himself, he'd have to admit he felt the same. Beneath the hostility that separated them now, the sexual attraction that had only increased after their lovemaking sizzled like a live wire. She knew that he still wanted her—more than ever. And she still wanted him. But until he could give up his stupid plan to land himself a socialite wife, there was no hope for them. Not as friends. Not as business associates. And certainly not as lovers.

Maybe by leaving him, letting him see that he couldn't get along without her—either professionally or personally—Holt would come to his senses. It was a chance she had to take. For her sake and for the sake of...

You don't know for sure that you're pregnant, she reminded herself. Just because you're regular as clockwork and your period is two days late doesn't mean a thing. And just because the home pregnancy test you took this morning was positive doesn't necessarily mean you're carrying Holt's baby.

But what if she were pregnant? Then all the more reason to force Holt into choosing between some stupid "perfect wife" plan and spending the rest of his life with her.

An insistent rap on the door brought Bennie's gaze into focus as she glanced up just in time to see Holt enter. He'd always barged in, never waiting for an invitation, so why should today be any different?

"I have something for you." Holt held out an eight-by-ten-inch envelope. "It's a letter of reference and your severance pay."

She accepted the package, making sure their hands didn't touch during the transfer. "I'm sorry you haven't found a new assistant yet, but the employment agency has promised to send over more applicants next week."

"Yeah, thanks for taking care of that for me." Holt shifted nervously from one foot to the other. "You'll let me know if you need anything."

"Thanks, but I'll be fine."

"Got another job lined up?" he asked.

"No, not yet. I'm going to take a vacation before I start job hunting."

Holt wanted, one more time, to beg her not to leave him. But dammit all, he had humbled himself just about as much as a man could and still call himself a man. Didn't she realise that he'd give her anything she asked for, if only she'd stay? *Oh, yeah, you'd give her anything—anything except the one thing she wants from you.*

When he offered his hand, she stared at it, reluctance in her eyes. "Well, good luck, Bennie."

His hand was a challenge. He knew it and she knew it. If she refused to accept, then he'd know she was afraid of what might happen when they touched.

Bennie placed her hand in his. Tingles of awareness raced up her spine and jittery nerves tap-danced in her tummy. When she tried to pull her hand out of his, he held on tightly. Their gazes met, a silent plea evident in both his eyes and hers.

"Take care of yourself, Holt. And I hope you get everything you want."

I want you, Bennie. I always have. But we'd only wind up hurting each other in the end. You'd eventually hate me because I could never love you the way you want to be loved. And I'd resent you because I gave up my sensible marriage plans in order to have you.

He had to get away from her before he grabbed her and kissed the breath out of her. Without another word, he turned and walked away.

She slumped down on the edge of her desk and let out a long, low sigh. He didn't want her to leave. And she didn't want to leave. But she was going. The only chance she had to make Holt realize he loved her was to let him try living without her.

With trembling fingers, Bennie opened the envelope, pulled out the letter of recommendation and read it. Glowing didn't begin to describe what Holt had said about her. *Irreplaceable* was the word that jumped off the page. *Irreplaceable.* Dear God, she hoped so.

Then she removed her severance check. She had

to look at it a second time to believe her eyes. She gasped when she noted the exorbitant sum. Was he out of his mind? A hundred thousand dollars? He didn't have enough capital to be giving away that kind of money! What was he trying to do, soothe his guilty conscience? Was this check a consolation prize? A reward for loyal service? Or was it a payment for services rendered?

She couldn't accept the check. She wouldn't! Even if he had that kind of money to spare—which he didn't—she had no intention of letting him get even one little bitty good feeling from having been so generous.

After tossing the glowing recommendation on her empty desktop, Bennie clasped the check in her hand and marched out of her office. Without bothering to knock, she stormed into Holt's office. He looked up from behind his desk, then rose to his feet.

"Is something wrong?" he asked, the puzzled look in his eyes verifying that he didn't have a clue as to why she was so upset.

She held up the check in front of him. "This is what's wrong!"

"Your severance pay? What's wrong with it? I thought I was very generous. I know I owe you more, but—"

"You can't buy me off, Holt Jackson. You're damn right you owe me more. A lot more. But it's not money I want from you."

She waved the check in the air, then while he watched, mouth open and eyes widened in shock, she ripped the severance check into tiny pieces and threw the fluttering tidbits into his face. Before he could respond, she flew out of his office and into hers.

Rene tried to speak to her on her way out and Holt called after her. But she didn't look back. She didn't dare.

Holt kicked back in his recliner and hoisted a beer bottle to his lips. While he downed the drink, he flipped through the television stations, searching for the Falcons game. He had thought about giving Tiffany a call to see if she wanted to go out tonight, but he hadn't followed through. Their last date had ended in disaster. He had asked her to stay the night, but wound up sending her home in a cab after their first kiss. The minute he'd kissed her, images of Bennie had flashed through his mind. Just having Tiffany in his apartment had suddenly made him feel as if he were cheating on Bennie. And that notion was downright stupid. Hell, he hadn't seen or heard from Bennie, except through Rene, in nearly two months. And all Rene would tell him was that Bennie was doing just fine.

How could she be doing just fine when he was feeling lousy all the time? He had hired and fired one new personal assistant and was now tiring out another. This time he'd asked the agency to send a man. But Wilson Houser wasn't Holt's ideal assistant. He and the man, who wore a suit and tie, drank cappuccino and didn't know a damn thing about football, had nothing in common. He supposed Wilson was competent, but the guy couldn't begin to fill Bennie's shoes. He didn't have her years of experience, her knowledge of the construction business or her winning personality.

Even his plans to find a suitable wife had gone up in smoke. He'd managed to secure a couple of dates with the right kind of ladies, with Bo Reynolds acting as a go-between, but both encounters had left him cold. He didn't necessarily expect any sexual sparks, but he thought it necessary to at least like the woman he married.

Holt figured Bennie would be delighted if she knew that his personal life as well as his peace of mind at the office had steadily deteriorated ever since she'd left him. He found it difficult to concentrate on anything except her absence in his life. He went to sleep every night remembering what it had felt like to have her lying beneath him, moaning his name. And every morning he awoke knowing that when he went into the office, she wouldn't be there.

He had driven by her duplex apartment at least once a week, but couldn't bring himself to stop and ring her doorbell. He'd played the scenario over in his mind countless times. He'd tell her he just happened to be driving by and thought he'd stop and see how she was doing. And she would tell him she was miserable without her job and his friendship. Then they'd kiss and make up. Well, maybe not kiss. Shaking hands on the deal would be safer.

Bennie tossed the pregnancy-and-baby book on the floor and made a mad dash to the bathroom. Morning sickness, no matter what time of day it hit, was the absolute pits! She prayed she was one of those women who wouldn't suffer bouts of nausea after the first trimester.

When she finished throwing up, she lifted her head and groaned, then wet a washcloth and cleaned her face and hands. Since she hadn't been able to keep much of anything in her stomach for weeks now, she had actually lost four pounds, even though she was two months pregnant. What a way to lose weight, she thought. Of course, during the next seven months she'd probably balloon into an elephant. Short, plump women usually gained weight all over and not just in their faces and bellies.

Bennie had decided that if Holt hadn't made a move to make things right between them before the end of the year, she would have to leave Fairmount. She couldn't stay in town and chance his discovering she was pregnant. She intended making a trip home to Montgomery for Thanksgiving and breaking the news to her mother that it looked like her only daughter was going to give birth "out of wedlock." Her mother would be outraged at first and she'd fret about what her so-called friends would think. But in the end, she'd stand by Bennie. She always had. Even when Bennie had broken her engagement to Grayson. Her mother might be the quintessential society snob, but she loved her children and grandchildren. Of course neither of Bennie's brothers had presented Mary Bennett with an illegitimate grandchild.

There were times, like now, when she felt so alone that she wanted to call Holt and tell him it looked like he'd have to marry her, after all. But in her saner moments, she knew she'd never go to him, never make the first move. If he wanted her back in his life, then he'd have to come get her.

Although both of his brothers had invited him to come for a visit during the Christmas holidays, Holt had stayed at home. He'd had it in his mind to ask Bennie out for Christmas Eve dinner—just as friends, of course. But when he'd phoned her, her answering machine had picked up. And when he'd driven by her house, her car had been gone. He wondered if she'd driven to Montgomery for the holidays. He knew she had a mother and a couple of brothers who still lived there. He really didn't know much about Bennie's family, only that her mother was a widow and that both of her older brothers were married and had children.

Holt prided himself on being a smart man. And a smart man always knew when to give up and admit defeat. He wasn't saying that he loved Bennie, not the romantic, hearts-and-flowers kind of love she seemed to want. But he had discovered one important thing during her absence—he couldn't live without her. Why it had taken him nearly three months to realize that if he married anyone other than Bennie, he'd be miserable, he didn't know. Maybe old dreams died hard. Even as a kid, he'd promised himself that someday he'd marry one of those fine society women, who wore pearls around their necks and possessed an attitude of superiority that could, without an unkind word, put others in their place. He had thought that, with enough money, he could buy himself one of those pedigreed hothouse flowers. He had wanted a business deal marriage that would by its very nature circumvent any possibility of divorce, once there were children involved. But what he *had* wanted wasn't what he wanted now.

If Bennie was willing to marry him, to take him and his kind of love without expecting more, then he was willing to put aside his old dreams.

But had he waited too late? Rene had hinted that there was someone new in Bennie's life, someone who was going to be around on a permanent basis. And when he'd asked Rene exactly how Bennie felt about this person, she had grinned and said, "Oh, I think love and a lifetime commitment are definitely involved."

On Monday night after Christmas, Holt drove by Bennie's apartment. When he saw her Grand Am under the carport, he whipped his Jag into the driveway and parked. But he sat there for a few minutes, garnering enough courage to face her. Get out of this car and go ring her doorbell, he told himself. If she slams the door in your face, you'll have your answer.

Ten minutes later, his stomach tied in knots, he rang the doorbell and waited.

Bennie opened the door. Her mouth rounded into a startled oval. "Holt!"

"Hi."

"Hello."

He nodded to the interior of the apartment. "Mind if I come in?"

"Oh, no...I mean, yes. Of course, come in." She stepped back to allow him entrance, then closed the door behind him when he walked into the tiny foyer. "Please, go on into the living room."

"I'm not interrupting anything am I?" He glanced around the room, checking to see if they were alone.

"No, you're not interrupting anything," she said. "I just got in from Montgomery about an hour ago. I went home for Christmas."

"Did you have a nice trip?" He tapped his fingertips on the sides of his thighs.

"Very nice."

Her warm smile hit him like a hard punch in the stomach. Bennie was so pretty. And tonight she seemed to be glowing. Looks like she hasn't been pining away for you, he told himself.

"Won't you sit down?" She waved her hand, motioning towards the sofa. "Would you care for a drink or maybe coffee?"

"Nothing, thanks." Sitting on the edge of the sofa, he dangled his hands between his spread knees. "How are you doing, Bennie? I've been worried about you. But you look great."

She sat down in a rocker across from the sofa, then placed her folded hands in her lap. The last thing she wanted was for Holt to notice she was trembling. "I'm fine. How about you?"

"I'm doing okay."

"Did you spend Christmas with—"

Holt shot up off the sofa and began pacing the floor. "I'm not doing okay. As a matter of fact I'm doing lousy."

"I'm sorry that you're—"

He rushed toward her. "Don't lie to me, honey. You're not sorry at all. You planned it this way. You knew that if you walked out on me, I'd never be able to get along without you."

Bennie's heartbeat accelerated at an alarming pace. "Rene told me that you've tried three different assistants since I resigned and none of them have worked out. Just give it time. You'll eventually find someone perfect for the job."

Holt stood right in front of her, his blue eyes focused on her face. "*You* were perfect for the job. I want you to come back to Jackson Construction."

"I can't. I—"

"I want you to come back to me, Bennie." He reached down, took her hands and lifted her out of the rocker. "I can't make it without you, honey." He pulled her into his arms. "These three months without you have been pure hell."

"I really am sorry that you've found me irreplaceable, but there's no way I can return to the company. Besides, once you're married, I'm sure your wife wouldn't like the idea that one of your former lovers is working as your assistant."

"What wife?" He tried to kiss her, but she turned her head.

"Your suitable wife," Bennie said. "You know, the one with the blue blood."

"I've decided that I prefer hot-blooded women over blue-blooded ones." Cupping her hip with one hand, he brought their bodies intimately together. "And since you're the most hot-blooded woman I know, I want you."

Bennie felt confused and bedazzled all at the same time. Was Holt saying that she thought he was saying—or was she, once again, reading him wrong?

"I'm afraid what you want isn't a top priority in my life anymore," she said. *Our child is what's important now.*

Grabbing her by the shoulders, Holt glared at her.

"So, Rene was right, there is someone new in your life, isn't there?"

"Rene told you that—" She realized Holt thought there was another man in her life. She barely restrained the smile that threatened her lips. "Yes, there is someone new. Someone who means a great deal to me."

Holt released his hold on her. "I'm not going to let some other man have you," he said in a deadly calm voice.

"Do you love me?" she asked.

"Is that it? You think this man loves you?" With the utmost tenderness, Holt cupped her face with his hands. "Can he give you the kind of love you want? All the romantic garbage people tell themselves to justify the reason they can't keep their hands off each other?"

"Do you think *you* could ever give me the kind of love I want?"

"Probably not, honey," he admitted. "You know how I feel about all that crazy love stuff. But I can tell you this—I want you and I need you more than anything on earth. And without you, my life isn't worth a damn. Since you left, all I can think about is you. I never realized how truly important you are to me."

"Oh, Holt." Tears welled up in her eyes. "You idiot. Don't you realize that what you feel for me *is* love?"

"Maybe it is." He shrugged. "I don't know. But

will it be enough? Would you marry a guy who can't say the words?"

"If I loved him and knew that he loved me, I could live without the words. At least I could wait until he was able to say them to me."

Holt closed his eyes and prayed that he wasn't too late, that whatever Bennie felt for this new guy wasn't half as strong as what she'd once felt for him. "Do you still love me?" he asked.

"I never stopped loving you for one minute."

He brought his lips down on hers, passionately, provocatively. When she wrapped her arms around his waist, he grasped the back of her head with one hand and deepened the kiss. The kiss went on and on, until they were both breathless.

Holt lifted her in his arms, then dropped down in the rocker and placed her in his lap. "Will you marry me, Bennie?"

Chapter 8

"I'll marry you, if..." Bennie smiled mischievously as she draped her arm around Holt's neck.

"If what?" He frowned, creating worry lines across his brow.

"If you'll take me to bed and make wild, hot, passionate love to me." She planted a quick, hard kiss on his lips. "One night with you wasn't nearly enough. As a matter of fact I'm not sure a lifetime of nights with you will be enough."

"Honey, you've got yourself a deal." Holt laughed, the sound boisterously happy.

He rose from the rocker, with her in his arms, and glanced around the living room. "Which way to the bedroom?"

"Left and down the hall."

The door to her bedroom stood open. Her unpacked suitcase lay on the floor by the closet. A table lamp illuminated the room with a soft, creamy radiance.

Holt set her on her feet beside her fancy iron bed, then slowly began undressing her. Her hands reached out for him, her fingers fumbling with the buttons on his shirt. Helping her, he shucked off his sport coat. It fell to the carpeted floor. Then he finished undoing his shirt. She spread the material back to reveal his naked chest. Laying her hands on him, she breathed deeply.

When he pressed his lips to hers, the kiss turned wild within seconds. Overcome with their sexual hunger, Holt and Bennie lost themselves to their desire. In between passionate kisses, they undressed each other. Aroused and ready, Bennie drew Holt into the bed with her.

"I want you," he murmured. "Now!"

"Then don't wait this time," she told him. "We have all night for slow loving, don't we?"

"We have the rest of our lives."

His mouth worked hers, tasting, licking and probing. She writhed against him, her hands skimming his body. The moment his mouth encompassed one tight nipple, her hips bucked up and Holt entered her quickly. He was hard and hot and filled her completely.

"I love you. I love you," she chanted as he drove into her with fierce pleasure.

He silenced her cries by covering her mouth with his. And just when he felt he couldn't hold off any longer, Bennie whimpered, then trembled, as fulfillment claimed her. Her release triggered his. He jetted into her, his big body shaking with the force of his completion.

They lay together on top of the damask cream-colored coverlet, naked and sated, his lips against her temple, her arm draped across his chest.

"When will you marry me?" Holt caressed her hip.

"How about this Saturday?"

"New Year's Eve?"

"Remember, I wanted to be married by the millennium."

"But what's the rush, honey?"

She curled his chest hair around her finger. "I think I've waited long enough for you. Five whole years. Besides, I have no intention of giving you time to change your mind."

"Won't happen," he told her. "I'm not going anywhere. You're mine now. For keeps." He cupped her chin with his hand, tilting her face toward his. "What are you going to do about this other guy?"

"Other guy? Oh, you mean the new person in my life." Bennie pursed her lips as if contemplating the situation. "I'm afraid you'll just have to take both of us—we're a package deal."

Holt shot straight up in bed.

"No way!"

Bennie smiled, then giggled and finally burst into laughter. Holt glared at her as if she'd lost her mind. She sat up in bed beside him, but when she reached out to touch him, he pulled away.

"Aren't you willing to share me with your son or daughter?" she asked innocently.

"No, I won't share you with—did you say my son or daughter?"

"Mm-hm. You see, I wasn't totally honest with you about the pregnancy test."

"You're pregnant?"

"Yes."

"Then this new person in your life is—"

"Your son or your daughter."

Holt grabbed Bennie, crushing her to him. "You really know how to torment a guy, don't you? Having Rene drop all those hints about your loving and being committed to some new person in your life. And all the while..." His big hand glided down over her rib cage and around to her belly. "When will you start showing?"

"Soon. I already feel like my stomach's bigger." She laid her hand over his.

"What if I hadn't come here tonight? Would you never have let me know about the baby?" The thought that he might have lost not only Bennie, but the child she carried, tied knots in his gut.

"I don't know what I'd have done," she admitted. "I didn't want you to marry me because I was pregnant."

"I'm sorry that I've been such a fool. When I think of all the time I've wasted holding on to a stupid idea about the ideal wife, I could kick my own rear end."

"You don't know how many times I've wanted to do that for you." Giggling, she hugged and kissed him.

He held her close, grateful that he hadn't lost her. Thankful that she hadn't given up on him long ago. She was more than he deserved and he intended to spend the rest of his life showing her just how important she was to him.

"About our wedding," she said.

"I suppose we could get married at the courthouse or possibly find a minister, but five days is pretty short notice. We can go tomorrow for blood tests and then get our license. I'm sorry we don't have time for a really nice wedding. I know things like that are important to you women."

"You wouldn't mind a fancy affair?' she asked. "White gown, tuxedo, lots of flowers and a limousine to take us off on our honeymoon?"

"Honeymoon! I'll take you anywhere you want to go. I can call tonight and book reservations."

She painted a trail of featherlight kisses down his

neck and across his shoulder. "You never answered my question about a fancy wedding."

Holt arched his neck and shuddered. "Whatever you want, but, honey, on such short notice—"

"Believe me, my mother can perform miracles on short notice," Bennie assured him, with a deviously satisfied smile on her face. "Why don't you leave the wedding and the honeymoon plans to me? I'll call my mother later tonight and tell her to get everything set for us and we'll come in Friday for a rehearsal before the big day."

"Aren't you asking an awful lot of your mother? I mean how can she come up with a dress for you, let alone plan a whole wedding?"

"She's always wanted me to wear her wedding dress, and considering I'm about the size she was when she and Daddy got married, I'm pretty sure it won't need alterations."

"Does your family know you're pregnant?" Holt asked.

"My mother does, but not my brothers." She ruffled his short blond hair. "I didn't want them coming after you with a shotgun."

"Your mother probably hates me. That's a fine way to go into a marriage, with a mother-in-law already despising you."

"If you make an honest woman out of me, she'll forgive you."

"Do you suppose we should ask Rene to the wedding?" Holt chuckled.

"As a matter of fact, I'm counting on Rene being my maid of honor and probably godmother to our child."

"Yeah, I suppose she deserves both honors, considering how hard she's worked to get us together."

Before Bennie could respond, Holt slid his hand between her legs. When he touched her intimately, she sighed and wrapped herself around him.

"Let's save the talking for later," he said.

And they did.

Mary Bennett was no middle-class housewife living in a split level home built in the fifties. She was, according to Bennie, one of the wealthiest women in the South, having inherited two sizable fortunes—one from her parents and one from her husband. And the home Bennie had grown up in was larger and more elegant than any of the houses where Holt's mother had worked as a maid.

Yesterday, when the iron gates to Roseland opened for his Jag to enter, Holt had asked Bennie if this was the country club.

"This is where we've having our wedding," she'd told him.

"Can your mother afford a place like this?" He had offered to pay for the wedding, but Bennie had told him her mother insisted on paying for everything.

"The owner is perfectly agreeable to our having thc wedding and reception here."

"Does your mother work for these people?"

"Not exactly."

"One of your brothers works for them?"

"No."

About that time the house had come into view and Holt had been temporarily rendered speechless.

The butler, who'd opened the door, had referred to Bennie as Miss Marianne. It was about that time when Holt started having a really peculiar feeling in his gut. Like he was walking into a trap and was powerless to escape.

"Marianne!" Mary Bennett had enfolded her daughter in her arms, then surveyed Holt from head to toe and offered him her hand.

After the introductions to Bennie's two older brothers—one a banker and the other the CEO of Bennett Industries—and their wives and children, Holt had lost all sense of reality. He did remember that Robert Bennett III had fathered three adorable little boys and his younger brother, Lloyd Bennett, had produced a set of equally adorable twin girls. Other than that, most of last evening was a blur.

But this morning he had awakened in a guest bedroom as big as his entire apartment and realized that not only were Bennie and the baby going to be his, but so was the fulfillment of a lifelong dream. His beautiful, smart, sassy Bennie was an honest-to-goodness blue blood.

She'd brought him breakfast on a silver try and asked him, almost timidly, if he forgave her for neglecting to mention that she was an heiress and was indeed a member of the DAR and could trace her ancestry back to the shores of England.

"I wanted you to love me for myself," she'd said. "Not my prestigious lineage or my sizable trust fund or—"

He'd tumbled her into his bed and reassured her with a ravishing kiss. But when he'd tried to persuade her to fool around a little on their wedding day, she'd told him he'd just have to wait until tonight.

Mary Bennett had performed a minor miracle in preparing her home for a small, elegant wedding. But then money talks and Bennie's mother had enough to shout from the rooftops.

Holt's brothers stood at his side. Bennie had put her foot down when Mary had said only one best man.

"Holt has two brothers. How is he suppose to choose between them?"

That was when Holt learned that his mother-in-law would never interfere in their lives. Bennie wouldn't allow it!

When he heard the music, performed by piano, harp and string quartet, Holt tensed. Leaning his head to the right, he whispered, "You've got the ring, don't you?"

"I've got it," his brother Jim said. "Just settle down. You're going to live through this."

Holt wanted to loosen his collar and take off the bow tie, but instead he stood ramrod straight in his black tuxedo and focused his gaze on the white velvet aisle leading from the enormous front parlor out into the hall. Bennie's four-year-old twin nieces, decked out in hand-smocked cream dresses, edged in heavy lace, scattered rose petals as they strolled down the aisle. Rene followed the girls. She looked as nervous as Holt felt.

A hush fell over the room and the crowd of friends and family stood in deference to the bride. Holt's heart swelled with pride at the sight of his beautiful Bennie.

Like something out of a dream, she glided down the aisle on Mary Bennett's arm. Her wedding dress, he'd been told, was not only her mother's, but her maternal grandmother's, as well. Apparently an hourglass figure was a trait passed down through the generations. The 1930s dress retained the classically chic lines of a wedding gown chosen without regard to cost. But the woman wearing the dress was the true treasure, one whose worth was beyond measure.

The minister performed the ceremony, per Bennie's instructions, allowing each of her brothers to read from a book of verse by Elizabeth Barrett Browning—Bennie's favorite poet. Their wedding, though small and intimate, was as special and romantic as Bennie had hoped it would be. Her mother had given her a day she'd remember forever as one of the happiest and most perfect in her life. She knew that Holt probably hated every minute of it and that the only thing on his mind was their wedding night. But he owed her this day, after all the time and hard work she had invested in him. Besides, he had wanted a society wife, hadn't he? Well, that's exactly what he was getting.

"And with the power vested in me by the state of Alabama, I now pronounce you man and wife," the minister proclaimed.

Before he could say "you may kiss the bride," Holt took her in his arms and gave her a breath-robbing kiss.

"Friends and family, may I present to you Mr. and Mrs. Holt Jackson."

They turned to face the people they loved and who loved them, those who had come together to celebrate their lifelong commitment to each other. Before they retreated down the aisle, Holt pulled her close and whispered in her ear.

"I love you, Bennie."

With tears of happiness glistening in her eyes, she replied, "I love you, too."

Hours later, alone together in the limousine that was taking them all the way to the Bennetts' seashore cottage on the Gulf Coast, Holt lifted his bride's hand to his lips and kissed her with tenderness.

"Happy?" he asked.

"Delirious. What about you?"

"Delirious."

They both laughed. Holding Bennie's hand, Holt fingered the two-carat diamond she wore.

"Are you sure this was the ring you wanted? I could have gotten you something more expensive. I noticed the size of the rocks both your sisters-in-law were wearing."

Bennie caressed Holt's cheek. "This is exactly the ring I wanted. It's perfect for me."

"As long as you're sure."

She grasped Holt's face with her hands, forcing him to look directly at her. "You're a rich man, Holt Jackson, and we can live quite nicely off the profits of Jackson Construction. I don't want or need more than you can give me. Do you understand?"

"Yeah, honey, I understand." He grinned at her. "But there's just one thing I want to know."

"What's that?"

"What in the world did a woman like you ever see in a guy like me?"

"Broad shoulders, big biceps and a tight ass."

"Now, I know—you married me for my body."

"Got that right," she teased as she began unbuttoning his shirt.

"We can't...not here, Bennie." Ignoring his protest, she continued her efforts to undress him. "What about the driver?"

She punched a button beside the minibar and a privacy shield came up between them and the limousine driver.

"This isn't a rented limo, is it?" Holt asked.

"It's Mother's," she said, tugging on his jacket.

"What the hell!" Holt laughed as he removed his jacket and shirt and then reached over to help Bennie out of her suit.

* * * * *

Legendary love comes to Whitehorn, Montana,
once more as beloved authors
Christine Rimmer, Jennifer Greene and Cheryl St.John
present three brand-new stories in this exciting anthology!

Meet the Brennan women:
SUZANNA, DIANA and ISABELLE

Strong-willed beauties who find unexpected love in these irresistible marriage of covnenience stories.

Don't miss
MONTANA MAVERICKS: BIG SKY BRIDES
On sale in February 2000,
only from Silhouette Books!

Available at your favorite retail outlet.

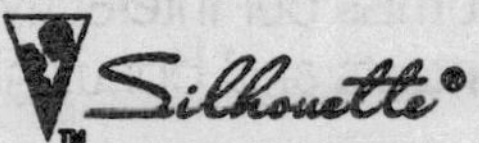

Visit us at www.romance.net PSMMBSB

Looking For More Romance?
Visit Romance.net
Look us up on-line at: http://www.romance.net
Check in daily for these and other exciting features:
Hot off the press
View all current titles, and purchase them on-line.
What do the stars have in store for you?
Horoscope
Hot deals
Exclusive offers available only at Romance.net
Plus, don't miss our interactive quizzes, contests and bonus gifts.
PWEB

SUZANNE BROCKMANN

continues her popular,
heart-stopping miniseries

They're who you call to get you out of a tight spot—or into one!

Coming in November 1999
THE ADMIRAL'S BRIDE, IM #962

Be sure to catch Mitch's story,
IDENTITY: UNKNOWN, IM #974,
in January 2000.

And **Lucky's story** in April 2000.

And in December 1999 be sure to pick up a copy of Suzanne's powerful installment in the **Royally Wed** miniseries,
UNDERCOVER PRINCESS, IM #968.

Available at your favorite retail outlet.

Visit us at www.romance.net

SIMTDD2

Desire.

These women are about to find out what happens when they are forced to wed the men of their dreams in **Silhouette Desire's** new series promotion:

The Bridal Bid

Look for the bidding to begin in **December 1999** with:

GOING...GOING...WED! (SD #1265)
by **Amy J. Fetzer**

And look for
THE COWBOY TAKES A BRIDE (SD#1271)
by **Cathleen Galitz** in **January 2000:**

Don't miss the next book in this series,
MARRIAGE FOR SALE (SD #1284)
by **Carol Devine,** coming in **April 2000.**

The Bridal Bid only from **Silhouette Desire.**

Available at your favorite retail outlet.

Visit us at www.romance.net

SDTBB2

Return to romance, Texas-style, with

ANNETTE BROADRICK

DAUGHTERS OF TEXAS

When three beautiful sisters round up some of the Lone Star State's sexiest men, they discover the passion they've always dreamed of in these compelling stories of love and matrimony.

One of Silhouette's most popular authors, **Annette Broadrick** proves that no matter the odds, true love prevails.

Look for ***Daughters of Texas*** on sale in January 2000.

Available at your favorite retail outlet.

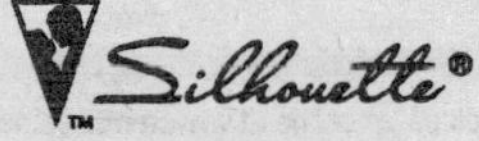

Visit us at www.romance.net

PSBR3200

FOUR UNIQUE SERIES
FOR EVERY WOMAN YOU ARE...

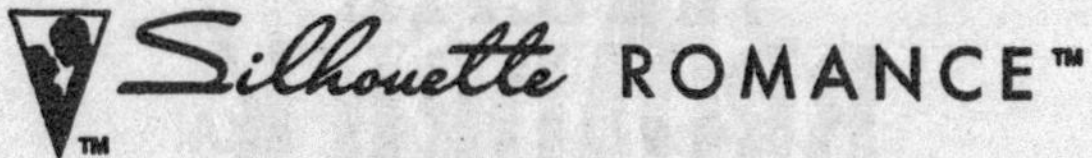

These entertaining, tender and involving love stories celebrate the spirit of pure romance.

Desire features strong heroes and spirited heroines who come together in a highly passionate, emotionally powerful and always provocative read.

Silhouette® SPECIAL EDITION®

For every woman who dreams of life, love and family, these are the romances in which she makes her dreams come true.

Dive into the pages of Intimate Moments and experience adventure and excitement in these complex and dramatic romances.

Look us up online at www.romance.net SGEN99

Special Edition is celebrating Silhouette's 20th anniversary!

Special Edition brings you:

• brand-new LONG, TALL TEXANS
Matt Caldwell: Texas Tycoon by **Diana Palmer**
(January 2000)

• a bestselling miniseries
PRESCRIPTION: MARRIAGE
(December 1999-February 2000)
Marriage may be just what the doctor ordered!

• a brand-new miniseries SO MANY BABIES
(January-April 2000)
At the Buttonwood Baby Clinic,
lots of babies—and love—abound

• the exciting conclusion of ROYALLY WED!
(February 2000)

• the new AND BABY MAKES THREE:
THE DELACOURTS OF TEXAS
by **Sherryl Woods**
(March 2000)

And on sale in June 2000, don't miss
Nora Roberts' brand-new story
Irish Rebel
in **Special Edition.**

Available at your favorite retail outlet.

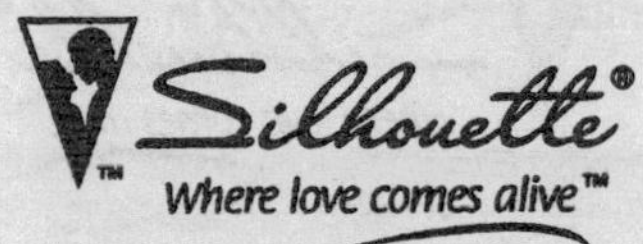

Visit us at www.romance.net

PS20SSE

Celebrate Silhouette's 20th Anniversary

With beloved authors, exciting new miniseries and special keepsake collections, **plus** the chance to enter our 20th anniversary contest, in which one lucky reader wins the trip of a lifetime!

Take a look at who's celebrating with us:

DIANA PALMER

April 2000: SOLDIERS OF FORTUNE
May 2000 in Silhouette Romance: *Mercenary's Woman*

NORA ROBERTS

May 2000: IRISH HEARTS, the 2-in-1 keepsake collection
June 2000 in Special Edition: *Irish Rebel*

LINDA HOWARD

July 2000: MACKENZIE'S MISSION
August 2000 in Intimate Moments: *A Game of Chance*

ANNETTE BROADRICK

October 2000: a special keepsake collection, plus a brand-new title in
November 2000 in Desire

Available at your favorite retail outlet.

Visit us at www.romance.net

PS20GEN